CITY HAUL

A Novel

Richard Little

This is a work of fiction. Apart from actual people, events, and locales that figure in the narrative, names, characters, places, and incidents either are the product of the author's imagination or are used fictitiously.

Published by Pepys2000 Writing
pepys2000.blogspot.com
© 2018 by Richard Little   All rights reserved.
Bellingham, Washington
"The Write Stuff"

ISBN 9780999848210
LOC 2018954168
Printed in the United States of America

Dedication

Austen to Zola, Faulkner to Ford, McMurtry to Mantel—the list goes on and on of the wonderful literature that's been laid at my door. I don't know about others, but I write because I read.

And to my parents, Katie and Dick Little, who surrounded us with books.

What we choose to fight is so tiny!
What fights with us is so great!

Rilke

‡

Salish County Superior Court Judge Scott Key was stoned. Very stoned. And drunk. He couldn't get a fix on where he was, let alone count to ten as the young sheriff's deputy asked him to. He wobbled on the cowboy boots he customarily wore—an affectation not particularly helpful in his present state. He muttered to himself as he fumbled for his license, red-eyed, his otherwise fashionable hair in disarray. One moment he'd grin and try to put a sentence together. The next moment, he'd sigh and lean against the car. He was confused, and the rational, totally together façade—the stucco wall behind which he usually hid shortcomings—cracked.

Dolores Key sat in the passenger seat. Dark-eyed and motionless except for fingering a diamond-encrusted Cartier cross displayed against her little black dress. One might suppose that her paralysis was due to fear for her husband's career as a sitting superior court judge and the resulting damage these circumstances could inflict on their personal commonweal. But that would not be accurate. She didn't move because she was beyond intoxicated, stupid drunk, which is why the judge was driving. Clear thinking was not in the cards.

His Honor—for the record "Francis Scott Key, Esq."—stepped farther to the side of the roadway and assaulted the dawn's early light, pristine in its quiet seaside slumber, with a rich mixture of bass-register retching and a potpourri of his stomach contents. Even the sheriff's deputy was impressed.

By now, the license and plates had been run and the lad realized who he was dealing with. A bright fellow, he didn't call in on the radio, but punched in a number on his personal cell. His boss answered, Sheriff Lucas Barkley. "Weaving all over the road, baggie in the glove box, sir. Car smells like Hempfest. Yes, sir, I'm sure it's him."

Sheriff Barkley congratulated the deputy on notifying him personally. Asked him to bring the report directly to him. Then, he fixed himself a cup of coffee and, in the emerging day, reflected on the vagaries of life. And smiled.

Part One

Gunk

Early Fall

1

On a splendid Pacific Northwest fall day, scattered sunrays poking through disappearing rain clouds, I turned my faithful pickup truck into my usual drive-through latté stand and pulled up to the window.

"Double-punch Monday, Matt!" Tiffany, the barista, grinned at me with her toothpaste ad smile. She leaned out of the booth. She wore a loose white peasant blouse, from which I averted my eyes as quickly as I could and handed her my Joltin' Joe Espresso frequent-buyer card. I ordered a tall doppio caffé mocha.

"Good morning, Tiffany." It was almost noon.

"You're lookin' sharp, handsome." It must have been the sport coat, the blue shirt with white checks, no tie. Tan Dockers and slip-on loafers completed my better-than-usual ensemble, but she couldn't see them.

"You lawyers."

"Well, it's what I do."

She turned and did whatever they do to extract coffee out of little spouts. Over her shoulder she asked, "Whip or no whip?"

"With, please."

She came back to the window and drizzled chocolate in little circles on the whipped cream. She stabbed the drink with a pink plastic straw and handed it to me.

"You used to do something else, right, Matt? Like, with the government?"

"Very true, Tiffany. I worked with the state legislature."

"So hey, I started community college this week."

"Hey, that's wonderful."

"And I'm, like, taking this class on government."

"Good for you." Barista Tiffany was pretty as a cheerleader, but why the turquoise swath across her blonde hair? And wouldn't one piercing in each ear have been enough? Jeez, I was old!

"And my teacher says if we don't like something the government is doing, we should write our congressman."

"That's good advice."

"Who is he? What's his name?"

"Her name is Jeanette Smith."

"A girl?"

"A woman, yes. Go online and you can find her address. So what don't you like?"

"Parking meters. I hate 'em. I went in for maybe three minutes to take back a CD my boyfriend was, like, bored of. And the grumpy lady in that stupid little car gave me a ticket."

"I'd be upset, too. Those people are vicious."

"Fifteen dollars! Who has an extra fifteen dollars?"

"Tiffany, here's what. It's not your congressperson you need to talk to. Parking fines are handled right here in Church Harbor at City Hall."

"Oh." She frowned.

"Yep. Just go down there and tell them your story."

"Will I have to talk to a real person? Can't I text them?"

"No, they won't let you do that."

A truck larger than mine and a car were now in line behind me. "Think of it as a learning experience," I continued. "For your class."

"You're the best, Matt." She punched my card with a flourish and handed it back. "Thanks, and bye-bye," she mouthed. Excellent customer relations, that gal.

On my way out, I spotted a spiffy green Jaguar pulling up to the opposite window. My stomach lurched. The vehicle, with its too-familiar café au lait leather upholstery, was piloted by a certain female legislator who was possibly the last person on earth I wanted to make eye contact with. The back tires of my truck caught gravel and spun as I left like a high school kid peeling out.

But as I drove away, what I thought about was neither the driver of the car I'd managed to avoid, nor the pained face of Judge Scott Key and his ongoing saga—once again above the fold on the newspaper lying on the passenger seat of my truck. It wasn't even the curious message on my cell from Canada about someone called "Gunk."

No, my mind instead lingered on barista Tiffany's turquoise hair and piercings, and my precious ten-year-old daughter Allie, who'd grow up—and not be caught dead wearing a fetching blouse, if I had anything to say about it.

If, that is, thanks to enough stupidity on my part to jeopardize my marriage and leave "visitation" with my daughter to the whims of her mother, my wife Ellen—up till recently my best friend; these days, hardly.

Back to something I did have control over, I weaved through late morning traffic on my way to the monthly Salish County Bar Association meeting. Tiffany got my past role "with the government" right, but now I was back to lawyering. And in my renewed incarnation, these dry-toast gatherings were part of the drill. It was important to let people know what I did for a living. As a lobbyist, I'd avoided blowing my own horn. (Government Relations Specialist, read my business card.) Even though my one and only client had been my very own hometown of Church Harbor, I'd tried to stay under the radar. I used to joke that even my mother didn't know what I did for a living. That's partly true. It broke her heart, she said, to learn that her son the attorney, in her mind bound for the US

Supreme Court, had decided to leave the legal profession, even briefly, and dirty his hands in the messy and unprincipled soil of legislating. Whether I'd moved up the food chain or down was not a question for her.

This did not mean I was embarrassed about the job, afraid to defend a lobbyist's role and deflect the stereotypical image that got headlines. If asked, I'd point out that there are notorious plumbers, dentists, accountants—and lawyers, for that matter. I just didn't advertise.

Unlike undertakers, say. The mechanics of what they're called to do is too grisly for me. I'm queasy about the occasional dead cat I run across—figuratively, that is. But morticians don't hide what they do for a living. Kiwanis Club or Rotary, church or casual get-together at a friend's home, they don't hesitate to tell people they're undertakers. Lord knows somebody's got to do what they do, but they have no qualms about letting you know. Walk into any service club luncheon and there he'll be, first name and occupation in bold on his badge, "Irwin Gray—Gray Funeral Home," hand extended, voice like a news anchor's, and a smile as big as a vacuum cleaner salesman's.

This train of thought occurred to me when I arrived at the meeting. As it happened, that day the program featured Undertaker Gray. He was on a panel along with an attorney and a CPA, each of whom specialized in estate planning. Irwin Gray is a fine citizen, dedicated, charitable, giving of his time, and by the way, successful. We knew each other casually, as businesspeople do in our town, and greeted each other, handshake and arms pumping.

The meeting itself was true-to-form—introductions, minutes, and perfunctory announcements—but Gray et al's presentations went okay. I even jotted down some notes. There was no chatter about poor Judge Key's ongoing misery, but I wasn't surprised. Scott Key's dark side had been exposed. But no attorney would disparage a sitting judge, especially around the not-always-friendly confines of a lunch table. He was still on the bench, after all. When there's doubt, better to say nothing, as lawyers are trained to do from Day One.

The room was warm and the meeting droned on, including an announcement of upcoming CLE (Continuing Legal Education) courses offered in the area. Maybe if there'd been a refresher course in marriage. Naw, wouldn't've helped.

My mind took a detour.

Ellen and I were well past the newlywed stage. I loved her and she loved me, even the times I played golf on Mother's Day. Still, I had no trouble recalling the first time I saw her—classy, not showy. Light brown hair cut short, she had on dark slacks, a white shirt, and a light green cardigan sweater, sleeves rolled up, a pair of amber-framed glasses perched on her head. Walking down the law school corridor, she carried a manila file, a pencil tucked behind her ear. "Serious efficiency" was my first thought. No, my real first thought was to resume breathing.

"Who was that?" two of us said at once.

"She works in the dean's office," someone said. "They hired her firm to do some publicity. Don't know her name."

I made it my business to find out. I nosed around the dean's office and spotted an inbox slot that said "Ellen Latimer." On a hunch, I asked the receptionist if Ms. Latimer was in. She said no, but asked if I had an article for the newsletter to drop off. Bingo!

One day, the same Ms. Latimer was coming toward me in the hallway. When she got closer, we did that stutter-step thing people do when they're walking toward each other and can't decide who's going to pass on which side—a dance for which I've never found the name. Only I wasn't trying to pass.

"Pardon me," she said.

"Not at all," I replied. I was close enough to see how blue her eyes were. She was tall, maybe five-eight, and in low heels.

"My name's Matt, by the way."

"Nice to meet you." She stepped aside and started to walk by. This wasn't going to be easy.

"Um, I wanted to tell you that I try to fall in love with a woman only once a week."

She looked at me like I was the guy on the corner you cross the street to avoid. She shifted the file she was carrying from one arm to the one nearest me, holding it like a shield. Figuring, I guess, that little harm could come of an encounter in a law school hallway, she said, "So?"

"Well, it's Monday and you've used up my quota for the entire month."

She didn't blink. "That's not a bad pick-up line."

"I'm glad you liked it."

"I didn't say that. Gotta run. Pleasure to meet you, Mark."

"It's Matt," I called after her.

The fellow sitting next to me at the bar association meeting interrupted my reverie with a nudge on my elbow. "They're making the pitch for dues." Since money—the getting not spending—was a major preoccupation for obvious reasons, I snapped back to reality. But nowadays, the reality of my situation was more reflected in the stunned look on Ellen's innocent face a few weeks back, her disbelief, and my lame excuses before the proverbial door hit me on the way out. The self-inflicted stab in my gut that came and went unbidden.

As soon as I could, I left. I avoided dessert with the certainty that it would have added an exclamation point to the horrid luncheon fare: chicken marsala covered with phlegm-like sauce, overcooked green beans with slivers I took to be mushroom pieces, and a lump of dry, brownish particles of rice. It would have been disingenuous, however, to complain.

Many of my meals living alone meant leaning over the sink, spooning leftover Chinese out of a carton.

Out I went, stashing my name badge back in the alphabetized box and leaving a modest stack of crisp, white business cards next to it. I climbed into my truck and started for my office. Bravely facing down bouts of self-pity, I was learning once again the daily grind, the quotidian business of earning a living at the practice of law. Such as representing someone called Gunk.

2

To date, "earning a living" would be stretching it.

I'd grown up in my small town just south of the Canadian border, but restarting a law practice, like beginning one, meant casting the net wide and dragging in whatever creatures ventured into it. Plus, there were too many lawyers around. (How Shakespeare would laugh!) Nonetheless, up went the proverbial shingle on stylish, shellacked cedar with black, custom designer script, hanging in front of my second-floor window facing the street, announcing "Matthew Archer, Attorney-at-Law." Sooner or later, so the mythos went, it'd lure a fine monthly retainer from a solvent corporation or the mega personal injury fee on which one could retire.

After the bar meeting, I drove back to my office, parked, and walked downtown to the Salish County jailhouse to follow up on the morning's phone call from a Canadian area code. The woman's voice message gave the name Willard Carlyle, aka "Gunk," and said he was in jail because he'd been arrested along with members of the notorious Bandolero motorcycle gang. Oh well, at least I had a client, even if it was an angry outlaw biker now staring at the world through the steel bars of our downtown hoosegow.

I knew about the Bandoleros. But a Canadian connection? I'd called in a favor from a friend in the Church Harbor Police Department, so I stopped by the station on the way to the jail

to pick up a copy of the police report of the arrest. I read it on
the way.

The pong of a drunk tank is unmistakable and universal—
disinfectant that doesn't completely mask the urine and stale
vomit aroma that wafts through the bars, plus the unique
bouquet of the particular individual you're meeting with.
With jailbirds as a cleaning crew, you're not going to get spit
shine. The gloom of the holding cell was lit by a gray shaft of
light from a slit window high in the wall, aided by a single
unshaded bulb hanging from the ceiling. On what passed for
a bed, there lay a disheveled veteran of the premises who'd
finish sleeping it off soon and would be back out on the street.
Another occupant was a young skinhead with tattoos and a
scowl, twenty-something and like many of his street-corner
best buds, looking like he had it all figured out.

The jailer motioned me to a table at the end of the hall and
brought out a third man, my client. This was Willard Carlyle.
He walked bow-legged to where I stood. I handed him my
card. He squinted at it and stuck it in his pocket.

"Call me Gunk," he said.

"I'm Matt." We shook hands and sat down.

"So, 'Gunk,' huh?" I asked.

"You know, the stuff you clean up grease with."

Gunk, duct tape, Velcro, and WD-40, all miracles of
modern science, traces of which will remain floating through
the universe after a meteor blasts the planet to smithereens.

"I know what it is. For a biker, not a bad road name, I
suppose. Beats 'Willard' all to hell, doesn't it? 'Willard Carlyle'
sounds like a hotel I used to stay at."

He was in his forties and grizzled, no doubt from years
astride a motorcycle and from who knows what all else. He
was unshaven, but his ponytail was in place and his eyes
were clear.

"So, who was the kid?" I asked, scanning the police report in front of me. I was referring to the "mule" who'd possibly set up the drug bust that resulted in my client's predicament.

"Does it matter?" replied Gunk.

"He probably spent at least a little while in that cell." I motioned with my thumb. "I thought you might have known him."

"Mule" is the term for the guy who is paid to hump the drugs across the Canadian border at night and into the States. It's usually a kid, hard up for the few hundred bucks he's paid. The actual seller and buyer don't soil their hands in this risky part of the venture. A delivery point is arranged at an out-of-the-way spot, the mule drops the contraband, and beats it back north to watch the Canucks on TV with his girlfriend.

Not so in the present case. According to the report, instead of hustling out of there like they should have, the gang had stuck around and partied. The noise and lights and music and the pot smoke perfuming the trees led the troops right to them. Drug Enforcement agents along with local cops and sheriff's deputies had caught the delivery boy, too, when they descended, en masse, on Gunk and four of his outlaw motorcycle gang pals and rounded them up.

I pictured the bikers scattering like schoolboys in a parking lot when the flashlights and yelling started—a half-dozen leather-jacketed, middle-aged Bandoleros running, while 150-watt torch beams flashed off tree limbs and glinted off drawn pistols and badges. And yelling, lots of yelling. Drugs or no drugs, the boys knew better than to argue with guns. They were cuffed and herded back to the highway. Gunk ended up here; where the others were, I didn't know.

We looked at each other for a bit, his face passive like he was assessing how much to trust me. I was trying to gauge who I was dealing with, an inexact science necessary when representing someone accused of a crime. Besides, this was a federal case—drugs across the border—not simple possession, now legal in our state. The stakes were high. No lenient, look-the-other-way enforcement; federal penitentiary versus state prison; no-nonsense prosecutors, and judges appointed by the US government.

"Why'd they let him go?" He meant the mule.

"Took him back, you mean. They'd have checked with the Mounties up north who had him on another beef and wanted to be sure he didn't run. He'll be back if the government wants him to testify."

"That's in the police report there?"

"Most of it. The rest is my educated guess."

He smiled. It was a good smile. "You're assigned counsel, right?"

"Actually, no. Someone named Sheila called me instead. If you hire me, I'll want a retainer. I won't rip you off. We can work something out."

"Okay by me. Unless I have to sell my bike."

According to the police report, law enforcement had taken along a van to haul away a few thousand bucks' worth of Messrs. Harley and Davidson's finest and much-loved products. They would be held as evidence or confiscated outright as "implements used to commit a crime."

"I'll give it a shot, Will ... er, Gunk. I'll see what I can do about your bike."

Gunk inspected his large paws lying flat on the table, hands that no doubt had cleaned many a cylinder head. Then he looked up and nodded like he didn't have much choice, which was pretty much the case.

"Sheila—the lady at that phone number—will have the money. So, why you doing this kind of work, Matt? You don't look like you just got your license to steal."

"I didn't. Long story. Plus, there's this thing about

responsibilities and other sappy words in the oath we take that I happen to believe in."

If I'd expected a reaction, I didn't get one. I flipped through the police report. "Okay, let's start with a little background. Bandoleros."

I meant it as a question even though I knew the Bandoleros were an outlaw motorcycle gang with chapters all over the country including in our state and county. Drugged up or not, a pack of bikers, wired up like dervishes, would blow people away blasting down the interstate, or out on a county two-lane, passing on the right where barely a shoulder existed. The full-throttle Harley roar would come up from behind, a six- or eight-pack in formation in black leathers and bandanas. You prayed they knew what they were doing in spite of being toasted, because there was no chance to get out of the way.

I didn't think they were into the drug distribution racket, though. But this time, the stuff in the duffle bags the Feds had seized was serious weed, celebrated "B.C. bud" (as in British Columbia) at its THC-dripping best. True, the state legislature on our side of the border had legalized marijuana for "personal use," but the US government had not. And neither government was okay with the quantity imported that night through the forest.

Gunk didn't add much to what I already knew. After we'd talked for an hour, I did get the impression he was going to work with me. I said I'd go see the bail bondsman and left. The jailer took him back to the holding cell.

Outside, I punched in the number from this morning's message. The woman who answered said she was Willard's "old lady." She had my retainer, but she was Canadian and had understandable reluctance about coming south given the events. Could I come her way to meet up? I said sure. Federal cases don't come along all that often, plus they carry a nice fee.

Traffic was light as I drove up to Park Woods, British Columbia, a town no more than a mile north of the border crossing. The Starlight Lounge turned out to be a run-of-the-mill roadhouse with a gravel parking lot and a tall neon sign advertising Molson's. What I didn't notice at first was a smaller sign below it saying GIRLS.

I parked and walked in, shooting a blast of sunlight into the dim interior before closing the door. The place seemed empty till my eyes adjusted and a duo of women motioned me over. Not hard to spot a Yankee in a suit and tie in that place on a Monday afternoon.

"Mrs. Gunk" turned out to be mid-30s, dressed in a prim white blouse, with her hair cut short. With her was her sister, unnamed. I nodded hello and sat down. As she started her narrative, I tried to pay attention. I really did, but there was a stage across the room behind her. The girl pole-dancing was stark naked except for a g-string and pasties. Long platinum hair, silver glitter placed where it wasn't intended to do any good, and athletic—one might say profoundly so. I swear I was listening, but I wasn't hearing. This was a first in my client-interview experience.

The music ended and the dancer left to a smattering of applause from somewhere in the darkness. I tuned back in. Gunk had used his one call to phone Sheila (she wasn't his wife after all), and she'd called me, running down "Attorneys" in the phone book. She didn't get past "A." So much for creative advertising.

Gunk hadn't told her any details, which was smart. She did have the money. I'd told her my retainer—fair, considering the exchange rate—but I was not prepared to be slipped a large envelope under the table. Roadhouse, nude dancer, unidentified onlooker, surreptitious cash. Did my favorite law prof tell me this part as he guided me into the legal profession?

I said goodbye and left, perhaps a little hurriedly. "Furtively" is a better word.

How guilty did I look driving back? There are laws about transporting large sums of cash across the border. The US-Canadian authorities guard the longest peaceful international boundary in the world. Friendly nations. "Children of a common mother" it says at the US side of the Peace Arch crossing which one million people use every year. On the Canadian side it says, "Brethren dwelling together in unity."

But do not be misled. All that international comity disappears if an agent at the crossing decides, with cause or completely arbitrarily, that you need to be questioned further. You get pulled into "secondary," asked to get out of the car and open the trunk, and sometimes are escorted to a windowless room and asked your life story.

Where are your rights? Where is your attorney? What are you being questioned about? Don't ask. Your job is to be beholden to whatever whims pass through the suspicious mind of your questioner. That is the law. It was worse lately because of terrorism and illegal immigration. All too often, no pretense is needed because the true object is drugs—interdiction of massive amounts of contraband targeted at the waiting markets in the US.

It was intimidating even though, instead of the busy Peace Arch crossing, I was using one of the more remote points of access because it'd be quicker. The crossing at Park Woods is little used, but something about the approach—the striped speed bumps, the black-and-white rail crossing arms, the row of orange barrels, and the gun strapped to the side of a border agent who steps out of the tiny kiosk—is chilling even on the most innocent of trips.

Besides which, I wasn't naïve. Even if I'd come by the cash legally, admitting that I had it could mean further questioning. What to say? "I'm being paid a bunch of money by the girlfriend of a motorcycle gang member who's in jail on US government drug charges. Did I mention I got paid in a strip joint?"

What to do? I hadn't thought ahead, so the manila envelope was still on the passenger seat. Try to act innocent? Hide it under the seat? Maybe I could sneak it into my briefcase. Surely, even a suspicious border guard would be unlikely to ask a lawyer, with ID, to open his briefcase.

My pulse rate was on its way up. I swallowed as the guard hut grew closer. The envelope was in plain view, and I wasn't about to pull over and remedy that a hundred yards away. I braced my knee against the steering wheel. My right hand shook as I unfastened the brief case, put the offensive package into it, and tried to drive at the same time. I may have swerved.

"Good afternoon, sir. What was the purpose of your trip into Canada?"

Better not lie here. "I'm an attorney in Washington and I was meeting with a client."

The agent, crisp uniform and all of thirty, peered into the car and into the backseat. He walked around the car. He stood in front and checked on the plates. Sure seemed warm for a fall day.

He walked back to my window and leaned against the door. "Bet it's some kinda drug case, huh?" he said with an uncharacteristic grin.

"Hey, attorney-client privilege and all that," I joked.

"Well, have a good day, sir," and he waved me through.

My bowels unclenched.

3

I stopped by the bank and handed off a bundle of colorful cash to a quizzical teller, who knew me better than to ask. Back at my office, I took the stairs, huffing and puffing up the last two; I simply had to get serious about an exercise program. That, and my domestic situation. Gunk's case would be interesting as well as remunerative. I'd get paid for defending the poor devil—which meant negotiating the best deal for him under the circumstances. They'd caught him and his gangster buddies with legendary and pungent "stinko" bud all over their hands, not to mention with the goods. What could go wrong?

No, the main conversations in my head these days were closer to home. Literally. A few months before, I'd spent my fortieth birthday sitting in a dimly lit restaurant in the state capital staring at a pretty woman not my wife, holding hands like a couple of kids on prom night, minus the tux and corsage. Nothing I'd ever have guessed.

But it had indeed been the selfsame pretty Senator Deanna Mackenzie in her flashy Jag at the Joltin' Joe drive-through that morning, a reminder, like a bookmark in a bad novel. It'd been her all right. Out my side mirror, I'd seen the back of a too-familiar head. She and I did still live in the same town. So did my wife Ellen, and so did our one-and-only daughter.

I opened the window over the street and dropped into

my creaky office chair. I clicked into denial mode. There was work to do, and I was about to get a lesson, a case study, in the truism that new attorneys attract, well, case studies. The day before, as I thumbed through the small pile of pink message slips on my desk left there by my part-time secretary, a familiar name had caught my eye. Tommy Thomason. The voice on his answering machine sounded right when I'd called back and left a message that he could come in this afternoon.

Tommy Thomason had been my shop teacher a hundred years ago. This had to be the same guy, or lots of Thomasons get nicknamed "Tommy."

There's an adage for beginning attorneys: "You don't get to pick the clients. They pick you"—especially when you can count them on the fingers of one hand. I was about to find out how true that was.

At the stroke of four, I greeted Mr. Thomason at the door. There he was, twenty-five years later and unmistakable. He must have been in his thirties back in the day when he conducted a combined wood shop, metal shop, and entry-level auto repair class. The goal was—let's be frank—to educate some less academically inclined boys in skills that might be bankable down the road.

I was in the class because the other electives were drama (girls and sissies) and ROTC (dweebs and budding militiamen). I was on the macho track even then. I did sports despite noticeable handicaps: big enough, but with pencil-thin ankles in wobbly football shoes with heavy spikes, a helmet that would spin around on my head every time I got hit, and a chronic aversion to pain. So, before I bulked up some, I ran track and swam even though they lacked the Friday night exuberance and overjoyed cheerleaders.

"Well, hello there, Mr. Thomason. How good to see you." We shook hands, and I motioned him to a chair.

"Very nice to see you again also, Matthew. It's been a long time. And please, 'Tommy' is fine."

He appeared to be in good shape for his sixty-plus years. Same tall, angular man with a tiny mustache, thinner hair, and, I guessed, he got exercise.

I said, "You look terrific Mr. Thom ... er, Tommy. Healthy, I hope."

"Yessir, Matthew. Take my walk every morning, eat right, and keep busy."

"I'm guessing 'busy' is why you're here."

"As a matter of fact," he said, setting a worn leather briefcase on the floor.

This was a time warp. The mechanical pencils in their plastic sleeve took me back. (Mechanical pencils—added to the other three P's of "nerdy": pocket protector, polyester slacks, and personality-free.) I couldn't shake the memory of the younger man wearing a full-length tan apron, striding from student to student, carefully monitoring our progress. Or in my case, lack thereof. Today, he seemed smaller; we do magnify things we knew as kids, and this was no exception.

I was hopeless in Tommy Thomason's class. Everything I tried in metal shop turned out to be an ashtray. In wood shop, other guys were making water skis. I managed a box for my mom. A box. It made her cry. I think my dad cried, too, for the wrong reason. If something required working with my hands, I was lost. No adept hands or eye-hand coordination. (I tried that excuse regarding after-dinner dishes; good luck with that.)

I'd taken the class for the easy grade, despite his storied bad breath. The one glitch in Mr. Thomason's otherwise salutary career involved driver training. He'd taken the job because it paid extra, plus no one else wanted it. However, I wasn't female. Thomason was relieved of driver's ed responsibility when parents of some of the girls complained that his instruction on a manual transmission was frequently too "manual." That was that. My buddies and I concluded that this had been his one opportunity to interact with the other half of the student body, and he kept taking his eyes off the road.

The driver training incident was even more serious than when Billy Williams took off the tip of his thumb sliding a board through the band saw. It was gruesome for those of us who were there that day, but not gruesome enough to place Mr. Thomason in a different curriculum. Besides, he was union.

I asked him in my office that day if by any chance he knew what had happened to Billy. He said he did, since he'd been genuinely concerned about the boy's well-being.

"I heard he is the head of neurosurgery back at Johns Hopkins," he said, shaking his head.

"You never know, I guess." I was equally surprised.

"Some people even manage law school," he added and laughed at his own joke. I gave him a courtesy chuckle.

"So, what brings you here?"

"A couple of lousy tenants I have, Matthew."

"Call me 'Matt,' please. The other reminds me of when I took your class." My turn for levity.

"I have some rentals around town," he went on. "One couple of jerks take the cake. They don't pay on time, they argue with me, they have crap lying around in the yard. They have cats!"

"What does your lease say?"

"What lease? Who has time? Never been a problem."

Mr. Tommy Thomason's face was getting flushed. I questioned my original "good health" diagnosis.

"How many rentals do you have, Tommy?"

"Three. Five, if you count that two are duplexes. This couple is on the ground floor of a duplex."

"What's the rent?"

"It's in the market." He paused. "Okay, maybe a bit low. Times are tough."

Tough for tenants, or tough for landlords trying to fill up marginal property? I kept my mouth shut. He would be paying me, I hoped.

"Tommy, here's the process. Without a lease, they're on a month-to-month tenancy. I expect you know that."

"I do."

"Are they current?"

"Did I tell you the one greaseball works on his outboard behind the house? Oil smoke to choke a horse. The other tenants, a law-abiding, clean-cut couple, complain all the time. And those foul, foul cats. The place smells like a sewer."

"The rent, Tommy?"

"No, they're a month behind."

"It goes like this. You give them a three-day notice to pay or quit. If they're still there, you file for an eviction with the court. The three days doesn't include the day they're served or weekends and holidays."

"Do I have to go to court?"

"If they don't leave, yes. You serve them again, this time with a seven-day notice to appear. If they don't appear, an writ of restitution is issued which you take to the sheriff's office."

"So, we're already ten days out, maybe, and more outboard motor smoke and cat urine."

"That's if they don't show up at the hearing and contest."

"Contest what?" Tommy jumped up and knocked the chair back. He waved his arms around and his hands were shaking. I tried to remain professional, safe behind my desk. Tried to picture my businesslike shop teacher with the mechanical pencils.

"I don't know. Premises not as advertised, disagreeing about whether the rent was paid. Or sometimes, just to buy time. The judge has heard it all. Your best hope is they get tossed out of court. Then the sheriff can toss them out of your apartment."

"Let me understand this," he said, beginning to pace back and forth to my window with the great view, glancing at the row of law books, then over to the door and back.

"Mr. Thomason. Tommy, please sit down."

He did not. He stood behind the chair with his hands on the back. Through clenched teeth, he hissed, "Unbelievable."

I kept my voice level. He couldn't see me wiping my sweaty palms on my pants legs beneath the desk.

I continued, "You came to me for legal advice. I don't make things up. Often, clients don't like the advice they get, and you can ask someone else if you want."

He walked around and sat back down. "Continue."

"You have to have a sheriff at the actual eviction. It's to keep the peace as well as to enforce your rights. The sheriff will want a $150 deposit or a bond. This covers his fees. Posting the writ, serving the writ, fee for standing by, mileage, and $15 for filing a return of service with the court."

"You have got to be kidding."

"Well, you do get to keep the personal property ..."

"Don't even tell me. It goes out on the sidewalk."

"You may do that. It's legal, much to the dismay of the city who has to get rid of it."

"Know what, Matt?"

"What?"

"My 'best hope,' as you put it, is this."

He reached down into his old leather bag and yanked out a .38 revolver. He slammed it on my desk. I jumped a foot. I tried to think of something to say—like it was every day I had a possible psychopath, armed, in my office.

We stared at the gun. We stared at each other. Outside through the open window, the sound of passing cars ebbed and flowed. It seemed to have a calming effect. With a measured voice, I said, "Tommy. Please put the gun away." Right out of a bad movie script. "And don't for a minute think of using it."

"I can use it fine," he mumbled. His tiny mustache quivered above his thin lips, but the angry alley dog had been cowed. He said, "I do have a permit. I even spend time out at the range with the boys in blue."

I made a mental note for Mick Malone, my friend the cop. I stood up.

"Tommy. Mr. Thomason, I won't say it's exactly been a pleasure seeing you again because you scared the shit out of me. But I do think I at least owe you this advice."

He replaced the gun and sat back. "Fire away." I think he thought that was a joke.

"As an attorney, I am what's known as an officer of the court. Regardless of his duty to his client, an attorney cannot condone, or fail to report, a breach of the law."

"What law have I breached, pray tell?"

"None, at this point, but even making a threat with a firearm is an assault in this and all other states. I will consider our conversation today within the ambit of attorney-client privilege. You haven't presently indicated your intent to assault anyone—at least, I'm willing to see it that way."

That sounded like a jury summation, and I was proud of myself. Maybe I hadn't lost my touch.

"You're not for hire, I take it."

"That's correct."

Mr. Tommy Thomason, age sixty-something and at second glance a lot older, ex-shop teacher and now slumlord, put his gun away, stood, and walked out.

Might never makes right, and I hoped it wouldn't come to that. I turned out the lights and pulled the door closed. I went for a walk.

4

I moseyed around for a while to get some fresh air and to cleanse my palate of Tommy Thomason—more than that, to be by myself and take stock of where I was. Gunk's arraignment was the next day. I'd need a clear head, to wit, not feeling sorry for myself.

I walked out to the far end of the old dock where a century ago Church Harbor's namesake, Ebie Church, erected his sign to attract passing ships to his mercantile venture. I found a weathered bench and watched a crowd of seagulls dart and squeal at each other over a piece of glop bobbing in the bay. A steady wind played the sailboat riggings in the harbor like a hundred wind chimes. The water in the bay was choppy and gray with scattered whitecaps like dollops of whipped cream.

I pulled my windbreaker tighter. Sitting on the dock, the music of the harbor in the wind was soothing. My hometown was part of me. And a part I'd been able to share with Ellen for years.

She hadn't made it easy at first. After my brilliant repartee with Ellen in the law school hallway, I let a week go by before I summoned my courage and went by the dean's office. Yes, Ms. Latimer was in, and I was directed to her office.

Ellen sighed, but motioned me to sit down. Right off the bat, she asked, "Are you seeing anyone for your disorder, Mr. Archer."

She knew my name, but she was indulging me—like a teacher might. "My dis—" oh, that. "Nope. Why would I?"

"Matt, I'll cut to the chase. I don't date students."

"I'll drop out."

"That's quite noble of you, but I'm serious."

"I am, too. Do you know that I love to read?" I'd noticed a copy of *Sense and Sensibility* on the credenza behind her. "One of my favorite authors is Jane Austen."

"That belongs to a friend. Right now, I'm reading a book by Richard Russo. Do you know *Nobody's Fool*?"

"Touché." I got up to leave. "Ellen. Ms. Latimer, we just had a conversation, which is more than I hoped for. I understand your rule. Would a beer after work be a chance to see if there's an exception?"

"I'll consider it, Matt."

Something in the way she said it, maybe a nanosecond's hesitation, or maybe how lost I was in her pastel blue eyes, I was sure something had clicked. I waited a respectable week or so (she'd say it was three days), and my patience was rewarded. We went out.

Ellen had a master's degree in communication and had been with a graphic arts company for a year. She was out-of-my-league attractive. I have everyday brown hair that usually needs cutting, and matching eyebrows, also bushy, over gray-green eyes. I was taller than she but not much and a bit blocky, hence my unremarkable career as a lineman in high school. My saving grace was a *thousand*-dollar smile—Ellen's clever words—with a tiny dimple on one cheek that continued to embarrass the hell out of me.

The first time we made love, in her apartment, I was stunned by her tennis pro's body and the energy that went with it. I had trouble keeping up. With arms and tendons strung as tight as racquet strings and legs from hell to breakfast, she moved like a sylph.

I told her I wanted lessons—in tennis, not sex. She did take me to a tennis court, once. I swung at lobs and volleys and slams in vain. Ellen said I looked like a marionette with a racket. In her deceptive little pleated tennis skirt, her aggressiveness made our "keeping company" (as my mother referred to it) all the more titillating.

She took me to meet her parents. They lived in a high-end suburb outside the big city. Her daddy, a dentist, was skeptical. Typical of many in the medical profession, he didn't much care for the one I was studying for. I was prepared to not like him; the practitioner in my youth was of the knee-in-the-chest variety, unpleasant regardless of the nitrous cocoon. But I drank Dr. Latimer's martinis and played golf with him. I let him beat me at cribbage and lost money I couldn't afford. We hit it off okay. Ellen's mom flirted with me.

As for my folks, they were captivated. Mom spent zero time worrying if Ellen was good enough for her boy. The two of them chattered away at dinner and Ellen helped clear the table. I heard them giggling and laughing over something in the kitchen.

Throughout dinner, Dad kept looking at her then back at me and shaking his head. When they sat back down, he finally asked Ellen, "You sure you've got the right house?"

My dad was good Irish-American stock and a man for whom wry humor was an art form. He began at a state college in the Midwest—the first in his family to attempt higher education—and found a summer job in the small town's print shop. He met my mom at the same college and they both quit and moved west, exchanging tornados and inexplicable heat for lots of rain. Using a loan my grandfather cosigned, Dad bought an existing business that was on the block because of the owner's unfortunate neglect of taxes.

Irish good humor and a fair bit o' blarney allowed him to bring the shop out of the red. In five years' time, by the time I was four, he had a dozen employees in two locations knocking out everything from business cards and stationery to black spiral-bound term papers, homemade memoirs, and by-god novels with glossy covers by local wannabes. The occasional hard-bound work for mainline publishers he contracted out to whichever press in the big city would give him the best deal and save his customers money.

He and mom lived in a comfortable split-level on a tree-lined street in a pretty Church Harbor neighborhood. I was an only child; "Isn't one of him enough?" Mom loved to recite on cue. However, according to a marital shrink I eventually patronized, perhaps trying to live up to my special status (or not!) explained a hole I kept trying to fill as an adult.

My mom worked at Dad's shop part-time and did Cub Scouts, church boards, Y volunteering, soccer coaching, and even a forgettable stint selling Tupperware in her spare time. There was also a duplicate bridge eightsome of ladies that met in our family room once a week and filled it with a mélange of coffee aroma, the smell of fresh scones, and enough perfumery to give a Macy's cosmetic department a run for its money.

They were great parents. Sports, books, and a healthy kick in the pants that got me accepted to college and instilled in me enough scholarship (to use the term loosely) to pull off law school, which made them very proud.

Wonderful folks, and grandparents-to-be, except that Dad died too soon. He contracted cancer of the bladder—printer's ink and attendant chemicals were prime culprits, and chemo did the rest. Sense of humor intact, he'd remark to friends that he was going to die not from some garden-variety cancer—lung, brain, skin—instead, from something original. Like him.

Every time I stand in front of a mirror to shave and rub my hand across my chin, I can feel the stubble on his cheek when I'd bend down to kiss him. I kept a death watch in the hospital for a week.

Mom never got over it. Her grief was so severe, she moved to another state—Arizona, where it was warmer. She came north once, when Allie was born, and she sent Christmas and birthday cards. Lonely, she found a "partner," she called him. She also called him Randy, which was his name. Yes, Randy. I flew to visit once and met him. He was okay. And they've been together for a while.

After graduation, on Ellen's birthday as it happened, I proposed to her. We got married after I took the bar exam and found out I'd passed. We'd waited because she is not an impulsive person. We honeymooned at Disney World. We moved to Church Harbor, I opened an office, and Ellen got a job at a graphic shop at an okay salary.

We bought a house and a few years later brought a beautiful little girl into the world, my relationship with whom I'd jeopardized ten years later. Now back home, the road ahead out the window was daunting.

5

Gunk's criminal arraignment the next morning could have been filmed—a caricature of a courtroom drama, except that for five of the participants, the stakes were real.

Imagine a police lineup with five men dressed in slacks: one with a sport coat on, another in a sweater, and the other three in ill-fitting long-sleeve shirts. Maybe they were trying for "frat boy" look, but couldn't quite conceal the "biker" inside. I couldn't help visualizing leathers and bandanas. But their act didn't quite work. "Facts are stubborn things," an eminent jurist once said. "You work with what you've got." We filed into the courtroom. There they sat quietly, hands folded, more like Vienna Choir Boys than *Boyz n the Hood*.

I sighed and rearranged papers in front of me. We were assembled for arraignment in Federal Magistrate Gerrit Hamstra's court. Persons accused of a crime in America cannot be held in jail indefinitely. Within forty-eight hours, a prosecutor must demonstrate to a judge that a crime has been committed and there's reason to assume the person in custody did it. Other issues can often be settled at arraignment such as bail, and sometimes technical objections are raised like a challenge of unreasonable search and seizure.

I didn't expect lofty Supreme Courtish matters to clog the wheels of justice this day. There they were, five Bandoleros, like kids sitting outside the principal's office after notes to parents had gone home. Busted in broad moonlight, partying with the contraband in plain sight. "Nailed, jailed, and bailed," the saying went. No, this appearance wouldn't overwork Magistrate Hamstra's capable brain cells. The night they busted Gunk with the "junk" had been one screw-up after another. A five-year old could've pulled it off. The moon was full. The drop spot was one the gang had used before and was at the exact place where the South Pass Road in the US veered to within two hundred yards of Canada. You might as well have given the federal posse a map. And the mule was a kid the bikers had never used before, so who knew about him?

Magistrates are sort of regional federal judges, part-timers. The US District Court, per se, is located in the big city to the south. Growth in case numbers and the length of trials has meant that District Court judges themselves hear cases there and don't have to travel to corners of the state such as ours. Arraignments are often heard before a magistrate. He or she can also take a guilty plea if a defendant agrees. The magistrate makes a formal recommendation to a full-time District Court judge who can, but rarely does, disagree.

Judge Hamstra was a practicing attorney of good repute in town. Over the years, he'd supported the right political candidates and had practiced in federal court. When the magistrate position opened up, no one was surprised he was selected by a panel of the District Court, particularly with a timely assist from a US senator.

As the arraignment commenced, soft gray light from windows to my left settled on polished counsel tables and chairs, the empty jury box, the court reporter's stand, and His Honor's high, imposing bench. I felt like I was on the set of an old black-and-white Perry Mason episode—in a cavernous room dating from that era, replete with tall ceiling, enormous mullioned windows almost as tall, with lower panes cantilevered out to let in fresh air that was moved around by antique fans that I guessed ladders no longer tried to reach to dust.

Things went smoothly. I signaled Gunk to come sit beside me; the other four defendants were seated behind the "bar," the wooden railing that separates the riffraff from we august personages doing the work of the court. That's what "passing the bar" means, an expression dating back some centuries. To most attorneys' ears, the word "bar" induces a stomach clutch and a mental video of a three-day exam hopefully never to be repeated.

The young man who'd carried the contraband across the border wasn't part of the proceedings. He had been escorted back north by his handlers, as I suspected. Seated behind the other Bandoleros were two jail guards. A deputy federal marshal stood next to the side entrance to the courtroom, firearm holstered at his waist. The chance of flight was miniscule, of course, but appearances matter.

Seated across the way from me at the other counsel table was Assistant US Attorney for the Northern District Lemuel Fish. Lem and I had gone to law school together and had litigated against each other prior to my taking the detour down the bumpy path to the state legislature.

He looked the part, spiffy in a standard-issue blue suit, red and blue rep tie, and mahogany wing-tips. Expensive togs, but I would not have traded for his caseload. He rode a circuit spanning several counties. Bad guys—"raw material" in his jaded phrase—abounded. No matter more and smarter cops, stiffer penalties, or prosecutorial zeal, they kept on popping up like crabgrass in the lawn. Today, Lem Fish was in our town. I didn't dare return the look he flashed me upon surveying the clientele.

On the other side of me from Gunk was Rebecca Murray, the appointed public defender, with four files stacked in front of her. Today, courtesy of the Constitution, she represented the other defendants at this stage. At some point, she would have to select one of the four for conflict of interest reasons. She wore a charcoal suit accessorized by a tasteful lemon yellow scarf at her neck, and her dark hair was short. I knew Ms. Murray to be very good at her job. Along with law review smarts, she was unabashed about aiming startling blue eyes at the most confident of government witnesses, the nonverbal equivalent of "bullshit."

I had suggested that she go first with her clients so I could watch the other defendants. My offhand question to Gunk at the jail about the identity of the young man humping the drugs didn't mean he was the only suspect for the role of snitch. It was just as likely that someone in the courtroom had recruited the kid and maybe even set up and coordinated the drop. The DEA didn't show up out of thin air. They had come in force and with reinforcements.

As one by one each of the other four came forward, I wanted to spot shifty eyes, hesitant speech, fingers crossed behind the back, some kind of clue. I was going to model a police show I'd watched at some point, problematic now that I didn't own a TV. My recent transition from lobbyist to law practice hadn't left time anyway, and the present state of my treasury ruled out the wall-mounted big screen a man like me deserved.

"All please rise," intoned the bailiff.

Judge Hamstra took his seat, banged his gavel, and we all sat.

"What is your pleasure, Mr. Fish," asked His Honor.

"Let's start with Stanley Lee Stanley."

"All right, Mr. Stanley, please come forward."

Stanley Stanley? What kind of parent saddles a kid with that moniker? Gunk and I exchanged a glance, and I thought I heard a brief snort from the peanut gallery. This was one of the few times the boys ever heard their real given names used. They knew him as "Stinky."

Tall and thin, Stinky's was not the body type I'd expect of a biker gangster; more like a farm boy, in from plowin' and cleaned up for supper. He was visibly uncomfortable—not odd, given the circumstances. His discomfort became plain when he started to speak.

In a thin, reedy voice he said, "I ... uh ... don't ..." He leaned down to whisper to Rebecca Murray. "Can you do this for me?" My guess was that education past eighth grade had been beyond Stinky's reach.

The judge said, "Mr. Stanley, I only need to know if you understand what I've asked you. Is that your name, and do you agree Ms. Murray will represent you?"

"Yes, sir."

"Ms. Murray, how does he plead?"

"Not guilty, Your Honor."

Not guilty is the obligatory plea to be entered at this point even if the accused was caught with a bloody knife in his hand, standing over the still-warm corpse in front of a roomful of witnesses. Why? Because the defendant is presumed to be not guilty? Sort of. Rather, it makes the government assume it will have to put on a case—witnesses, evidence, a cleaned-up defendant sitting blameless as a choir boy in an ironed shirt and new haircut.

It also gives his attorney time to muster extenuating circumstances and present them, along with an eventual guilty plea to a lesser offense. Facts such as, that his mother didn't hold him enough as a child, or held him too much, or that his older brother beat the crap out of him on the way home and threatened him with worse if he ratted. Any of the myriad other ways by which we of the opposable thumbs and big brains have managed to do the dirty to each other for eons.

If I'd thought Stanley Stanley was a mastermind of anything more complicated than breakfast, I'd have thought again. Mr. Stanley's not guilty plea was duly entered.

"Mr. Stanley is in custody, I see. What do you recommend regarding bail, Mr. Fish?"

"One hundred thousand dollars should be adequate, Your Honor."

"Your Honor, we think that is excessive," argued Rebecca Murray. "Mr. Stanley is married and is not likely to flee the jurisdiction."

"I set bail at a hundred thousand dollars."

As the judge knew, a bail bond could be had at the usual 10 percent of the amount stated, and security for same could be a pledge and title to a motorcycle worth at least ten thousand. This was a safe bet.

"Next, Mr. Fish?"

"Let's do Prescott Earl Endicott."

Where were we, here? Back Bay Boston? Over six feet with curly brown hair, Mr. Endicott walked confidently through the gate and went to stand beside Rebecca. He looked nothing like the model of a bad biker. The bespoke outfit he wore fit him. So, too, the natty tan sport coat. His slacks were pressed. Somehow, he'd gotten a haircut. More than this, he was magazine-cover handsome with stark blue eyes and nice teeth. Gang name, "Pissy."

Mr. Endicott's answers to the questions were as crisp and precise as he appeared. I dismissed him as a suspect. No nark looked that good. If this guy was in trouble with the Mounties up north, it was for tax fraud. Or maybe a bunco rap. I pictured a broken-hearted divorcée in South Vancouver softly weeping into her handkerchief while Constable Gordon took notes.

Same plea routine. Same one hundred grand set as bail.

Daniel Ray Higginbotham went next—"Butthead" for sure, as described in the charging documents. More quiet snickers.

What I observed about Mr. Higginbotham didn't help. Nervous, but responsive, he stared straight ahead at Magistrate Hamstra.

My mind wandered to my three long years of law school, back in the day. A lawyer friend of my dad's had warned me: "Son, first year, they scare you to death; second year, they work you to death; third year, bore you to death." Thus it transpired that in my final year I played too much poker in the student lounge and skipped Trial Practice class, where I might have learned cross-examination techniques for moot court.

How long ago all that seemed compared to the scene in Magistrate Hamstra's courtroom. We seemed a long way away from The Majesty of the Law; a long way from the eminent English jurist Sir William Blackstone who wrote his "Commentaries" in the mid-eighteenth century. Blackstone traced British common law back before the Middle Ages—before John Lackland (known now as Bad King John) capitulated to the Magna Carta in 1215. In spite of current twenty-first century events—catchy headlines and unsavory political back-and-forths—things hadn't changed much since the Anglo-Saxons invented the gig many long years ago.

Therefore, in spite of the assemblage that day, I had to summon up the noble purpose of being the line of defense between all that legal majesty, the United States Government, and Willard Carlyle.

Gunk snapped me out of my reverie. "Did you hear what he just said?"

"No. What?"

"He said, 'I plead not guilty *ipso facto.*'"

"He did not!"

"Look at the lady."

He was right. Rebecca Murray, Esquire, was no doubt happy she hadn't had a mouthful of Coke which, by now, would be shooting out of her nose. She recovered herself, and added, to an amused magistrate, "That's 'not guilty,' period, Your Honor."

"I accept your plea, Mr. Higginbotham, both *ipso facto* and *post facto.*" Thereby was recorded the one attempt at humor in those chambers in the memory of anyone present.

Last went Mitchell (no middle name) Scruggs. Now there was a righteous biker. He walked with a limp and could have been a centerfold for Chopper Magazine. I had no trouble divesting him, in my mind, of the clean Levis and gray long-sleeve shirt he wore and placing him instead in greasy black jeans, heavy boots, an open-necked lumberjack shirt, and bad biker vest with a patch that said "Bandoleros" on the back. His fingers were stained yellow, and I wondered how long it'd been since he'd had a cigarette.

It might have been my imagination, but I thought Ms. Murray stepped a bit farther away from Mr. Scruggs when he arrived next to her. The jailhouse stench, maybe, or simply his overall aspect, was daunting. If he'd have pulled a switchblade, I wouldn't have been surprised.

I leaned over and asked Gunk, "How's it with this guy?"

"What do you mean?"

"Are you friends, other than in the gang?"

"I don't invite him to my birthday party, if that's what you mean."

I made a mental note to be sure I picked up Scruggs's rap sheet from Lem Fish.

"By the way, Matt." Gunk leaned toward me. "It's not a gang."

"What's not a what?" I whispered.

"Bandoleros is a club. A motorcycle club, not a gang. You and the cops and the papers all say 'gang' and that just grates. Would you say the Kiwanis gang or the Rotary gang?"

I decided that this was neither the time nor place to parse outlaw street jargon and turned my attention back to club member Scruggs.

The fellow did nothing unexpected in his brief encounter with the federal judicial system. The same procedure ensued and with the same result. Remanded back to custody until such time as $100,000 bond was posted.

Four up, four down. All four gentlemen were escorted from the courtroom by the dour jailers. Rebecca and I nodded to each other, and she followed them out.

"Willard Guy Carlyle" stood up next to me as his name was called.

After a not guilty plea, Lem Fish addressed the court. "Your Honor, I've spoken with Mr. Archer, and I believe it's safe to release Mr. Carlyle on his own recognizance."

Judge Hamstra frowned.

"Your Honor," I said, "Mr. Carlyle owns and operates his own nursery business in the county and has no prior offenses."

"I guess if you both agree, I won't object. Mr. Carlyle, you do understand that departing the jurisdiction of this court without approval will result in a warrant for your arrest, and that will not reflect well on the outcome of your case."

"I do, Your Honor."

"Court shall be in recess." Magistrate Hamstra rose, as did we, and he, the court reporter, and the US Marshall left.

Lem Fish came over and sat down.

"So, what do we have to work with here?"

"Lem, meet Willard Carlyle." They shook hands.

"As I told you, Lem, Willard owns and operates a successful flower and garden shop."

"Honorable community businessman, of course."

"This is a first offense."

"That we know of, at this point." Fish shuffled through a file. "What else?"

"I plan to investigate further, of course. Right now I've only read the arrest report."

"Matt, I'll cut to the chase. Is there a superlative for 'red-handed'? 'Red-handedest'?"

"Lem, he earns money and pays taxes by working hard."

"By day and by night, it seems. Works with his hands. Does he teach Bible study on Sundays?"

"We can arrange that."

"I'm serious, Matt. What about innocent drivers scared shitless by these guys! And now this. I will throw the book at 'em without blinking an eye."

Silence. A pause. I couldn't think of a reply to the tirade.

Then from Lem, "I'm sorry, I must have dozed off."

"Very funny."

Through all this, Gunk was watching us, back and forth like center-court at a tennis match. To his credit, he didn't say a word.

"What's not funny, Matt, is that I will have to stand up in front of a judge and with a straight face give my recommendation. When you come up with something that'll allow me to do that, give me a call. Otherwise, see you in court."

Lem rose, shook my hand, and gathered his files. He nodded to Gunk and left.

"My," I said. "That went well, dontcha think?"

6

Gunk and I walked out of the courthouse; the sky had darkened to an ominous slate gray. The unmistakable metallic smell of rain meant that the light drizzle the day before during my harbor reverie was about to cut loose with a vengeance. Gunk's arraignment hadn't left me with any clues, let alone any brilliant insight about how to help him. We parted, but he was due back at my office after lunch.

The wind picked up and it started to spit rain. Fall downpours would soon be upon us in earnest. I was hungry, but my lonesome abode didn't call to me. Nor did my empty refrigerator or bare cupboards. I sought out a familiar haunt, The Lunch Bucket.

It was busy as usual, but there was space at the counter, a long, polished slab of old-growth cedar accessorized by a row of cracked vinyl stools. A vintage pass-through into the kitchen, past the display of pies, was loaded with orders on the check wheel. Both waitresses, in black skirts and traditional white aprons had their hands full, literally. I wanted noise around, people chattering and dishes clattering. White noise. No company.

Good luck with that. A person slid into the booth next to me and jabbed me in the ribs. Pepper Martin was a reporter for the local newspaper, the *Church Harbor Light* (or "*Lite*" as detractors would have it), who'd been a big help to me during the late, unlamented legislative session. He'd tracked down information which I'd used, questionably but guilt-free, to seize an advantage for my client, namely, his and my town. I wasn't going to tell him to buzz off.

Pepper and I were friends, which was unusual. Lawyers, along with politicians, say that "reporter friend" is an oxymoron. But Pepper and I had known each other a long time. When we'd get together we'd stay on safe topics—books and back-country hikes and baseball. Speaking of which, the name "Pepper" was as close as his baby sister could get to "Peter," confusing it with the spice she'd heard mentioned at dinner. The name stuck, abetted by his lifelong love of the game and honoring the Pepper Martin of the fabled Gashouse Gang, St. Louis Cardinals in the 1930s.

Sitting beside me this afternoon, Pepper was practically salivating—and not because of the generous aroma of burgers and french fries, which we both ordered.

"Any comment, Counselor?"

"Are you on the clock or just making conversation, Pepper?"

"How little you know about the news racket, Matt. The clock is never off." Turned out he wasn't snooping about my bad-guy client. He meant the latest item about our sorry local jurist, Scott Key. He handed me the newspaper. I handed it back. True, superior court judges don't get busted for drugs every day, but the delay in any resolution, plus slow news days kept the feeding frenzy alive. No matter how trivial, the story remained fodder for sleepy minds fetching the paper from wherever on the front lawn the newsboy had tossed it.

I knew the basic facts. But since getting back to town, I hadn't paid much attention to Scott Key's problems. I didn't think I needed to. I had my own. But, curiosity got the better of me enough to ask, "What's taking so long? Scott's, uh, adventure on the other side of the law is so last summer."

Pepper noshed, then shook his head. "Nobody's talking. Hints of there being more to the story."

I knew the state Commission on Judicial Conduct had sent an officer to town for a preliminary "discreet investigation," the first step in a disciplinary process. There'd been nothing public since.

Intrepid Pepper Martin surprised me yet again. "'The wheels of justice grind slow, but they grind exceedingly fine,' Chinese dude said a couple thousand years ago," quoth Peter "Pepper" Martin, Ivy Leaguer.

Scott Key and I were acquaintances, not friends. Lawyers and judges seldom cross that line. I knew his wife Dolores, too, as a participant in the social dance that is typical of many communities. She'd be with Scott at a reception or seated next to me on the dais, and we'd have the meaningless conversations that are the lubricant of such events. Her hair was jet black and she was attractive. From unremarked-upon local beginnings, she'd gained some refinements, though my overly critical eye always perceived a feral quality no matter how nicely she dressed or styled her hair. Attractive or not, it didn't surprise me that she'd been intoxicated, too, along with her husband the judge, the morning they'd been nailed. Turned out it was more complicated than I thought.

I tsk-tsked about the crummy publicity Scott Key's story was still getting but watched how I said it, since Pepper Martin's daily rag was helping stoke the fire. Munching a french fry, I mumbled something about the continuing body blows to the reputation of a judge I respected, and changed the subject.

"And hey, there was a Bandolero bust!" said Pepper, sniffing the air like the newshound he was. He slid another piece of paper over to me, Gunk's police report.

"Sheesh, you work fast."

"It's publish or perish where I live, Matt."

"You're flattering yourself, Pep. That applies to profs up at the university."

He ignored the slam. "Bushel bags of pot, outlaw bikers, South Pass Road by the border, dogs, lights, every law enforcement outfit except the Marines."

I returned his gaze with as much reserve as I could muster; he had struck a nerve. The profile was high, hence the risk of looking like a fool. I told him to put his notebook away, said I'd been retained, and confirmed the miscreant's name. I knew I was taking a risk dangling pieces of raw meat in front of a reporter and expecting him not to fire up the barbecue. But maybe he'd be of assistance down the road.

He asked for more, but respected my courteous "no comment." We went on to neutral ground—safe topics that allowed our careful friendship to continue: the latest Man Booker prize winner neither of us was likely to read; the legislature having slashed the state parks department's maintenance budget on the spurious logic that in a state with a nationwide reputation for forests and wilderness, money to protect them was low-hanging fruit; and, the usual misery of the baseball team in the big city south of us.

"Did you watch last month's lame imitation of a professional sport? Those guys commit larceny picking up their paychecks."

"Nope. It's times like these I'm glad I don't own a TV set anymore." I picked up his tab and went back to the office to call Allie.

This is how my life had gone for months. Family counseling, visitation (a horrible word I'd always associated with the supernatural), being a supportive noncustodial (horrible word number two) parent, and keeping my eye on the prize—prizes, plural, namely my wife and daughter, loves of my life. Since the breakup, the three of us hadn't gotten together as a "family." After a couple of months working at it, we were still at a base-level of cordiality. Ellen had met with a lawyer about divorce, but she'd agreed not to file anything right away. After finances had been agreed to, things would stay status quo, except that I had found a place to rent.

The focus was all on Allie and doing no more to disrupt her childhood than I had already done. Ellen's rock-solid commitment to her daughter's well-being was all she cared about. My honey-haired daughter, a little tall for her age and with my gray-green eyes, sported jeans and T-shirts more often than dresses. I'd met her teacher, who described her as being as cheery and bubbly as ever. How much of that was compensating for her being collateral damage from my screw-up, I didn't know. The slightest look on her face or tone in her voice that might be a sign of what she felt or how much she knew made my heart literally skip a beat. But I was too afraid (read, guilt-ridden) to ask.

Her mother had seen to it that counselors and teachers knew what had happened, hopefully the sanitized version. Counseling, Ellen's and mine, was ongoing and all adult parties were paying close attention. Plus, and sad to say, there was no shortage of other children from so-called non-intact families. Allie seemed to get it. She knew Mommy and Daddy had had a really big fight and that was it. She didn't know what about. Ellen had told her it was about grown-ups and for the present, at least, Allie didn't press it. Maybe being surrounded by plenty of kids in her situation helped. She was now in Column B rather than Column A of twenty-first century family arrangements.

I stretched out on my beat-up sofa and punched in her number.

"Archer residence. Allie speaking."

"Hi, honey, it's me."

"Hi, Daddy. You remember about Friday, right?"

"Of course. Wow, you sound so grown up."

"I am grown up, Daddy. I've answered the phone my whole life."

"Oops, I forgot."

A little bossy, for sure, but I clung to the ten-year-old voice in my ear like it was the last conversation I'd have.

"Very cool. How's swimming?"

"Okay, I guess. Yesterday was really gross. This girl threw up."

"Not in the pool, I hope."

"In the pool."

"Yuck. Where were you?"

"In the pool also. But not in her lane."

"I'm sorry I asked."

She changed the subject. "Hey, Daddy, I asked Mom about you-know-what."

"Is she standing right there?"

"Sorta. In the next room."

"What'd she say?"

"She said, 'If your dad wants a dog, tell him he can get one.'"

"Figures."

"So?"

"We can talk about it later."

"That's better than Mom. She said not to bring it up again."

Neither of us said anything for a second.

"I miss you, honey."

"Me, too, Daddy." A pause. "Did you just hiccup?"

"Uh, no. Something caught in my throat."

"I guess I'd better go. Wanna talk to Mom?"

"No, that's okay. Tell her hi, and I'll see you later."

"Yay! Bye, Daddy."

"Bye, Allie."

I pushed the off button, found a paper towel, and blew my nose. Gunk was due any minute.

7

Gunk showed up right when he'd said he would, leather jacket and helmet dripping wet. He made apologies for the precipitation, but I waved my hand to indicate the elaborate furnishings and told him to have a seat. Getting him released on his own recognizance without bail had impressed him. It was based on a promise—mine, to Lem Fish—that he was not a risk to abscond. Lem and I knew each other well enough that it hadn't been much of a stretch. Getting his bike back so quickly after the arraignment impressed him even more—a bit of magic I performed right after court thanks to the evidence custodian at the jail whose wife had been Allie's kindergarten teacher. Small town.

Gunk hung his rain-soaked jacket on the doorknob and I handed him a towel from the cupboard. He was dressed in Levis and a dark blue corduroy shirt. He seemed surprisingly at ease. We exchanged pleasantries.

My workplace was not elegant but it had a killer view of the bay even when the weather was lousy. The islands were silhouetted in the distance and downtown's picturesque buildings were in the foreground. In addition to my old sofa, I'd retrieved from storage a secondhand mahogany desk and two chairs. A knock-off antique table by the window held a vase of dried flowers; a catch-all cupboard by the door contained my stash of energy bars. I'd installed enough law books in an old bookcase to make my ad in the phone book look legit. Two framed Winslow Homer reproductions from Target hung on the walls. My antique computer and printer sitting on another table that served as a credenza completed the ensemble. Other tenants in the building and I shared a conference room. The secretary was part-time from a temp agency downstairs. She made my pleadings and memoranda presentable. She also did my letters and bills.

Bare bones, but as I said, the view was good.

"So, Gunk, what all do you do to keep body and soul together?"

"I have a day job."

"I know that. Tell me how that's going?"

"I run a business."

"Are we playing Twenty Questions here? I sense hesitation. Tell me about the nursery."

Long pause. "Oh, wait." I snapped my fingers. "I get it. A nursery with plants and grow lights and suspiciously large electricity bills."

"No way. Why would I hang out there like that when the shit ... er, marijuana comes across in waves these days. Besides, B.C. bud's better than anything down here."

"I see. Instead of growing your own which is too much trouble, you stay under the radar by racing down the interstate on real loud hogs dressed like the outlaws you are with signs on your back saying 'Bust me!'"

"Hey, we all have our recreational outlets."

"I'll let that one go. What's the business called?"

"'Florganica.'"

"Florganica! Tell me again the part about not having your own backyard grow operation. No, never mind. I don't want to know. Where's the shop?"

"It's on the frontage road off the interstate, at the last exit this side of the border."

"Okay, I'll buy that. Honestly, Gunk, I wouldn't have been more surprised if you'd told me you ran a beauty shop."

"That'd be Pissy."

"*What?*"

"You know, Prescott Endicott."

"That is some bad-ass motorcycle name. You guys are a laugh riot." I paused to write on my legal pad.

Gunk added, "'Prissy' wouldn't work, with an 'r' in it, now would it? Not that we didn't try. Nonstarter."

"I'm afraid to ask. What's the name of Pissy's beauty shop?"

"The 'Head Gasket.'"

Oh my God. "And that brings in customers?"

"He's booked solid. More haircuts than perms these days."

"Gunk, you are a truly unique individual. Now, tell me who else was out there? Anyone other than the four of you and the kid, the mule?"

"Uh ... not really."

"Not really, what? Don't be cute here, Gunk."

"There was supposed to be *Mongo.*"

"Mongol? Like the hordes?"

"No, *Mongo.* No L. Remember *Blazing Saddles*? Alex Karras."

"What about Mr. Mongo?"

"He was supposed to be there but he didn't show."

"Know why?"

"Nope."

"What's his real name?"

"Leonard Smart."

"Smart."

"Uh-huh."

"Tell me why Mongo's his gang, er, club name."

"You'll know when you meet him."

"When's that?"

"Anytime you want. I've got his cell."

He punched in a number and stepped out into the hall.

He stuck his head back in. "Mongo'll meet us this afternoon."

"Deal," I said, and named a place outside of town called Betsy's Breakfast Bar.

I watched out the window as Gunk made his sodden way to his bike, then I locked up. I went to the gym to detoxify.

It wasn't long before I found myself lying on a narrow bench, back slippery, staring up at a pair of obsidian eyes grinning down at me. A hundred and eighty-five pounds of metal on a power bar rested against my chest, supported by my clenched hands.

"That's it," I whined.

"C'mon wuss, one more."

My friend Yuri Brodsky reached down and inched the bar off my chest. The weights wobbled, so I grunted out one last press before clattering the bar onto the standards over my head. I lay there.

"I didn't come in here to spot you while you lifted soup cans," Yuri said.

"I didn't come in here to entertain you, loser. Your turn."

If Yuri, midthirties, was not the buffest guy in the room, he was close, due to regular visits to the gym. He was remarkably good-looking, and single. He wore his black hair long but not shaggy. His eyebrows were dark like his hair. The rest of his face, cheekbones, nose, and mouth were movie-star quality, making more than one woman tell Ellen she wanted to adopt him and take him home like a puppy from the shelter.

We traded places. Yuri straddled the bench and lay back while I loaded up another twenty-five pounds on each end of the bar. He popped off a dozen reps while I watched from behind his head. I didn't have to touch the bar.

Yuri Brodsky was a local success story, a feel-good tale you couldn't make up. His mother and father were Russian Jews who'd emigrated to the US from Minsk in Belarus. When the Soviets temporarily relaxed emigration rules, David and Rebekah Brodsky saw an opportunity and ended up in the Pacific Northwest. They hailed from a land where people repaired shoes rather than toss them to the back of a closet or shunt them off to Goodwill, so Yuri's dad opened a shoe shop in a quaint Dutch Reformed community in Salish County north of Church Harbor. He was good at what he did, plus well-liked. Rebekah helped in the shop, and they became wealthy by local standards. No Dutchman worth his *appeltaart* would argue with that.

Yuri came along and his good Jewish parents took him to the YMCA early on. It turned out that Yuri was good at basketball. Quite good.

By the time he was in high school, he was a starter and was team captain his senior year. Not quite six feet, he had springs for legs and could slam dunk whenever a lane opened—often over guys he gave away more than a few inches to. The weapon he used most of the time was a two-hand set shot the likes of which hadn't been seen since the days of an NBA superstar named Rick Barry. His astonished defenders would lose a step watching him instead of crashing the boards for a rebound—which most often never came anyway.

Yuri made his name when he took his team to the state championship. They knocked out a top seed in the first round and went on to take it all. Yuri had forty-one points in the final game, and all he did afterward was praise his teammates for setting picks.

A full ride to a national hoops powerhouse with an assist from a four-point GPA lured him out of state. After college, he tried law school for a year but found it boring, so he came home and went to work as a private investigator for the county prosecutor. Said he preferred "hands-on" work in the legal field, not the dry toast of the courtroom. When he saw there wasn't much P/I competition around, he went out on his own.

It wasn't long before he'd moved past sitting in dark cars across a street with binoculars or peering in motel windows hoping to catch hubby in flagrante delicto. He could tap a phone with the best of them. After a while it wasn't to listen to wifey planning to raid the bank account. More often, it was an undercover gangbanger reporting in or a crooked insurance agent choreographing arson. In my first go-round as a young attorney, Yuri and I had worked together on a couple of cases.

More importantly, we'd become close and hung out a lot—Ellen and Allie included. My extramarital shenanigans and the separation from Ellen put Yuri smack in the middle, especially regarding Allie, for whom he'd stand in front of an oncoming locomotive. I had put all of that to the test. Thus far, the friendships had held somehow, all of them.

My turn back on the bench, I suffered Yuri's torment till I was sweating like a plow horse. I hollered uncle and we bumped fists in that macho way in case anyone was watching. While we toweled off, I told him I was once again in need of his nonathletic skills. (It was not lost on me that he rode a motorcycle. A righteous machine.) He didn't say no, so I filled him in on Gunk and the arraignment—all I had, so far. He didn't seem to find the bikers' names amusing, or the whole situation as harmless as it appeared to me.

"Mongo." He said it, but his eyes skittered away for a second, which I took to mean he knew more than he was letting on.

"Gunk seems a pretty mellow guy. Can I keep you posted?"

"Do that, Matt. Please. Bandoleros aren't on the FBI list for their skill at checkers."

"So, should I hire you?"

"You can't afford me and you know it."

He stayed in the weight room to punish himself some more, and I went to shower. Out on the street, I flipped open my vintage cell phone.

"*Beep.*" I listened and frowned. Dolores Key of all people wanted to talk to me. I could guess the subject, but why me? I wondered. Could I meet her soon?

I texted her back that I was pretty jammed but I would have time the next afternoon. She got back to me saying okay, so I named a time and a coffee and sweet roll place at the mall just outside the city limits.

Off I went to meet the mysterious Mongo at a place called "Betsy's."

8

I'd chosen Betsy's Breakfast Bar because it was out of the way and seemed like a good place to meet this character Mongo. I'd also gotten to know the proprietor, Megan, not long after moving back to Church Harbor. The eponymous Betsy was long gone. She'd gotten fed up with the Northwest rain and moved to New Mexico.

I'd found the restaurant one morning when daylight was sneaking around the edge of my drawn blackout curtain and prickling my sleeping eyes. I gave up trying to sleep, stumbled out of bed and went looking for someplace different to have breakfast.

A tidy little bungalow with a red-tiled roof and a neon-sign coffee cup atop a pole by the parking lot called to me. I pulled in, took a seat in a booth, and opened the menu. The sun was clearing the trees across the street and making the vintage gingham curtains in the windows transparent.

A waitress came to my table and set down a glass of water. It said MEGAN on her nametag. She wore her auburn hair pulled back with a pair of barrettes, restaurant style, long enough that it swished when she turned and walked the length of the counter to bring back a coffee pot. She leaned a hip against the seat opposite me, studied a moment, then said, "You look like you could use some of this."

"That bad?"

"I'll cut you some slack. It is morning." When she smiled, her face lit up like the studio photo we all hope we'd take. "Ready to order?" It took me an embarrassed second too long before I answered. A pretty face in the morning is a gift. Plus, friendly female companionship had been nonexistent for me since moving home. Down the aisle, two diners hollered "G'bye, Meg," and left. The one other creature in the place was a quietly mumbling fellow at the counter. From the kitchen came the clatter and sizzle of cooking.

"Megan." I read her name tag aloud. "My mom's a Megan." What a killer line! Sometimes I amazed myself. I recovered, "My name's Matt." I motioned with my hand and risked, "Have a seat?"

She slid in across from me like she owned the place, which it turned out she did. She was in her twenties; in her restaurant, she was in her element and confident. She had on a full-length apron that didn't flatter her, but pretty, pale blue eyes that more than compensated. *I* was flattered, feeling mostly woebegone in those days and hardly star-quality.

I ordered bacon, eggs over easy, hash browns, and toast. Megan put the order in, then came back. She might own the place, but she saved on payroll by waiting tables herself. We covered the weather (pleasant for fall), how long she'd been in Church Harbor (two years until her boyfriend left), where each of us was from (she, Sacramento). I did tell her what I did for a living but omitted my marital situation. We watched each other from time to time, not staring, and shared a giggle at "Mumbling Herb" at the counter who was a little slow, she said, but harmless. She was funny. She said she'd been waitressing so long she hollered "corner" at home going from her living room into her kitchen.

Nothing more than that. Just a hint that I still might have a life. She got up to seat some folks and take orders, then brought me my breakfast.

I finished eating, folded my napkin, took another swallow of water, and dawdled a bit. Another waitress showed up and donned an apron and took my money at the register. Megan and I exchanged waves as I left.

The day of the meeting with Mongo, I got to Betsy's first, then Gunk arrived. We sat outside on the deck overlooking the river and the evergreen forest beyond. The day had cleared up, in the mercurial way of fall, and the sky was cloudless. Fluctuations in atmospheric conditions in our part of the world outwitted weather-guessers all the time, sending them scurrying back to their algorithms. We watched juncos hop and scratch around under the shrubbery.

After some small talk, I noticed that the sun had disappeared behind a cloud—except there was no cloud. It was Mongo. The man was huge. He was a tree with legs. The ground didn't shake as he walked up, but it should have.

"Mongo, this is my lawyer, Matt. Matt, Mongo."

His head scraped the fringe of the table umbrella as he bent to shake my hand which was like a six-year-old's in his. He pulled a chair over, swung a leg over the back of it, and sat down. He had that catlike agility that some big men have.

He and Gunk did one of those arm-wrestle grip handshakes.

"How you doin', bro?"

"Okay, I guess," said Gunk.

Mongo had reddish-blond hair that curled down past his shoulders. His biker regalia consisted of the usual black leather jacket with the Bandolero brand on the back. He had a confident look about him, but I detected a faintly hunted mien that was often the result of the turnstile that is a life of crime and punishment. His biker-tan face broke into an ingratiating smile. He had all his teeth and they shone white. As the "missing person" at the drug bust, yet someone Gunk seemed to defer to, I was all about meeting him.

He said, "You takin' care of my man here, Counselor? How can I help?"

"Well, for starters," I began, "how come you missed all the excitement out on the South Pass Road?"

"Easy one, Matt. I live not far from there. I rode out to the end of my driveway. I intended to join the party. Just in time I saw not one or two, but four vehicles of unmistakable pedigree racing past me toward the rendezvous. I chose discretion over valor."

Maybe biker jargon included words like "rendezvous" or "pedigree" and phrases like "discretion over valor," but something seemed a bit off. The waitress brought coffee—not Megan, another gal. Mongo ordered iced tea.

"The arraignment was pretty pro forma," I filled him in, inserting some of my own lingua franca on purpose for fun. "No surprises. A not-guilty plea, of course. We talked awhile with the US Attorney. Gunk's got no record, which helps, so a plea bargain ought to be reasonable. Maybe a little jail time, probably most or all of it suspended, plus a fine."

Mongo frowned and looked at Gunk. Gunk frowned and looked at me. I frowned at both of them.

"That's it?" said Mongo. "A plea deal? Jail?"

"Okay, you two. Even with this state's lax view of marijuana enforcement, bringing bulging bags of weed across an international border is a no-no. Not to mention outlaw bikers. Did I mention that under federal law the stuff's still illegal, hence the DEA?"

I went on. "Plea bargain is what it's going to be. That's what we do when the culprit is guilty as sin. My job isn't to get Gunk off here." I eyeballed Mongo. "It's to get him a better deal than he'd get by himself. What part of this isn't clear?"

"What about the snitch?" asked Mongo.

"What snitch?"

"Don't you think you should inquire?" There it was again, that un-biker jargon.

I said, "I can ask around, but you two—just a guess—have better sources."

The biker bros looked at each other. Mongo's iced tea arrived, he took a couple of gulps, and we sat for several minutes. No one spoke. Stalemate, like chess. That, I decided, was that. We were wasting time.

I clattered my spoon into my coffee mug and made to leave. Gunk started to say something, but caught himself like it wouldn't do to take sides. I refused Mongo's offer to pay. He left his glass half-full and we walked out. I marveled again at his avoirdupois. Astride his bike, he made a fully-loaded Harley cruiser look tiny. Like me, maybe, sitting on a child's toy fire engine. If I'd hoped for a word with Gunk, it wasn't going to happen. He mounted his ride and rumbled off behind Mongo. I stuck my head back inside. By the clock behind the counter, we'd been there all of twenty minutes. Gotten nowhere.

9

Feeling very lawyerlike and, I suppose, a little cocky, on a hunch I drove to our, or rather Ellen and Allie's house. There was no sign of Allie—soccer practice or something— but Ellen was home and didn't seem to mind that I'd shown up unannounced. I slipped my shoes off and hung my jacket on the coat rack by the door, like old times. I followed her into the kitchen. She cleared a glass and a plate off the kitchen counter and set them in the sink.

"I'll get to them later. Coffee?"

I said I'd pass.

We went into the living room. I sat on the sofa. I truly missed that house—three bedrooms, an ample kitchen, living room, and dining room, and a backyard that opened onto a city greenway. Needless to say, I couldn't grumble about having to lease a place, assuaging as much guilt as I could, tablespoon by tablespoon.

Ellen sat across from me, one leg tucked under the other, in an oversized chair. Backlit by the afternoon sun, it was hard to gauge her mood, though I did see she still wasn't wearing her wedding ring. Without make-up and her hair un-fussed over, she looked, well, erotic, in that first-thing-in-the-morning, "Hi, honey" way. The way it used to keep us in bed and make us scramble to get to work on time. I missed her so much. The easy way we had: her mock exasperation as she held out a missing sock, her glistening eyes when I hadn't forgotten our anniversary, cuddling on the sofa, well-taught, she kicked my ass at cribbage. We'd been a team, she and I, and then Allie, against the world.

"So what's up?" she asked.

I snapped back into reality. "Not much. Just in the neighborhood," I lied.

We chatted, the fall weather, her job. Master's degree or not, Ellen enjoyed working for a downtown graphics design shop. She wrote a weekly advertising flyer, the kind you picked up on the way into the supermarket or found in your mailbox—sort of an advice column for shoppers where she could flex her post-graduate writing skills. She made even the mundane format interesting. Her boss hung onto her like glue. I told her about my run-in with erstwhile shop teacher Tommy Thomason.

How pretty she was. I took a plunge.

"Listen, Ellen. Don't answer right away, but do you think that you and I could go out to din—?" She didn't even let me finish. Her pleasant mood vanished.

"Forget it!"

"Okay, okay. I only wondered if ..."

She snapped. "You being around is important for our *daughter*, and I thank you for that. But an emphatic no."

"I'm only asking about dinner. Maybe Allie would get a kick out of it."

Wrong thing to say. Her eyes flashed a killer, azure-eyed stare.

"Don't you dare play the Allie card with me. I invited you in this afternoon because I'm trying very hard to erase memories—that oversexed bitch you played with! Who can compete with a fucking cheerleader? Tits and ass!"

I started to stammer something but gave up. How do you follow that statement anyway? She didn't give me a chance.

She had both feet back on the floor and leaned forward, glaring at me.

"Sneaking around! The embarrassment. I have to show my face in this town. And Allie's! It's sickening. Makes me want to throw up. Goddamn it! You son of a bitch!"

By this time, I was nailed to the chair. Or a cross. I didn't move. Couldn't. Except for my hands, which I noticed were shaking. This was a year's worth of profanity for Ellen. Overhead smash. No lob, no volley. It was really weird. I sat there watching myself watching Ellen, and with not a clue how to react or what to say.

My mom and dad never fought, at least not in front of me. I'm sure they argued; what couple doesn't? But I recall one time, an evening—I must have been ten or eleven—when I came downstairs to snag something to eat from the kitchen. I looked into the family room and something was up. Mom was obviously upset, like she'd been crying. Dad had his jaw set and I remember him grinding his teeth.

I didn't say anything, just took it all in, in an instant like you do. These were my folks. It was like a foreign country, a foreign language; beyond my understanding. I was just a kid and these were grown-ups in their grown-up world.

That's what this felt like with Ellen. Not a ten-year-old, but my forty-year-old self looking at the two of us having a horrible disagreement. Maybe one of those out-of-body experiences people talk about, or like I was on some other planet. What should I say? Apologize, certainly. Again. Feel awful about what I'd done to her, and want her not to hurt anymore. Say I'm sorry I brought up dinner, and leave? Tell her I love her? Who were we, this once happily married couple acting in a play someone else wrote?

Ellen and I sat there for maybe the five seconds it took me to have those thoughts. She had her face in her hands. How I wanted to go to her, hug her, fall on my knees. Apologize till I was hoarse. The nightmare was continuing. Of course I deserved it, but how long and how much penance? I thought I'd been taking steps, day by day, small ones. But it was clearer than ever that I'd destroyed the trust in our marriage—sacred, unquestioning faith. Maybe it would never return.

I did the only thing I could think of. I stood up. "Ellen, please. I'm sorry I misjudged things. What …" My voice caught in my throat. I started over. "What can I do?"

She looked up. "Matt, leave. Just go."

I walked to the entryway to let myself out.

She called me back. "No, wait Matt. I'm sorry. Don't go yet. Sit back down. I'm sorry."

I retraced my steps, shoes in hand and one arm in my jacket sleeve, but I didn't sit. She sniffled and wiped her eyes with the dishtowel she still held. "Even with all the time in counseling, talking to people ... I'll calm down." She took a couple of deep breaths. "Jesus, Matt, you get me to say things, to think things I …"

I stood there on one foot and then the other, then said, "No, I'm sorry, Ellen. Unbelievably and unforgivably sorry. I mean it and don't know what else to do about it. I'll go. Thanks for letting me come in."

I started to slip on my shoes.

"Matt, please. Wait another minute."

Uh oh, I thought. There's more.

"Matthew, I just need to say, I don't consider myself unattractive by any means. For having a child and oh, time doing its thing—I mean, I'm not …"

I walked back in the room. The air was calmer.

"Ellen, what happened wasn't about competition," I said. "Christ, you look fantastic. I assume one or more members of my sex have told you so recently."

"Matter of fact, I went to dinner with one guy a couple of

times who will go unnamed. I let him kiss me good night at the front door. Once."

"Oh, who was that?"

"None of your business. Do I ask you who else you're seeing? Come to think of it, ick! Men! Why do you want to know that? I sure as heck don't."

"Because you think the worst of me, for good reason, and the reverse isn't true. And for the record, I'm not 'seeing,' with quotes, anyone."

We let that sit a minute. Ellen draped an arm over the back of the chair. It was a lovely effect. She said, "Actually, there was the lawn boy the other day."

"The *what*?"

"I wore shorts and a halter top when I went to hang up laundry. It was warm out."

"Wow."

"A very tame halter top. He was eighteen." She giggled.

"Did he notice?"

"He didn't turn down the iced tea I took out. After he drank it, I know he took more time than he needed to putting the lawn furniture back. I showed him where it went. I do think he took his time."

"He sure as hell did."

"Yes, he did. We're not going any further with this, Matt."

She got up and walked with me to the door. I didn't even think about a hug. She shut the door behind me firmly but without slamming it. I was halfway to the truck when she came back out.

"Oh, hey, Matt."

"Yes," I answered. Not more about the eighteen-year-old kid, I hoped.

"I forgot to tell you. Dolores Key called here for you this morning."

"Huh? Did she tell you what she wanted?"

"I wasn't about to ask, needless to say. I gave her your cell."

"Thank you. I guess."

"Bye, Matt."

I got in the truck. Dolores Key being persistent. I was sorry that she and Judge Key were in it up past their eyeballs, but that was old news. At least whatever my problems were, they weren't splashed across the front page of the paper.

I let out a long breath I'd been holding and started the truck. I was exhausted.

10

A s I drove home after the scene with Ellen, I reminded myself that a journey of a thousand miles often begins with a single misstep.

I was worn-out. It had been a long couple of days. A pistol-packing landlord, then the arraignment and Gunk and Mongo—their poker faces staring back at me across the table at Betsy's. I thought about Yuri's caution. Maybe this was no penny-ante drug case. Maybe I should have paid more attention to the words "Drug Enforcement Agency" before being so eager to grab a few bucks. Maybe I should stick with traffic court. And what was up with Dolores Key tracking me down?

With my mind was flapping around like a lunch wrapper on a playground, I headed home rather than fall asleep at my desk in the office.

As I passed the CHURCH HARBOR HISTORICAL DISTRICT sign, it occurred to me that I could blame the predicament I was in on this very town of mine.

The name, Church Harbor, had nothing to do with churches. Not that there wasn't the usual array of denominations like in many an American town. But the town used to be Church's Harbor, named after one Ebenezer Church.

In the 1890s, young Mr. Church had hightailed it out of the booming city to the south that hoped to be the West Coast terminus of a transcontinental railroad. On Church's heels were two uncles of a young lady of questionable virtue—at least that was Church's view of the matter—whose "family situation" they sought to address. Her avengers weren't interested in quarreling about the characterization. All that mattered was that the putative father had refused to legitimize things and had skipped town.

Ebenezer Church escaped to a place that was hardly even a town, alongside a modest river that emptied into a bay. There was a lumber mill, a saloon, and a clutch of cabins that housed mill workers. Salmon were running, lumber was everywhere, and the bay was large enough to accommodate small vessels. The pursuers never showed up.

There was no general store. Whatever supplies folks needed they fetched from out of town or foraged for. Ebie Church knew the mercantile biz thanks to his father, who'd followed gold to California and fed hungry miners rather than break a pick. Ebie figured that coastwise traffic would come up the straits to the excellent harbor he'd stumbled onto. He went down to California, got a grubstake from the Old Man, and came back north. His gamble paid off. More fishermen and loggers and their families began to fill the fledgling town, and after a year he moved out of his original one-room dwelling and storefront and built "Church's Mercantile" down by the harbor. A logging dock extended fifty feet out over the water. Sign painters were in short supply, so Ebie hand-drew CHURCH on a big piece of sheet metal in letters large enough to be read by boats rounding into the bay. He mounted it at the end of the dock, and "Church's Harbor" the place became.

The town grew. Commerce thrived. Travelers and merchants came, waterborne and by coast road. A lively fishing fleet soon fed two canneries. The final "s" in the town's name was dropped.

Ebie Church became a prosperous man. He took his next

risk in the 1920s and got married. He and his wife decided that the town, with then upwards of three thousand souls, needed a music hall. The boisterous times demanded it. An architect who specialized in such things back in Boston was hired, for the unheard-of sum of ten thousand dollars plus expenses, to come to Church Harbor to design a theater.

Gawkers, scoffers, and amused passersby spent a fall and winter watching an ornate brick and stucco building rise out of the ground. It was finished on the Fourth of July. Opening night was captured in a black-and-white photograph of Model Ts and horse-and-buggies parked on the wet street in front, men wearing bowlers and an occasional top hat, and ladies in finery strolling outside with umbrellas. A hurdy-gurdy man with monkey spun his song at the corner of Pine and State Streets. Two little boys were at the entrance offering to wipe shoes clean of mud for a penny. The evening was a resounding success.

Ridiculed no longer, the Pine Street Theatre featured a fifty-foot white obelisk on the roof at one end, topped by a yellow gilt dome with a star on top. The words "Pine Street Theatre" ran down its length. At the other end, farther down the block, was a forty-foot proscenium, giving the whole building a faint resemblance to a sailing ship with its mainmast too far forward. Transposition of the two last letters in "theatre" from the usual spelling was an affectation suggested by Ebenezer's wife, whose Brahmin upbringing in the sophistication of Boston demanded nothing less.

Inside, the Moorish décor, all shining red and gold gilt lacquer, was breathtaking. A balcony and plush loge seating accommodated several hundred people. The *pièce de résistance* was a genuine Wurlitzer pipe organ shipped from the East Coast that rose up out of the stage on hydraulic pistons. Nothing like it existed north of San Francisco. Soon there came movies—silents and talkies, black and white, finally Technicolor. Touring companies continued to make stops.

As a youngster, I didn't know a day when bicycling or in the car with my mother that I didn't see or pass the Pine Street Theatre. It was and is an icon in Church Harbor. The upper balcony was where an eighth-grade fantasy was fulfilled when, giddy with a barrel of buttered popcorn and a giant Pepsi, Melanie Sugarman and I giggled and played touchy-feely, oblivious to whatever movie was playing.

Dial forward, and I could name Ebie Church's theater as the root cause of my domestic trouble. The old Pine Street Theatre needed a major renovation. A downtown urban renewal project was planned. Ellen and I had decided I would accept the city mayor's offer to take a leave of absence from my law practice and set off to the state capital, Franklin, to bring back money. A "city haul," we joked. Other cities in the state were getting their share of state money, why not Church Harbor? Plus, it couldn't hurt that our local state senator, Deanna Mackenzie, who I'd helped get elected, chaired an important committee. Surely, she'd help.

I pulled in the driveway in my modest neighborhood. I'd found the house I was renting by checking ads posted on a corkboard in the grocery store. It had a fenced-in backyard and a front yard as low-maintenance as it got. A lawn to mow to be sure (not in fall or winter) and rhododendron and Oregon grape along the side yard. There was a five-foot Japanese maple out in front, now having shed most of its leaves. In spring, some daffodils and tulips might show up, planted by my predecessor or maybe by my landlord—not named Tommy Thomason.

Inside, there were two bedrooms, a dining area off the kitchen, a full bath, and a living room with a fireplace I hadn't tried yet. Allie picked out gingham curtains and a pink shag area rug for her bedroom. Her bed had a Cinderella coverlet. There was a bookcase she'd talked her mother out of, with books in it and assorted geegaws on it. On the wall was a poster of a pretty young woman called Taylor Swift.

Furnishings in the rest of the house? "Spare" is the word. A discount store had stolen money from me in exchange for a sofa and coffee table. At a consignment shop, I'd found two end tables that matched in low light plus a lamp that I set on one. I replaced the shade on a floor lamp I had and put it across the room.

I made it as far as the sofa, but not before my phone beeped. A phone message from Ellen and a pleasant surprise. The next day, a Wednesday, school wasn't happening for some reason. Could Allie spend the day with me? "Of course," I messaged her. Her voice on the phone had been pleasant. I must have survived my botched visit.

I'd already told Gunk I was going to pay him a visit. Why not take Allie along? Next morning, I picked her up, and we went out for breakfast.

11

S he said, "Fish McBites? What will they think of next?" Her question was accompanied by a perfect, preteen eye-roll. Ten years old and already a social critic. At a McDonald's.

"I think it's kinda clever. Whoever thought something called a Sausage McMuffin would sell?"

"Mom buys Cheez Whiz."

"Chuck E. Cheese?"

"Cheez-Its."

"Jungle Juice."

"What's that?"

"I made it up."

"Stop!" She covered her ears, dislodging an earbud.

"Ever heard of a hula hoop?"

"Of course, Daddy. Who hasn't?" Another eye-roll. Wordplay with a ten-year-old. I prayed silently: Please God, let her stay this age forever.

Allie said, peering up from her smartphone, "And what's this man called we're going to see? He's a 'Band-o'? 'Band-row'?"

"I think you should tell him that. His name is Gunk. It's a nickname."

The ambience of a McDonald's pretty much defines what this country's about: unhealthy supersaturated food, at prices less than the daily wage in a number of Third World countries, served by sullen teenagers supervised by laid-off computer techs with degrees from Google University online. How could I complain, though? Two Egg McMuffins for $3.89 each, coffee in a plastic travel mug from home with a washed-out San Francisco 49ers logo for me, and an orange juice for Allie fit my budget. The aroma of what I assumed were the Fish McBites took a lot away from the savory pre-cooked perhaps-Canadian bacon, mouth-watering hard-cooked egg, and limp English muffin. I persevered.

So did Allie. "Whatever," she said. "It's better than cafeteria food." Maybe she'll work for *Bon Appétit.* Today she was humoring her dad by going along on a "business trip" instead of wandering a beach investigating tide pools. This would be fun, I'd told her. Do other little girls get to visit crime scenes with a guy who rides an outrageously tricked-out motorcycle?

A red-headed boy, a few years older than Allie, came over and offered to clear our tables. "Trying to enhance your dining experience," he said, wiping his hands on a fairly clean apron. Maybe I'd misjudged the workforce.

"Thank you, sir," said Allie.

The young man—"Jacob" it said on his nametag—actually winked at my little girl, which she ignored. Then he took our trash away. We got up to leave.

"Keep the shotgun locked and loaded right inside the front door," advised an old codger across from us as we got up to leave. "Where it's in plain view," he added.

The clean restrooms were a welcome surprise, then we were on our way.

A frontage road parallels the Interstate and we drove on it once we were out of town. It was straight, with little traffic, and we passed pastureland with dairy cows and wide fields with flocks of black crows and seagulls foraging. Hawks here and there lurked motionless on telephone poles, alert to the telltale rustle of dry grass below and the unwise appearance of a hapless rodent. Hoops of raspberry canes were coiled in rows because winter was approaching. Lombardy poplars lined the road. So did stretches of barbed wire and patched wooden fence posts. This was the rural land I loved, the reason I lived here. A ten thousand-foot dormant volcano towered in the distance, and soon would be much whiter after the first snow hit.

Up ahead was a sign that said FLORGANICA, in bold black script. It sat atop a white pole in a planting strip circled by an in-and-out gravel driveway. The shop it announced was picturesque, with flower boxes along the front and beside the drive. The boxes were painted in different pastel colors and were empty because of the time of year.

We parked and went in, tinkling a bell over the door. Gunk came out from behind a parted green curtain, wearing a full-length brown apron and wiping his hands on a towel.

"I'd shake your hand, but I've been potting tulips." This was one unusual biker.

"Tulips in the fall?"

"It's called 'forcing' them. They'll be in stores around the county by the first of February. Who's this delightful creature?"

"I'm Allie. You're Gunk, huh?"

"Bashful child, as you can see," I explained.

Gunk did that good smile again. "Look around. I'll clean up."

We did. A kaleidoscope of gardening paraphernalia displayed here and there. Seed packets on a revolving rack. Ubiquitous hanging ferns, planters trailing indoor geraniums and fuchsias, sparkling new trowels, forks, shears, clippers, and pruning saws. An array of shovels and rakes hung along a wall beneath a shelf of colorful flower pots.

I strolled outside, being nosy. Doing my job. Aha! Attached to the side of the building was a large electrical junction box. A thick black wire looped out to the utility pole by the road. On closer inspection, I noticed that the conduit exiting the side of the box was empty. I'd been jumping to conclusions about excessive power use. A separate, ordinary electrical wire ran from the pole to the front eave of the shop, the same as at any residence.

I went back inside to fetch Allie who was fumbling through a bin of bulbs, why, I couldn't guess. Gunk came out and offered to help her. The curtain to the back room snagged open, and I saw a bed and dresser and an old wooden armoire. Gunk lived here.

He locked up. We walked around back to an unpainted wooden shed. He opened it and sunlight shone in.

"Wow. That's the awesomest motorcycle I've ever seen in my life, Gunk." We even stepped back a few steps. Allie was right. She stared at the fully loaded roadster, swirls of black and purple and turquoise lacquer painted on the tank with yellow and orange flame racing back along it. A ruby red taillight sat on curved fender behind the seat. The big main seat and smaller rider's seat were glossy leather. Up front was an enormous headlight. Lots of shiny chrome—pedals, foot pegs, sissy bar, bulging gearbox, and handlebars with jet black grips at the end. It was one serious machine.

"I'm glad you like it. Want to sit on it?"

He wheeled it out. Allie put one foot on the tailpipe, her opposite knee on the seat, and launched herself onto the bike. She bent forward and wrapped her hands around the handlebars. Gunk glanced at me.

"Matt, I think I see problems ahead."

"You're telling me."

"Do you think she'd like a ride?"

"No, she wouldn't."

"Matt, it's … I'm totally safe with this."

"Gunk, I really don't think …"

"Daddy, please, please. I'll be careful," delivered with the killer grin.

"Just out the parking lot and back around, Matt. It'll be okay."

I stepped back. Gunk lifted Allie off, got on himself. Then, God help me, I lifted her up behind him. She wrapped her arms around his middle like he told her to, and they moved down the parking lot. Slowly.

I pictured the Family Court petition: "He put his ten-year-old daughter on the back of an enormous Harley-Davidson motorcycle and let her ride off holding onto a member of the criminal Bandolero motorcycle gang, who will be standing trial for a federal felony for running drugs."

Gunk sped up a little, but he didn't turn around and come back. He left the parking lot. My stomach clenched, and I didn't breathe. They sped off. Holy Shit! I am fucked!

Farther and farther away they went. Oh my God, a car was coming toward them. No, a goddamn farm tractor pulling a wide, rickety hay trailer, chaff flying in every direction. The tractor and my only daughter were closing at who knows what speed. The trailer was way over into Gunk's lane and swerving. I made myself watch. How could I not? Now Family Court was the farthest thing from my mind. If she'd been sliding into quicksand and I couldn't reach her, I couldn't have been more scared and helpless. What the hell had I been thinking?

I watched the bike clear the tractor and trailer with room to spare. Didn't help. Maybe a mile down—it could have been two hundred—Gunk swung around, and they thundered past me at what looked like sixty miles an hour. I was waving my arms like crazy. Allie's ponytail was flying. Her face was pressed against the back of Gunk's leather jacket. She held on for dear life, and her knees were forward like a pro. They slowed, did another U-turn, and came back.

I was fuming.

Allie was jazzed. Her face was flushed, her eyes watering. She climbed off and ran to me, threw her arms around me, and planted her face against my sternum. She bounced up and down on the balls of her feet and giggled. When she looked up,

I was glaring at Gunk. Bright-eyed Allie standing there kept me from wringing his scrawny neck.

"Daddy, don't be mad. It was my fault. I told him to go faster."

I waited for my heart rate to slow. The plea deal I had in mind for him went out the window.

Gunk read the look on my face, my teeth clenched, and my fists clenching and unclenching.

"Matt, I promise I didn't go past twenty-five."

"Right." I walked to the truck and the other two followed. Allie squeezed in between Gunk and me, and we went to find the scene of the crime. No one spoke. Allie had her earbuds back in place, but she was quiet.

12

The eastern two-thirds of Salish County is mountainous and heavily wooded, a duly designated National Forest. In the flatlands to the west where we were, surveillance of drug traffic and illegal immigration consists of cameras strategically placed, sensors in the ground to pick up footsteps, and cooperative farm owners. There is an almost constant patrol of nearby roads by agents in vehicles. In the United States, it's the Border Patrol, the US Department of Agriculture, the Drug Enforcement Agency, and the Salish County Sheriff. In Canada, the Canadian Border Services Agency and the famed Royal Canadian Mounted Police stand guard, as it says in that country's national anthem. The wary armada on both sides of the invisible line is pretty effective where the sightlines are clear and roadways are conspicuous. Not so where the farmland becomes foothills going east.

We came to a lone two-lane highway that approaches Canada. It veers northeast and into dense forest, and curves within a scant two hundred yards of the border. It's called South Pass Road, which is odd since it's as northernmost as our county gets.

What isn't odd is that contraband interdiction becomes exponentially harder here. Try wandering through an untracked forest at night with a flashlight, trying to see past numerous trees and branches and hanging moss and boulders and cliffs.

The result is that drug trafficking is plentiful, and nabbing miscreants is more often the result of a tip-off, not vigilance.

So it was in the present case. The usual pattern is that a snitch—also called a nark—has gotten himself in trouble and faces charges, so he's offered a deal. In exchange for participating in a bust, he gets a reduced or suspended sentence. Of course, this was well-known to drug dealers; trust among thieves was at a premium. The system was most vulnerable, therefore, in finding volunteers, as it were. The bad guys would recruit, and later so would the enforcers. It was a zero-sum game. One side won, the other lost.

This information was meandering across synapses in my brain and creating a disconnect. The same jerk, my client and a felon, had just scared the shit out of me. He'd recently begun to seem like an okay guy and was already a pal of my only child. Off we were driving to the scene of his crime with him sitting by the passenger door with my daughter next to him. I was confused.

I took a left on a dirt road Gunk pointed out. We left South Pass Road and bumped along for about a half-mile until we got to a clearing about the size of an extra-large backyard. A rock escarpment about twenty feet high rose on one side, a creek burbled along out of sight, and forest was everywhere around. My young special assistant dubbed it a perfect picnic spot, getting out of the truck and pointing to a grassy plot bathed in sunshine. A light breeze overhead slipped through the branches high above, a precursor of frigid nor'easters yet to come. Where we three stood, it was peaceful and quiet.

I love the forests of the Northwest—"lovely, dark and deep," like the poet said—an arborist's dreamscape. Douglas fir and western red cedar are everywhere, along with Sitka spruce and hemlock. The girth of these trees, especially old growth, is amazing, and their height soars out of neck-craning view. Heavy moss (*bryopsida*) wraps around long upswept branches and decaying logs. Here and there a Pacific madrone with long twisting limbs reaches out, broad leaves splayed to capture scarce sunlight. Its peeling, red, papery bark is unmistakable. So dense and plentiful are the woods that visitors from elsewhere in the United States don't understand what the problem is with logging—until they see an entire mountainside scalped by clear-cutting.

Where we stood, pine needles and grass and clumps of mud had been disturbed, messed up as if a herd of deer—or a band of outlaws and cops—had scuffed and skidded and rooted around a lot. Evidence of the foolishness continued in several directions and led away into the trees. Allie identified a burrow of some critter and knelt down to investigate. I asked Gunk to show me the direction his bagman had come from. We followed the remnant of a trail and crossed a ditch no more than three feet across. We were in British Columbia, Canada.

It was a strange sensation to step over an unseen boundary line into another country. It felt illicit somehow. In the days before heightened security, neighbors from two nations hailed one another across backyards and held barbecues and their kids played together, oblivious to sovereignty. No longer. Same forest, same trees, same neighbors, more contraband.

We retraced our steps. I didn't know what I'd find. I didn't expect much, since the DEA folks had searched the area and snarfed up any bits of evidence they found. I was following the advice of a revered professor of mine. "Ladies and gentlemen," he'd said, flicking his tongue around his lips in a reptilian way, his hands clenched and one forefinger jabbing the air, "never, never give advice regarding a real property matter without going out and looking at the ground." Something akin to suggesting that a weatherman take a peek out the window before going on the air.

Gunk and I split up. I bushwhacked and occasionally called to Allie to be sure she was okay. After a bit, I happened to snag a shoelace on a piece of root and bent down to untangle it. There, under a patch of moss, I spotted a round corner of shiny, dark plastic. It was barely visible, like it was almost waiting to be noticed. I nudged it free with the toe of my boot and saw the tiny red dot of a cell phone blinking at me. It'd been tossed away during the bedlam, I assumed. Gunk and Allie were out of sight, so I picked it up gingerly with a large fallen leaf and slid it into in my pocket.

We didn't stay much longer. I signaled the end of the search. Before we got in the car, Gunk pulled me aside.

"Matt, I'm sorry. Back at my place, I didn't know I'd scare you that bad. If she'd been scared, I'd've stopped. I wasn't thinking about you."

"Man, if you only knew ..."

"In fact I do. About kids, I mean. "

He looked away, through the trees into Canada. "Do you know how lucky you are?"

I waited. Gunk turned and leaned against the front fender of the truck. Allie was already inside, refastening her listening apparel.

"You met Sheila."

"Your wife."

"We're not married."

"Who is she?"

"She's my old lady. She's the mother of our son. She came up with the money to pay you."

"I didn't bother to ask her. She must care about you."

"She does, and for our son. Name's Gordon. We paid you out of the child support I send her."

That made me feel just dandy. I couldn't help but glance at Allie fiddling with her snazzy phone.

"Want to tell me more?" I felt like a father confessor.

"Sheila and I have been together a long time. She isn't one

of those righteous biker gals folks like you think of, skanky, loose, tough. She was—she is—a lady."

This was consistent with the woman I'd met, first impression.

"She loves to ride with us—the escape, the being a little wild—and we are good together. I love her hanging on in back, arms around me, wind whipping past."

Not your run-of-the-mill family, but I was moved. I started to say something comforting. He didn't let me.

"When she got pregnant, we went ahead and had the kid, but decided we weren't going to get married. She was afraid it might spoil things. Had to do with her own folks, she said."

"Okay, so why's she up north and not down here?"

"She went up to visit her folks a year ago. Took the boy. He was born in Canada but we hadn't done his paperwork, didn't know we had to register him or something to be a US citizen. So they stopped her when she tried to come back. Refused to let her in; worried that people come down and stay illegally. Now she's afraid to try."

"That can be fixed, Gunk."

"Not what we heard. So, the boy sneaks across."

"My God! How old is he?"

"Eight."

"Jesus Christ!"

"We—he and I—we jump the ditch. Hang out."

"Gunk, I'm very sorry. Let me do this. I'll check into it when this drug thing is over. See what I can do. No charge."

Allie called from the truck, "C'mon you guys. I'm thirsty."

Duly summoned by the voice of authority, we obeyed.

We stopped at a cafe. Allie and I had a Diet Coke and Gunk had a beer. We dropped him back at Florganica and started for home.

"Daddy, I don't think Mommy would have let me ride that motorcycle."

"I think you're right, sweetheart."

Her wheels were turning.

"I think maybe I won't tell her … unless you think I should."

Oh, perfect. Tell my daughter to lie.

"Listen, Allie, sometimes your mom and I …"

"That's okay, Daddy. Sometimes you make her angry, sometimes she makes you angry. I'm ten years old. I'm not, like, totally stupid."

I noticed that Mr. Drive-with-one-hand, elbow-on-the-windowsill had been gripping the wheel with both hands, staring fixedly at the road, and willing myself to keep my mouth shut. Hard for any parent.

"I just won't tell her," she said.

Yeah, kids figure out adults way before we think they do. "Grown up" is a relative term whether you're ten or twenty-one or forty. We came to a stop sign. I reached across and ran my hand along the top of Allie's head and gave her ponytail a tug.

On down the road we went. Allie put both earbuds in, looked at me, then went back to her tunes. Next thing, she was bopping along. We got back to Church Harbor in the middle of the afternoon and I dropped her at Ellen's. There was a birthday party later.

"See ya later," she said, and ran into the house.

"I love you, Daddy," would have been asking too much for a grown-up ten-year-old to say. Even I wasn't, like, that stupid.

13

I was going to meet Dolores Key at the mall. Malls depress me. People with elevator music looping through their brains purposelessly trek through commercial oblivion, wandering a Mobius strip of shops. Worse yet, from the standpoint of a struggling city's downtown core, this monument to vapid marketing was a giant mega-mall anchored by major chain stores, a Starbucks, and franchise jewelers, and featuring tropical planters of fake flora, 'rubbery shrubbery,' indigenous to no place on this planet. Perched outside city limits, big malls have "mauled" many a city's faltering downtown by hijacking the tax base.

Making my way through the recycled air, I dodged mall-walkers wearing garish tennis shoes, striding resolutely, heads up, talking little, puffing. I'd told Dolores to meet me at a small munchery called Cinnamon Corner. There was one table and she was already seated at it. We shook hands. I bought coffee, refilled hers, and sat down.

The composed and turned-out Dolores Key I was used to was a flipside of today's version. She'd obviously been crying.

"Matt, we need your help."

"That's what you said." I admit I sounded a bit snippy. I wasn't trying to be unfriendly, but again, why was she talking to me?

"Luke Barkley is going to ruin us."

She proceeded to flesh out the sordid tale I'd heard part of in Franklin during the legislative session, part of which I'd then shamelessly used to achieve my objective. Their story had been all over the papers for weeks, plus the inferences and rumors which ferment in a small community. I was puzzled that for some reason the prosecuting attorney still hadn't moved on the reports, but I hadn't been paying much attention. Sitting there and listening, with Dolores filling in the details, was like being trapped in someone else's bad dream.

Some of the background I knew. Lucas Barkley, Salish County Sheriff, was the kind of senior lawman any community wanted. Tall in the saddle and intelligent, he was tough on crime but not a wacko. He'd paid his dues in the department, even served a stint in the state senate. But he'd soon tired of making the laws and had gotten himself elected sheriff eight years ago to enforce them instead. He'd gotten re-elected, unopposed.

Luke did have a dark side some knew of and the general public did not. Underneath, he was an angry man. When crossed by someone he couldn't control—an abrasive defense attorney, an erstwhile partner in a gillnetter they fished, and on one occasion a state auditor's staffer—his practiced self-control was a mask behind which lurked fury. The stories of these encounters were passed along by a few folks, then either forgotten or chalked up to a man with a difficult and public job.

According to gossip, Sheriff Luke had been married to a Stepford wife for a few years, but they'd split up. She'd gone back East to wherever home was, and Luke never talked about it. There didn't seem to have been any women in his life since, despite being unattached. In a small county like Salish, that was remarked upon. Odd too, I always felt, was Luke's crassness in private with intimates of which, for some reason, he considered me one. Still.

Dolores paused and sipped her coffee.

I tried to be gentle. "Dolores, Scott was busted for possession of drugs and DUI. He was loaded. He's a judge. What do you expect a sheriff to do?"

She didn't answer. She was going to cry again.

I continued, "Scott's in plenty of trouble, true, but it's a first offense. There are AA meetings and community service, for example. He won't go to jail. Yes, he's got the state judicial commission to reckon with, but ..."

"There's more," Dolores interrupted. "More."

Tell me, I thought, but didn't say.

"Matt, Luke's not recommending deferred prosecution or anything like that. He wants to nail Scott. He's going to use some uncharged offenses from before to put him away."

I chose not to correct her misunderstanding of charging procedures, or explain the statute of limitations. "What offenses?" I asked.

"This wasn't the first time. Scott's been stopped before. This was the third."

"I see." I did. This I knew, also. I hoped I had on my attentive, neutral attorney face. "What happened to the other times he was caught?"

"Scott phoned Luke and was never charged. The calls were to Luke directly, after we got home. We had his personal number."

"Dolores, I'm dense, I know, but I still don't get it. Why doesn't this blow back at Luke, too?" The thought had occurred to me when I was in Franklin and first heard the tale. "You're going to tell me why this is more of a problem, correct?"

I wasn't being cruel. I'd connected the dots down in Franklin, and already knew what was coming. Dolores Key, ordinarily a picture of a dutiful politician's wife and a not-unattractive one, that morning looked like she'd been caught lying to her mom. I handed her a napkin. She blew her nose and took a breath. Dolores closed her eyes.

"Luke and I had an affair."

There it was.

To hear directly from Dolores Key that our upstanding Sheriff Barkley'd had an affair with her of all people still stunned me, even if it was the same information Pepper Martin and another friend, Jack Tulio, had dug up during the session.

Dolores's voice caught in her throat and she didn't look at me. She went on. "Scott and I were having problems. Luke gave me a ride home one of the times. The next day he called and we met at a place out of the county for coffee and then we ..."

I held up my hand to stop her. Now, I didn't want to hear more.

She said, "Matt, I knew what I was doing. He was a port in the storm, which sounds trite, but I was angry. Scott sometimes is so, so ... Anyway, it ended quickly. I ended it, but Luke didn't. He kept on calling, then threatening. He'd say, 'You know, you're still mine.'" Her voice was shaking. "He's not a nice man. He'll ruin us."

The mall Muzak was hurting my ears. The cloying aroma of cinnamon swirled around us. I tried to concentrate. Of course evidence of prior drug or alcohol incidents would be damaging to Scott, but why not also at Luke's expense if it all came out? I asked that question and waited for Dolores to continue. She moved her cup around on its saucer.

"It's probably his ego. It's the two big dogs thing. He's willing to risk his reputation. He was providing solace to a wife of a druggie. He can say I'm in love with him. He can say anything he wants. We all know what people like to believe, and judges make enemies. Either way, there's enough here to keep the papers crazy forever."

"How much does Scott know about all this?"

Dolores said, "All of it. We started to patch things up. We committed to make our marriage work. We were trying to."

I wasn't convinced. And I had another question.

"Um, I have to ask, Dolores. Scott was high on pot as well as drunk. Seems that would be something even Luke Barkley would have trouble deciding to conceal. And was it each time?"

Her eyes avoided mine, but only for a second. She looked back at me. "Why does that matter?"

"Maybe it doesn't. Forget I asked." I went on, "Dolores, I'm very sorry. This is awful for you, but why me? What can I do?"

"Scott trusts you, Matt. You've known each other a long time. You've been out of town and don't have any cases in front of him."

"Where's Scott right now? And why are you talking to me before he does?"

"He's embarrassed. He asked me to meet with you first."

I leaned back, took a breath, and put on my grown-up responsible-attorney voice. "Dolores, I just don't think …" That was as far as I got.

She started sobbing, face hidden in her hands. Her shoulders shook like they wouldn't stop. I could think of nothing to do or say and just sat there blank-faced and clueless, and not quite convinced about her reason to involve me. Or other parts of her story.

I did tell her I'd think it over. She gathered herself. We walked out of the mall, which by now was quieter, except for Kenny G relentlessly reminding us that raindrops keep falling on our heads.

I liked Judge Scott Key. He and I had sparred in court from time to time—he was the judge and it came with the territory—but it never got messy. He was a good-looking man, my age, blond with a mustache, nicely trimmed, graying a bit at the edges that extended beyond the corners of his mouth. Not tall, he looked very judicial in his jet black robe.

Before ascending the bench, Scott Key was a good lawyer,

plaintiff's cases for the most part. He gotten local notoriety when he'd sued a New Age-y mortuary that had come to town, called "Remains To Be Seen," for mistakenly interring the wrong decedent's body before her sobbing next of kin noticed the error. "Almost interring" is a better way to phrase it. If the family had chosen cremation, who would have known? But, a peek into the coffin, requested by the deceased's husband, before it was to be slid off the gurney and lowered into the loamy earth revealed the horrible error. Why the old gentleman hadn't said his personal good-bye back in the viewing room wasn't clear. The coffin had been closed, but still.

Abject sorrow, was the stated reason, but little explanation was needed. Given the likelihood that a jury would have sat open-mouthed, dabbing eyes, and sniffling if it had had to listen to testimony, prompted the insurance company to settle. Which it did after one deposition, for an astonishing sum of money. The irony of the new business's aim to steer people away from cremation, not to mention its name, was no help to the defense. The malefactor's sign was removed one silent night and the owner slipped out of town. Gray's Funeral Home, community stalwart, continued its well-deserved monopoly in Church Harbor to the relief of everyone, including, to be sure, its good-natured proprietor Irwin Gray.

Scott Key was an unsurprising candidate for judge. Endorsed by the local bar association, he won handily. His opponent, a relative newcomer, didn't stand a chance. He'd run too soon. It wasn't his "turn," and Americans don't like people who jump the line.

Judge Key's interesting trademark was the row of frown lines across his forehead, actually two of them. Expressive furrows on his brow oscillated like lines on a seismograph whereby a seasoned attorney could gauge how his argument was faring while His Honor's eyes flicked up, then down to the memorandum in front of him. Frequent habitués of the courtroom suspected that the judge knew exactly what he was doing and enjoyed the reputation.

Scott had served honorably and was considered fair and impartial. That said, the judicial bench is a solitary outpost. A judge had to careful about who his or her friends were. Conversations had to be limited to the everyday, the weather, sports, tulip harvests. Cases and recent developments in the law were off-limits—more so in a small town like ours. One must be wary out in public, display proper demeanor at all times. Therefore, though Scott Key's choice of recreational diversion was a bad one, and the exposure possibly ruinous, it wasn't hard to understand.

On one occasion several years ago, I was surprised when the constraints about privacy were relaxed. Scott and I were riding together to an out-of-town conference. (He even agreed to suffer my truck.) Away from the bench, Scott was buoyant, like a guy selling health club memberships. This day was no exception.

On the way to our destination, we found a restaurant by the water and went out on the deck to eat. The sun on the back of my neck was a warm balm. A breeze from below carried a musk of seaweed and sea critters up and over us. We stared out over the stillness of several thousand miles of open ocean. From where we sat you could see Japan. I traced with my finger a Kiwanis logo on the wooden railing in front of us commemorating the life of "Jim Spano - Fisherman" whose purse seiner was up yonder "working God's herring bed."

Earlier conversations had always been to inquire after family or vacations or discuss safe local news. Then, out of the blue, Scott had said, "Matt, you got any idea what it was like growing up with a name like 'Francis Scott Key'?"

This was a statement not a question. For some reason, he wanted me to hear this.

"Along about fourth grade, we learned the Star-Spangled Banner and the rest, so they say, was history. I didn't mind 'Scott'—it's not bad and a helluva lot better than 'Francis'—but the 'O say can you sees' followed me forever." He did one of those laughs that aren't meant to be funny. Kids are cruel.

He paused as our waitress—Sweet Charity, it said on her nametag—dropped off burgers and refilled our drinks. On the stretch of beach below, a kid flung a tennis ball for a black lab that flew like the wind down the sand and splashed into waves that had been breaking for, well, ever.

"Matt, I don't want this to sound like a sob story, but I'd like to tell you a little about me. Judges are pretty insulated from people in town. Away from there, I feel I can open up a bit."

I ate while he went on.

"My dad is a tulip farmer. Maybe you know that. He was from Frisia in Holland. He left the Old Country and came out here like a lot of the Dutch did, having heard about the bottomland and endless rivers. He changed his name to "Key" because no one could pronounce "Kooy." He started to make money, married my mother, and soon they had me and then my little brother."

I couldn't imagine where this was going.

"I went to college and beyond. My folks were so proud. Then, with no warning, my mom up and left. Kaboom! Found a place in the county and moved out, just like that. My dad never got over it. Completely clobbered him."

I winced and said I was sorry. Scott started in on his burger like he hadn't seen food in a while. He patted his chin with a napkin and went on.

"In my last year of college, I got a call one night from a deputy sheriff. They'd found my dad sitting behind the wheel of his old Chevy, parked on the bridge over Devil's Passage, right in the middle. You know the place."

I did. One of our local wonders. An engineering tour de

force several hundred feet in the air, the scary bridge spans a quarter-mile gap above a wicked tidal flow caused by large pieces of ocean moving between two promontories.

"I raced up and pushed through the gawkers. I slid into Dad's truck from the passenger side, and the only word my sixty-something dad said was 'Helene,' my mom."

Scott continued, said his dad was not a jumper. He hadn't decided that night to free-fall into eternity, but had been thinking about it. He was a stubborn Dutchman with calloused hands who'd found a nice Dutch girl to share his life with, and who'd then left him for no reason he could see. Lots of changes he'd accustomed himself to. Supermarkets sold tulip bulbs in bulk and forced daffodils in December. A barista, whatever that was, sold cups of coffee strong enough to etch steel for a dollar fifty a cup. Young women, including his niece, wore clothes like in the windows of Amsterdam. Everything from frozen dinners to cars with power windows to phones you didn't dial troubled him. He used to unattach and reattach the Velcro on the sleeve of his windbreaker just to watch.

I wiped my forehead and took a sip of diet cola. "Scott," I began. I didn't know what I was going to say next. Sometimes when you're supposed to be listening to someone, you get hijacked by your own thoughts. They race off with you like a getaway car. I was starting to have trouble concentrating but Scott kept talking. It was a sunny day, plus the view.

He must have sensed I was getting squirmy. He said, "Sorry, Matt. I'm almost done. I was getting to me and Dolores."

He cleared his throat and took a swallow of soda. "I followed Dad home from the bridge, fixed us some macaroni and cheese from a box, found the aquavit stashed behind the detergent in the mud room. I poured him a tumbler with ice and put him to bed.

"I called Dolores and proposed over the phone. We'd tried

to hold it together after high school even with her out of state. University of Texas, of all places. She'd gotten interested in another guy, so it ended. It hurt, but I'd been surprised in the first place that she seemed interested in me. I was one of the 'brainy' guys, not a jock. Then one day she was back home and called me.

"Her folks liked me, but the clincher was how she was with mine. She charmed my dad, and she found out my mom liked decorating ceramics. One day she went out to see her with a shopping bag full of goodies she bought at one of those do-it-yourself studios. They spent a whole afternoon painting plates and cups and saucers. After we were married, she bought a kiln. We still have it in her studio at our place."

I spied the waitress and made an elaborate motion looking at my watch. We split the bill and paid up. Back at my truck, Scott Key said, "Oh, and guess who the deputy sheriff was that night who found my dad? None other than the head guy now, Sheriff Luke Barkley."

14

I put Dolores and Scott Key's tales of woe on a back shelf—not my problem, that I could see. Gunk and Mongo, yes. And oh yeah, Allie and Ellen. Possibilities and personalities were smacking around like balls on a pool table. Somewhere in the dim reaches of my mind, some bits of information felt linked together but they flitted away when I tried to look directly at them.

There was one urgent problem to deal with, namely an electronic object that constituted evidence of a crime sitting wrapped in a baggie on a chair in my living room, its little red light still flickering its warning at me. Tampering with evidence, chain of custody rules, duty to disclose—all of them either legal or ethical proscriptions—were time bombs, but I'd decided to fudge a bit. I needed more of a clue what I was dealing with, before I'd turn it over to the police.

I called Yuri and told him I was coming his way. He lived in a converted boathouse on one of our picturesque local lakes. It was far enough away from the owner's main house for privacy, but near enough to enjoy its reflected affluence. Both dwellings were white with green trim, had brick chimneys also white, and distinctive plantings on the grounds. The owners, transplanted Cape Codders to the bone, left Yuri alone in the time-honored way of old New England money.

His unassuming abode was spare—living room, kitchen,

bath, and two bedrooms, one of which doubled as his office. Ellen referred to the decor as "Early IKEA" which meant nothing to me, but I didn't think it was derogatory. There was a long dock stretching out into the lake and a rowboat tied up next to it. A level stretch of beach the size of an oversized ping-pong table completed the scene. Allie loved it. The darkest gray clouds never kept her from throwing down a towel, adjusting her dark glasses, zipping up her parka, and stretching out like it was the Riviera.

On a redwood plank deck was a pair of orange-and-yellow striped canvas beach chairs, a round wooden table between them, and a shiny black pot-belly barbecue for oysters and burgers. Yuri and I adjourned there with coffee. I set the purloined cell phone between us, still blinking in its polyethylene container. I brought him up to date on Gunk's case. Yuri was good at his job and let me finish.

I slid the baggie toward him. He let it sit, elbows on his knees and index fingers pointed like a steeple beneath his chin. We watched a pair of mergansers out on the lake glide along, then submerge and pop up yards away.

I broke the silence. "Do you know what to do with the sim card or whatever it's called?"

"I do, Matt. Private Eye 101. For that matter, Pre-teen 101. Allie has one." He gave me a what-are-friends-for shrug and picked up the baggie. He slipped it into his pocket like a kid shoplifting cigarettes. He said he'd check it out, then turn it over to Detective Mick Malone when he was done.

We finished our coffee, then walked around back. He couldn't help showing off his two-wheeled ride, even though I'd seen it many times. In a sheltered lean-to, the bike was impressive: a shiny, tricked-out Harley-Davidson Sportster, a quarter-ton of midnight blue and chrome splendor that he'd taken as a fee from a wannabe weekend warrior whose wife had put her foot down.

The bike had been lowered and had after-market straight pipes and medium high bars, but was street legal. It had not escaped my thinking that it could turn out to be excellent cover for the case I was now in up to my eyeballs. The bike might not get him invited to the next bad biker round-up, but it could allow him entry past nervous security if he went. At least that was what I was thinking, plus other connections he might have access to.

I man-hugged him, shoulder wedged against his chest, biker style. I thanked him, returned to the truck, and left.

On the way back to town, I decided to take a detour—give myself a break and go for a drive, take some time to think. The enormous, monolithic white mountain in the east of Salish County had beckoned. I swung by home, grabbed my backpack and a day-old sandwich and a soda, and hit the road.

The highway was clear. Plows were still hibernating until winter. The highway twisted and wound for five thousand of the big mountain's ten thousand feet. Native Americans called the peak White Sentinel, and it stood alone, dwarfing ranges below and around it. I found a roadside pull-out I liked and parked the truck next to a cut bank. I zipped up my windbreaker (it was chilly at altitude) and yanked my dorky watchman's cap down over my ears. My backpack was behind the seat and I strapped it on.

Down a curved path was a wooden bridge that crossed the river. Picture-postcard foliage, shrubbery and seedlings and tall trees, wild berry bushes and pastel rhododendrons, crowded the banks upstream and down. The Cascade Range comes by the name honestly: full, frothing rivers race out of the mountains all four seasons of the year. Despite the warm flatlands below that day, there must have been an early freeze; tenacious crystal icicles hung in rows from bridge railings and struts like roof-line Christmas decorations.

On the trail beyond the bridge, away from the roar of the river, the silence was a whisper. My tramping must've flushed a hawk or a raven, but I didn't see it, just heard the sudden, heavy flutter of wings. I got to a clearing near a bluff, swept pine needles off a tree stump, and sat down to eat. The view was magnificent. A half mile away loomed untold tonnages of solid, white, quiet volcano, so close I felt I could reach out and touch it.

I sat and stared. I was glad I was home. I needed more of this. Maybe things would start to heal. The jumble I'd made of my life and the swirls and eddies around me would be manageable. Even the challenging case of a hapless motorcycle jock had a beginning, a middle, and soon an end. I was making too much of this guy Gunk and his Bandoleros. He did the crime, he'd do the time, blah, blah. I'd get him a plea deal, and it'd be over. Simple. Life would go on, and with it a wife and daughter I loved. Ellen and I would work something out. The other stuff—Dolores, Scott, Luke, new law practice, odd clients—was background noise.

Across the hills from me, clouds around the mountain's peak were starting to drop. A breeze picked up; sundown happened sooner and sooner in fall. I hiked back out, drove home, and planned to go to bed early.

After a stab at the crossword puzzle, the difficult one from the weekend, I wasn't sleepy. There were a couple of biker mags that I'd checked out of the library and I sat on the sofa reading. The floor lamp at my side was on low. I was hoping I'd start to yawn.

What were these biker guys about? What was their world? I was getting nowhere. I heard an ominous roll of thunder outside, odd for fall. Maybe it was alerting our corner of the continent to think about hunkering down for winter. Perhaps the clouds in the distance I'd seen up on the mountain meant business. When the nor'easter whistles down our way from the Arctic via Alberta and British Columbia and sneaks in past the neck of the finest parka, residents congratulate their freezing selves that they don't live in, oh, Calgary. Living as far north as our Salish County, and during the months when darkness takes up two-thirds of a twenty-four hour day, one often remembers that the entire nation of Canada is even farther north of the continental US—even Fargo and Minneapolis, of weather-statistic fame. More thunder, a rumble getting closer.

Then the roar wasn't thunder at all. The sound of a Harley-Davidson motorcycle is unmistakable—high compression ratio, V-twin engines, unmuffled straight pipes, and the distinctive "hubbada-hubbada" sound. I pulled a corner of drape back. Two full-on hogs, headlights blazing, slammed into my driveway and skidded to a stop.

I had on pajama bottoms and a ratty sweatshirt, slippers on my feet. I was half out of the sofa when the door burst open and two very large, very ugly bad guys started for me. I managed to stand up when the first guy put a meaty fist into my chest and knocked me back onto the sofa.

"What the fuck!"

"Hello, Matt."

"Fuck hello. Get the hell out of my house!"

"This won't take long. Time for a little conversation."

"The only conversation will be with the cops."

"Don't jump to conclusions, wiseass."

I was shaking like a scared little kid. The guy doing the talking sat down on the coffee table facing me, black chaps, knees apart, his black boots pinning my puny moccasins to the floor. His arms were huge and tattooed. He wore a wine-red bandana on his head and a skin-tight T-shirt under a black, sleeveless leather vest. I hadn't been able to see the patch on his back, and I couldn't see his partner's who wandered around the room, jumpy and distracted.

Visitor Number One had eyes that may have been dilated, they were so dark. They swept the room for a second or two at my meager surroundings and his mouth did something that passed for a grin. He had bad teeth and a droopy mustache. He was a caricature of a bad biker.

"You're quite the interior decorator, Matt."

"Fuck you, and get out."

"The sooner you shut up, the sooner we're gone."

His breath came at me in waves, sour and sickly. The irony occurred to me for a second of life imitating art, what with biker magazines open beside me. Was I hallucinating? No, and I decided to decide this wasn't funny.

"We simply want to make the point, Matt, that it would be better for all concerned for you to quit the Charles Darrow routine and go plead out your pal Gunk like a good boy."

"Charles Darrow?"

"Who the fuck ever. You're wasting a lot of your time. And some of mine. Worse, you're wandering into a swamp where there are very bad alligators."

Goon Number Two hadn't stopped pacing, peering into the kitchen and down the hall, then looking back at Number One and me. His vest and shirt and pants were like his associate's, and I still couldn't see what tribe they belonged to. He had the same stringy hair, and all the way down both arms tattoos, "sleeved out." My breathing was returning to normal. They were just trying to act tough.

"Tell you what," I tried to sound gruffer and sat up straighter, "you take care of the drug business and I'll take care of the law business."

That earned me a whack alongside my head I hadn't seen coming. I snapped back against the cushions. I wasn't hurt or even scared at that point, just crazy enraged.

"Matt, Matt. This *is* the drug business. Are you lame? Do I need to draw you a picture?"

"What do you want?"

"I already told you. Gunk and the boys got nailed dead to rights. What could be simpler than finding him a little home down in the pen in Morton for a stretch, courtesy of the US Government? You're making a federal case out of this, if I can make a little joke."

"I'll think it over. Now get out."

"Thinking is what we don't want, Matt."

The other ape walked over to the mantle and picked up my picture of Allie in a silver frame. His mouth hung open like a trapdoor to the empty attic where his brain should have been.

"Who's this?" he wheezed.

"That's it, motherfucker!" I jumped sideways off the sofa, leaving my moccasins behind, and lunged at the guy. I bulled into his midsection shoulder first and heard a satisfying *oof.* It knocked him back but not far enough. Not far enough for me to dodge his knee as it jerked up into my chin. Down I went. He unfastened a chain hanging from a belt loop in a flash and swung his arm back. I covered my head and face. Goon Number One grabbed him and shoved him away. Black boots next to my face, he growled, "Get up, loser."

Pain and a sliver of common sense kept me on my knees. There's brave and there's stupid. There was a white-hot blaze behind my eyes and a ringing in my ears.

"Matt, listen up. This really isn't that big a deal. We want you to understand we're serious. My pal here gets carried away sometimes. He's a little crazy, as he's the first to admit. Lemme give you a hand."

"Fuck you! Get the fuck out of my house and take that baboon with you," I wheezed. "And don't even *think* of going near that little girl. Don't even think it. Think only what I'm going to do if I ever hear …" I got up.

"I think we understand each other, Matt," said the mouthpiece.

"Did you hear me?"

The futility of this threat was all too evident, but what was I going to say? I lunged for the picture. He tossed it at me.

"Pretty little girl," he said. His partner yanked him back and away before I got to him again. I looked for something to throw or any kind of weapon, but they retreated and slammed the door on the way out. I did see a flash of red and white on his patch. I watched from the window. In the streetlight as they roared away, I might have seen the glint of a red Maltese cross on one of the bikes.

I was into my bedroom and dressed and out the door to the truck while their pipes were fading in the distance, the heavy two-stroke throb. In no time, I skidded to a stop in front of Gunk's place spraying gravel and jerked the hand-brake. After repeated thuds on his door, I saw a light come on inside. Then another one in the main shop. He opened the door. He'd been asleep.

I shoved him back with all the force my pent-up anger could muster and smashed him in the face. I hadn't cooled down a bit on my way out. He ricocheted back against the cupboard with the flower pots on it and slid to the floor. Crockery, trowels, and other clutter scattered around him along with an expensive ceramic vase that smashed into smithereens, its lid spinning around and around before settling to the floor.

I didn't hit him again. He was smaller than me and I'd hurt him. A trickle of blood dotted the corner of his mouth and he touched it with his finger.

I slowed down. The catharsis had helped.

"Who were they?"

"Who were who?" Gunk lisped.

I slid a chair over in front of him and straddled it backward. Gunk sat up and leaned against the cupboard.

"What two of your fuckwad amigos came over to my house tonight, broke in, and knocked me around?"

"Matt, I can't imagine…"

"Well, start imagining. They threatened me and brought Allie into it."

"Jesus!"

"Get up. I won't hit you again."

Gunk pulled himself up, found a stool, and sat on it. I got a paper towel from over the sink, wetted it, and handed it to him.

"Here."

I couldn't get my head around to thinking this not very big, not very threatening, nice-seeming guy was capable of the violence I'd been subjected to. Or any violence, for that matter.

"I promise, I swear to you it wasn't one of our guys. That's not what Bandoleros do these days."

This made no sense. If my attackers were for certain bad-ass bikers from B.C., what did they care what these Bandoleros did, pale semblances of their former selves?

"Let's start here, Gunk. How many guys in your troop?"

"On a good day, maybe a couple dozen."

"Twenty-four." I put that into a frame of reference. "As in, about a football squad, offense and defense."

"On a good day."

"What's a 'good day'?"

"Oh, like last spring we went down to Shuksan County for the tulip festival."

"Chaps, vests, headscarves, loud hogs, two abreast, passing scared motorists, messing up the parking lot full of SUVs and hybrids . . . to wander through the tulips."

"They've got great barbecue."

Gunk got up and went into the back room. He came back with two 7Ups and cracked them open. I took a swallow, thought about Allie, and went outside and threw up. It was colder out than before. When I went back in, Gunk looked at me with the sympathy of a well-meaning pastor. I took another swallow and sat down again.

We stared at each other. Gunk dabbed at his mouth.

"Gunk, I'm sorry I hit you."

"Don't blame you. What did they want?"

"For me to plead you out, send you off to do prison time, and back off trying to figure out who set you up."

"Set me up?"

"Gunk, how does it happen that your small band of desperados, out for a good time and scoring enough pot to last a month, gets crosswise with some genuine felons? And how'd the DEA get wind of it? You have to have asked yourself that."

I waited for him to answer.

"I have."

"Is there someone besides the four associates they caught with you who could have been leaned on? Have you wondered why Mongo just happened to not be there?"

Gunk nodded with each question.

"Does that mean you have an idea?"

"No."

"Well try like hell to think of one. Now go back to sleep."

"Are you gonna be okay?"

"Yeah, but I'm buying a gun. And escorting Allie to and from school for as long as it takes."

Gun? Wait, perhaps I didn't need one of my own. I had a good buddy who carried legally. Which made me remember, driving back, that my intruders hadn't said anything about a cell phone.

Back home, I was shaking so badly I had to hold the door key in both hands to let myself in. I turned on all the lights and sat in the kitchen for a long time. There was no alcohol around, which was a good thing.

I drank water and applied a cold washcloth to my

jaw, all the time trying to decide what to do next. Allie was my first priority of course. I needed to let Ellen know what was going on. That would be no picnic. Allie's school, too, needed a sanitized explanation. I was at a loss to imagine what form those conversations would take.

Despite a long shower, I was still awake at four. I did get to sleep; not before, however, writing two names on my bedside notepad to slow the spinning of my brain: Yuri Brodsky and Detective Mick Malone, Church Harbor Police Department.

Part Two

City Haul

Earlier that year

15

The story of my legislative misadventure in Franklin, the state capital, could be seen as a Creation myth—apple, snake, Eve, et cetera. But I could also trace the beginning to another sort of garden the previous year; to the impossibly green rolling fairways of Salish County's finest golf course.

Emerald lawn stretched away in a rolling valley between rows of aged trees and on toward immaculately groomed flat grass—manicured greens surrounding eighteen consecutively numbered flags on thin poles. Another myth was my ability to play the game of golf. In the venerable Greek tradition of hubris laid low, I persisted despite inevitable, Sisyphean results.

Our foursome stood on the fifth tee, a par three, and consisted of Yuri Brodsky, my attorney friend Jack "Hand Me Your Wallet" Tulio, and Everett Riley, former city councilman. These days, Ev was Church Harbor's mayor, having been appointed to that lofty position by his peers. Ev's predecessor had quit suddenly. The chap raised dairy cows out in the county, and the best story making the rounds about his recent ignominy had to do with his skill at animal husbandry—until they caught him at it one night. Old joke, and probably not true. He let the rumor mill run with it because, as I and others suspected, it covered up a far more ominous truth that had to do with a sealed indictment a grand jury had handed up.

My three buddies were taking practice swings, all

professional-like: Jack, svelte and trim and wiry; Yuri, almost my height and sculpted; and Ev Riley, a bit on the pudgy side, with tufts of red hair escaping the sides of his golf cap. Dress him up and ditch the hat and he'd look positively mayoral.

We waited for the threesome ahead of us to move along, three old guys slow as molasses. "Slow play," the bane of all golf courses. What did they think this was, the US Open? It was late summer, still fragrant with Douglas fir and pine, rhodies in bloom like on a postcard. I sat in the golf cart reflecting on the Meaning of Life, which—again, despite my best efforts—continued to elude me.

"We're up. Finally!" yelled Jack Tulio, interrupting my profundities.

Far and away the best in our group, Jack sent a tall arcing drive straight and true. It soared two hundred yards up and away in the azure sky before looping down for another fifty yards and rolling even farther. I loved watching Jack play. Duffers were commonplace; Jack made me feel good.

Yuri was next. All-around good athlete, his drive likewise split the fairway almost as long as Jack's.

Up stood "Mayor Riley" as we now delighted in calling him. He was the one in our group who might make me look good. Sure enough, he topped it and the ball skidded and rolled about fifty yards sending up a rooster tail of spray through the dewy grass that spouted a tiny rainbow in the sunlight. Ev buried the head of his club in the soft sod of the tee box and mouthed an expletive having to do with an obscene act with a close personal relative.

My turn. I teed up a Top-Flite X-Out that wasn't too scuffed; good golf balls stayed home, awaiting the day I'd play in a tournament. The miscellany rattling around in my golf bag were remnants of someone else's bad luck and saved me a fortune in new golf balls. No stand of nettles too thick, no viny copse too thorny, no precarious wet slope by a rushing stream ever hampered my search for white, round, dimpled treasures.

I surveyed the fairway like a pro, hand shielding my eyes, and took a couple of practice swings. I approached. I waggled my club. My drive sailed away the usual one hundred eighty yards, and this time safely down the green expanse.

The newly anointed mayor and I climbed into the golf cart, and I motored us down the asphalt path while he wiped mud from his driver with a blue and white cloth that said "St. Andrews."

His second shot was respectable. I walked to my ball and hit. While we waited for the other two, Everett turned to me.

"How's the practice?"

"I don't get to the driving range much. Maybe you noticed."

"I don't mean golf, I mean the legal biz."

I could have bluffed or dodged with the usual "fine, why?" but I decided to give him the honest answer. Business was okay. I was paying the rent and could afford a legal secretary. My law practice hadn't reached the comfortable point of a steady flow of dollars into the bank account. But landlord-tenant, adoptions, an incorporation or two, and naturally divorces kept us afloat—the usual fare of a run-of-the-mill attorney. There was a lot of competition in town even though I was a native. Wife Ellen's job at the graphic design shop was dependable.

I gave Everett the abridged version, then asked "Why?"

"Ever think of being a lobbyist? I think the city could use one."

I didn't answer right away. We watched our cohorts hit, then I punched the accelerator. Ev Riley knew I knew something about lobbying. I'd dabbled in government and politics before, in fact had worked on Ev's campaign for city council. Despite merely okay grades at the university, I'd landed an internship for a summer with the local congressman in Washington, DC, and liked the work. My stint in DC led the next summer to having an actual paying job in Franklin as an administrative assistant to a legislator I'd met in DC who'd gotten elected to state office. I admired the people who put themselves out there to run for office in the face of typical armchair negative opinions and op-eds. Did egos abound? Of course. It takes a thick skin to deflect the slings and arrows launched by one's opponent, also those by one's own partisans, including disappointed single-issue voters. No way I could do it, but I believed in the process.

"Tell me more, Ev." I tried to sound nonchalant, just making conversation playing golf.

"We're one town out of many in the state, Matt. The bigger fish gobble up most of the goodies the state passes out. We get leftovers, scraps at best. We need a presence. If you're not at the table," he continued the old saw, "you're not at the table."

Lobbying, as a full-time job as suggested by Mayor Riley, would mean living one hundred and fifty miles to the south and spending several months away from Ellen and almost ten-year-old Allie. I balanced that against the picture in my mind of a check signed by Everett Riley arriving like clockwork in the mail every month. Also, medical insurance, out-of-town apartment, and per diem to cover meals, phone and miscellaneous other accoutrements.

"Let me think it over, Ev. Discuss it with Ellen, of course."

Hizzoner landed his third shot a foot from the hole and carded a four. Yuri and Tulio had putted out for threes. I ended up with a six, courtesy of the jumble in my brain and a sand trap. Yuri commiserated, blaming it on the gawdawful shirt I was wearing. This confused me. Didn't all golfers look like they got dressed in the dark?

On the next hole, the three old guys ahead of us were standing midfairway one hundred and fifty yards or so ahead. There seemed to be some disagreement, something very important like whose turn it was to hit, until one of the geriatrics bent down, picked up a ball, and heaved it into the trees. He climbed into his cart and motored away, up the path and out of sight. We would have applauded, but after all this was golf, the polite sport. The good news was that play was speedier thereafter and we wouldn't be held up again.

Back at the clubhouse, we settled up—meaning Jack would treat himself to a fine dinner out. Yuri and I drove back to town. I tried to be casual and mentioned Everett Riley's offer. Yuri wasn't fooled. Neither was Ellen when I got home.

"Maybe your ego could use the boost, honey. The one and only Matt Archer carrying Church Harbor's water in the state capital, hobnobbing with all those elected officials, laurel wreath when you hit a home run." I ignored the mixed metaphor. Ellen added, "It wouldn't hurt our bank account either."

So the decision was mutual and came to pass that I took a detour from law practice. I sent the few open cases I had to a colleague, printed up new cards, found an apartment in Franklin a couple of blocks from the Capitol campus, and moved there shortly after the beginning of the legislative session. Two years, that's all, I'd told the mayor.

Turned out it was one. Turned out one was plenty.

16

My new employer, Mayor Ev, gave me one assignment, period: find a way to wrestle a bundle of cash out of the state budget to renovate Church Harbor's iconic Pine Street Theatre; perhaps even more to make improvements to adjacent sidewalks, streetlights, bollards, concrete planters—the full-on, downtown-amenities treatment. The city's role in the development would fit hand-in-glove, not at all by coincidence, with a wealthy entrepreneur's plans to overhaul a building he owned across the street, where he'd lease out condos, boutiques, and a rooftop restaurant. That the developer had contributed major dollars to get Riley a seat on the city council in the first place was no secret, but "downtown renaissance" would play well in campaign ads when re-election time came around.

There was a hitch, however. State law did not allow a town to use citizens' tax dollars, the money that replenished the state budget, to assist private sector ventures. Rather than spend time debating that issue with the State Auditor and her clever attorneys, I had in mind a safer solution. A creature of statute called a Public Facility District allowed public and private dollars to commingle in certain specified circumstances. As the law stood, those circumstances did not include work on theatres (regardless of how spelled) even ones on the National Historic Register.

Laws can be amended, however. That's what legislatures do—legislatures with a committee chaired by Church Harbor's very own Senator Deanna Mackenzie. So I headed off to Franklin, good-guy white hat firmly on my head, and drafted up a teensy little amendment for Senator Mackenzie's sponsorship that would do the trick: "… funds for improvements to a building or other structure *which has been listed on a National registry of historic places.*" Brilliant! Thomas Jefferson stand aside. Rookie or not, what could go wrong?

Deanna liked the idea and only had to wait for a propitious moment to move to amend the appropriations bill—the mammoth legislation that funded every state agency and also distributed money to counties and cities and transit districts and ports and legislators' pet projects statewide. I tried to be patient as time moved along, but my carefully crafted literary brilliance languished in limbo as we neared the end of the session. I got nervous. Larger issues occupied lawmakers' time and the end-of-session clock was ticking away. Not long, and everyone'd go home—me with my tail between my legs, the main chance lost.

I was leery of badgering Deanna Mackenzie, however. Not that I didn't enjoy her company. The two of us went back a long way. I was four years behind her in high school. As a senior and a cheerleader, she cemented her image, indelibly and unforgettably, on the retinas and libidos of all of us—lately pubescent, sitting in the wooden stands, transfixed. We'd jab each other in the ribs like the dorky teenage boys we were and watch Deanna's shoulder-length blonde hair bounce, her face eager with hometown pride and exertion, pompoms dancing in the air. What a stage! Blinding lights on tall stanchions, the green-and-white-striped field, goalposts dim in the shadows—Friday nights at their most vivid. Exuberant parents on the verge of nervous breakdowns yelled at volunteer refs. The pep band whose acquaintance with even The Star Spangled Banner was tenuous, struggled along, the tune recognizable because the tuba player's first four bars drowned out everyone else.

Deanna Mackenzie was pretty as a prom princess, one of which she became. Passing her in the hall walking to class, I'd try not to stare at her electric blue eyes. I spent troubled nights imagining her parking somewhere with her obnoxious football hero boyfriend—the quarterback, of course, whose voice had changed and who already shaved at least twice a week. My friend, wide receiver Rick "The Rabbit" Abbott (a freshman!) who ran like the wind, carried the ball, and caught passes and routinely got hit, told me that his damage-averse quarterback's room-temperature IQ made him often forget the count at the line of scrimmage. We'd sigh after the game and watch Goddess Deanna flounce away into the night in her short, pleated skirt, hand-in-hand with the jerk.

I didn't know what happened with Deanna and the boyfriend, but several years later she was standing on my front porch and selling real estate. Ellen and I were renting and were shopping for a house. Deanna said she remembered me, but was being polite because she couldn't have. By my senior year, long after she'd graduated, I was no longer a skinny freshman. I was over six feet and had gained enough poundage to anchor the end of an offensive line and catch a pass or two. Deanna was unchanged and pretty as the old days. I gave her our landlord's name and invited her in to look around. She didn't stay long, but left me her card and sent us a sheet of listings.

Ellen and I bought a house through a different realtor, but Deanna and I bumped into each other again. At the Bayside Coffee Shoppe and Patisserie, a regular haunt of mine, I offered to buy and we ordered. She asked for a "double-short non-fat, decaf latté with a pump of almond, no foam, leave room."

"Now, how's he write all that on the cup?" Flush with an uptick in my lawyering business, opening my own office, suit and tie, I was feeling cocky. The barista scribbled on a cup, tossed it away, and started on new one.

"At these prices, I'll order what I like."

"I think they raised their prices."

"Must be after they added a 'p' and 'e' after 'shop' and then 'Patisserie.'"

For six dollars and fifty cents, I'd put up with snarky. We sat down and exchanged the usual background information. No marriage for her, never the right guy. She was too independent, she explained. I remembered some of her backstory. The folks she called mom and dad were in fact an aunt and uncle. "Mackenzie" was their name. There was nothing sordid about it, just a sad story: her real dad had abandoned the family when she was very young and her mom died sometime later. Tragic as such circumstances would be, Deanna was lovingly cared-for and was gregarious and happy as far as anyone could tell. Being pretty didn't hurt. She even took on law school, passed the bar, but decided it wasn't for her after giving practice a try in a small firm.

I told her about me—Ellen and I, and how we met, and Allie. We caught up on people we might have known. I asked her how selling real estate was going, and learned why the snide comment earlier when we ordered drinks. Her otherwise assured face lost its glow.

"I'm sick of selling real estate."

"Tough, huh?"

"The whole deal. Evenings and weekends shot to hell. So's the market. Matt, you have no idea what's inside some people's houses. Or what they smell like."

This wasn't a subject I'd given much thought to. Any, actually.

"Deanna, I'm enjoying my afternoon mocha." I gave it a noisy slurp. "Jeez, what you must have thought about the place Ellen and I had."

She laughed, "I remember driving away and wondering if you even owned a lawn mower. I won't mention the travel trailer in the side yard."

"It was the landlord's. And I won't mention the get-up the real estate company had you wearing." Today, she was in civvies—a white blouse, navy slacks, and a maroon cardigan sweater. Her next comment made me think maybe we hadn't run into each other by accident.

"Matt, you told me once you were interested in politics."

"As an observer, yes. Why?"

"I'm thinking of running for office. The state senate."

That was a surprise, indeed. I'd paid enough attention to know that there was an open seat—the incumbent had had enough, he said—but impulsive career changes, even without jumping into the political campaign arena, were fraught and too often a mistake.

"It's a rough gig, Deanna."

"I get that, Mr. Archer, but I'm not kidding." Her attitude was back. The word "ballsy" crossed my mind.

But I said, "Yes, Ms. Mackenzie, you'd be a natural. Smart and energetic, and you're good with people." I did not remark upon the "voter appeal" of the photo on the campaign flyers. Her hair was shorter but still shoulder-length, professional, I thought, and she did, indeed, clean up good.

She pulled a yellow pad out of her briefcase and smiled, ballpoint poised. I filled her in with my experience albeit from the sidelines, which was more information than she had. We talked for over an hour. She convinced me she might just pull it off.

She gave notice at her real estate firm, and I enlisted a campaign manager for her, a twenty-two-year-old law student who'd done some research for me. He'd majored in political science and had been class president in high school. We both knew that the young man had never run a campaign, but he was a quick study and up to the task, it turned out. Deanna's opponent got into the race too late, and she won going away. She got re-elected in a walk, and now, midway into her second term, she'd snagged a committee chairmanship. Just in time for my sortie to Franklin.

The legislative session had a time limit, per the State Constitution, for a reason. The idea was that citizen legislators, not full-timers, would spend much of the year back home in touch with the Real World. When not in session, they'd have real jobs. The idea harkened back to the time of the Roman leader Cincinnatus, a historic model of civic virtue who twice "returned to his plow" after serving a term slaughtering enemy tribes.

For the most part, the concept worked. Legislators kept their noses to the grindstone and stayed out of trouble. Visibility and perception, of the good kind, are an elected person's stock in trade. Avoiding unsought publicity is axiomatic. But a paradox is that the capitol compound ran on gossip like an alcoholic runs on booze. Long months away from home, powerful and attractive men and women, egos on full display, duplicity perceived as a necessary virtue, winning at all cost, midlife crises—all were powerful reasons to rationalize that "what happens in Franklin, stays in Franklin." The most trouble I got into was over-time parking tickets. Daily, I'd dislodge rumpled yellow envelopes, one atop the other, from under my windshield wipers.

I found the day-to-day work of a lobbyist to be a curious mix: tour guide, chaperone, lunchroom monitor, designated driver, entertainer, seer, and public speaking coach. I arranged lunches and dinners and trips to ballgames. Wayward city council members tried to stray onto the Senate floor when they visited. I found Mayor Ev a shop to repair torn slacks, introduced Mrs. Everett Riley to a Northwest art exhibit, and more than once persuaded a woozy legislator to let me drive him home.

Most of the hours of a day were mind-numbing. Legislative hearings, not liquored receptions aboard expensive yachts, occupied my time. I was a Good Guy, working for a local government, not someone working for evil corporations. More than that, when I stopped long enough to think about it, I could get a little misty-eyed. Winston Churchill famously said something like democracy being the worst form of government there is, except when compared to everything else. I should add that for a political junkie like me it beat practicing law.

Things got tense in Franklin, too. "All politics is local," said the late US House Speaker Tip O'Neill, and his famous *bon mot* was unquestionably true. Why? Because lawmakers quavered like bad sopranos whenever an angry citizen of importance came to town in person to harangue and chastise deviation from The True Way. Legislators do a lot of throat-clearing when face-to-face with local stakeholders, i.e., voters. Labor unions, business groups, Native American tribes, environmentalists, farmers, nurses, teachers, state employees, cops, firefighters, colleges—each professed to be The Public.

So, why lobbyists? one might ask. Because, if they didn't exist, you'd invent them. The average citizen has a job at home, working, earning a living, and can't take the time to travel to the seat of government and plead his or her case. Lobbyists do the necessary educational footwork and advocate for their clients. A cardinal rule, however: Do not to cross the line into misrepresentation. Memories are long.

17

Days passed. The weeks went by uneventfully. I went to meetings and attended hearings on everything from Tribal fishing rights to shoreline protection, or local taxes, always a hot button issue. I sometimes had trouble staying awake. Nonetheless, I introduced myself everywhere, continued to work my way up the learning curve, and figured out who to trust and who was blather. I spread Church Harbor's historic theater gospel to any who would listen. I carried paper around and drank a lot of coffee. I was confident that the fix my city needed was securely in the back pocket of my favorite legislator, even if larger issues occupied lawmakers' time.

It was not all drudgery, though. As the session ground along, there came a pleasant diversion. I snagged Deanna Mackenzie as she came out of a hearing.

"Say, this may seem sudden, Madam Senator. The Governor's Ball is coming up. Do you have a companion?"

"A date, you mean?" She pretended to frown.

"Well, yeah. Someone who would walk in beside the one and only you and try to look like he belonged."

"Matt?"

"What?"

"You're lobbying me."

"Oh."

"You don't have to, I don't, and I'd love to."

Every four years, the newly elected or re-elected governor threw a bash—come one, come all, public invited. Deanna and I met at the door and presented our invitations. An array of enclosed tents surrounded the impressive, domed capitol building. Inside, the massive rotunda echoed with loud conversation and music. Down the halls and out under the tents, there were bands, solo instrumentalists, and groups of singers. Table after table was covered with food with lines five or six deep waiting for more oysters than a person could eat. The state's signature wines flowed.

It was declared to be "formal" but was tailored, as it were, to the casual boutique and haberdashery unique to the Northwest. Tuxes and gowns, of course, but also here or there was a down vest over a shirt and tie for him, a standard little black dress for her.

Deanna was a knock-out. She wore a black satin blouse with ruffles down the front under a waist-length open blazer. She had on expensive slacks and heels. Gold earrings, long dangly things, sparkled through her hair. In an ordinary dark suit, I looked like the guy they hired to escort a beauty pageant contestant. At least I had on a clean tie.

We passed into the building and Deanna handed her jacket to the attendant in the foyer. Without giving it a thought, I rested my hand on her waist as a courtesy to allow her to precede me into the hall. Zowie! Completely out of the blue, the feel of her skin under her thin blouse ran up my arm like an electric jolt. I disengaged rapidly, my head sort of buzzing at the unfamiliar sensation. We separated and Deanna headed off through the crowd to greet guests and fellow legislators. I bee-lined for the food, tucked into some canapés featuring native steelhead, and noticed that my hand was shaking. A Diet Coke helped somewhat, bubbles stinging my throat.

There were formalities to be observed, of course. The governor gave a little welcome from an impromptu podium as did the leaders of the House and the Senate. The audience, all too familiar with this folderol, was polite but unimpressed— casually attentive at best. Here and there, I did see a mom or dad holding a child's hand and paying attention; or a pair of teenagers, rapt as much by the celebrity as by the admittedly awesome ambience.

Later, dancing took place in a large canopied area that made for a ballroom. This was the Governor's Ball, after all. Deanna showed back up and took my hand. The Governor and her husband, like a bride and groom, led off … to Bruce Springsteen!

This tested my formidable negotiating skills. I had danced once before, at a very dangerous party in college and again at my wedding. Dancing to rock-and-roll? Deanna dragged me onto the crowded floor.

"Matt, you look like a priest in a brothel." The woman was observant.

"You definitely want to do this, huh?"

"Yes, and so do you."

After no more than thirty seconds of my attempt at hip, slick, and cool, Deanna said, "Okay. Do this."

She shifted back and forth from one foot to the other, shoulders sort of rocking along. I did as she asked.

"What do I do with my arms?"

"For now, bend them out in front of you and move them back and forth along with your shoulders. Can you snap your fingers?"

"Oh, shit."

"I'll take that as a yes. Now look me in the eyes and imagine that no one in here is remotely interested in you. Which happens to be the case."

That was good advice and it was bad advice. She was right. No one would be paying attention to me. So I kept right on staring since it was permitted under the circumstances. Body contact, even casual, I told myself, not a good idea. Besides, the choice of music ruled that out. Above all there was a hard and fast rule: Lobbyists do not mess around with legislators. The risks were well known, manifold, and the material for many a cocktail party conversation.

We didn't stay long. Back in the Capitol building, we dazzled a few of our mutual associates, retrieved Deanna's jacket, and left. It had started to drizzle, so Mr. Gentleman draped his coat over her shoulders. We walked the few blocks to her apartment building. We did the quick peck on the cheek thing and I walked back to my place in the rain. I dismissed any unchaste impulses I might have had. Flickering teenage memories, banished. No apologies did I make to myself for being an unreconstructed heterosexual male. Attractive women can be admired without possessing them, like a pretty flower, a Vermeer, or a new set of golf clubs.

Nor did I give a second's thought to a photographer at the Ball who had been posing folks. Or that I'd taken Deanna's arm and blithely stepped in line whereupon the guy took two: the first, a standard couple, demure, her arm in mine, saying "cheese." In the second, she mugged by leaning against me, body against my arm and gazing up adoringly. Her fingers were interlocked on my shoulder and a pretty, bare arm pointed at the camera.

The calendar over the desk at my apartment the next morning gave me a jolt. Had I lost a week somewhere? Fewer than five days left in the session! The end was approaching like a tsunami storm surge. When it hit the shore, it could submerge and drown my penny-ante attempt at law-making if something didn't happen soon. My anxiety level shot up, eclipsing the naiveté that had sustained me the first months. Despite the warm and fuzzy evening before, I took myself over to the Capitol with Senator Deanna much on my mind—for professional reasons.

The Capitol building itself was and is an impressive, spacious place. Built in the 1920s when public works of such scale were still possible, it rises out of a classic Georgian pediment to a dome many stories high. Inside, solid granite walls are polished to a shine with heavy oaken doors set in them. Marble pillars vault upward in the style of the US Capitol. Several tons of chandelier hang down from the apex suspended by strong chains and spread like an inverted hydrangea bloom thirty or so feet above the floor.

The place was swarming with lobbyists, several hundred of them busy in the muffled thunder of democracy in action, jazzed by the adrenal fix that happens when the finish line is in sight. They jabbered loudly to one another or quietly into cupped hands around cell phones in order to be heard, plus doing plenty of nervous standing around.

The vast, open interior creates an acoustic like the inside of a giant conch shell. In the closing weeks of a legislative session, this is how the *res publica* was conducted—not too much of a stretch from the pandemonium of the Greek *agora* where the democracy thing all started. It's a clumsy, noisy, and messy process. A teacher trailing a passel of elementary school students squeezed past me and wove through a gaggle of my compatriots. "Boys and girls," she said as they craned their necks. "Those pillars are fifty feet tall, and the chandelier hanging up there is the size of a Volkswagen bug." Gasps, and they moved on.

At the door that led into the Senate Chamber, I sent in a note and waited for Deanna. I could hear the pandemonium inside. Talented Senator Mackenzie was regularly called upon by her party's leadership to honcho floor debate on tough bills. They could've sold tickets to sit in the Senate gallery some afternoons and watch her launch opponents' lame attempts at debate over the straightaway center field fence. She was that good.

She came out and pulled me out of earshot of the rabble. She was enervated.

I stepped back. "You look feisty."

"*You* look terrible. Did you sleep in those clothes?"

"You're in there, inside the *sanctum sanctorum*. It's air-conditioned, and you're hobnobbing with forty-some fellow wizards. Meanwhile, I'm out here in the mosh pit and can't hear myself think."

"And you love every minute."

"I'd love it more if you told me they're about to move our little bit of legislation any time soon." I was whining, I knew. "I feel like one of those primeval mammals dodging brontosaurus feet. You know the saying. It takes a hundred reasons to pass a bill; it takes one to kill it."

"Stop, Matt. I'm about to cry."

"I don't hear that as reassurance."

"Don't worry, dear boy. I have an idea."

I leaned closer.

"Let's go for a hike."

"What? "

She told me that House and Senate leadership, with a kick in the backside from an impatient Governor, had given everyone the rest of the day off so higher-ups could huddle and try to get things moving before the closing bell. Deciding I had little choice, I shrugged and said I'd meet her at her place. I left and bought sandwiches and a couple of cold sodas. She picked me up. I put my daypack in the backseat next to her painting gear, and we set off for the trail to the summit of Jacks Peak, a landmark outside of Franklin.

18

This was my first ride in Deanna's sleek Jaguar, polished and gleaming like expensive jade. Spoke wheels glistened. A fine specimen indeed, not new; the only indication of its age was the faint craquelure in the *café au lait* upholstery. The steering wheel and gear shift knob were shiny and brown as autumn chestnuts, as was a decorative wood-grain trim along the dashboard over the vintage radio to the glove box. The engine purred like a contented feline.

Top down, Deanna was radiant, her hair streaming behind her and face flushed by the wind. My confident chauffeur, in maroon leather driving gloves, floored it on straightaways and took the corners like a grand prix pro. More than once she caught me holding on and mashing a nonexistent brake pedal. Sure, she was showing off, but why not? I was the guy who'd helped to launch her up the ladder into income security out of her days flogging fixer-uppers and duplexes in our then-depressed real estate market.

She might also have been commenting on my own aging pickup truck—faded blue (painted by the previous owner), dented fenders (two), timeworn dashboard, dinged front window, lumpy seats (premier scuffed Naugahyde), and roll-down windows with black handle knobs that hung on by sheer will. (Allie'd forget herself and look for a button to push, like in her mom's car, then flash me an annoyed look and begin cranking.) My beloved beater had been an impulse buy from a fellow down the street who did informal automotive work curbside. Despite having rolled off the Ford assembly line two decades earlier, it hadn't failed me yet. It had seatbelts, and the mileage was respectable. The turn signals worked as did the heater. The price I gave the dude still embarrasses me. What Deanna had paid for her luxurious ride was none of my business.

To get to the trailhead, we followed the Pinchot River, home to more bald eagles per acre than any place outside of Alaska. The Pinchot Valley had remained pristine. A hard fight in the '70s had blocked a proposed nuclear power plant on the river, one of six facilities of the ill-fated Western Public Power Supply System ("Whoops" as it came to be known). Now, dammed farther upriver and technically not "wild," the Pinchot teems with rafters, anglers, birders, hikers, and campers who consider it theirs.

From the state highway, we wound our way up a Forest Service road and through switchbacks to 4,300 feet. We parked among a dozen cars baking in the late morning sun and closed up the ragtop. The summit was still a mile and a half away, another 1,200 feet above us. We shrugged off an array of early spring insects on a strenuous climb. Patches of valerian surrounded us, white on slender stalks, along with just-blooming paintbrush and budding thistles here and there. We hiked past pink phlox leaking out of cracks in ice-age granite. Now and then a solitary red columbine leaned up from a ridge and nodded in the breeze, framed against the gaping backdrop of peaks of the Cascade Range far in the distance.

At the summit, we stood together near a cairn of stones and stared. The feeling of space—open, silent, unhurried and timeless space—was palpable and humbling. The pretty senator pulled off her baseball cap, turned it around, arranged her hair under it, and collapsed back against her daypack. She was relaxed and content. Ambling along the trail behind her reawakened synapses from the night before; neurons carefully sequestered over long, frustrating months felt like they were given permission to at least sit up and take note. But no, the rule was The Rule. Not to mention The Marriage!

Deanna rummaged in her pack for her supplies, set up shop, and went to work. Turned out she was a good watercolorist. She held her paintbrush at arm's length, thumb on the ferrule, and closed one eye in the clichéd way of artists.

"It works, you know," she observed.

I moved and stood behind her watching her sketch.

"So I've heard. I don't understand why, any more than that thing golfers do when they hold the putter in front of them and squint at the hole."

"Sweet boy, I'm not speaking of the paintbrush. I was talking about, um, 'influencing legislation.' You know. The outfits? Feminine wiles?"

An interesting conversation starter. A reply eluded me.

"That slime bag Hooker, for instance." She meant a fellow senator. "For all that down-home rectitude, he can't talk to me without starting to drool. So I get a teensy bit closer and stand up a teensy bit straighter, like this."

Remaining seated, she mimicked the effect. In her T-shirt and shorts, it was an effect all right, how much for my benefit I hadn't a clue. I moved away and sat back down. Why was she vouchsafing this intelligence to me? I told myself again where the boundaries were and moved to safer ground.

"Seriously, why do you hold the paintbrush out like that? Other than to look good."

"Matt, did you ever take geometry? Does the word 'perspective' ring a bell?"

"Yes, I took geometry. After the final, the teacher called my mother at home. Told her she'd pass me instead of flunking me if I'd promise never to take a course from her again."

Deanna ignored me, resettled her hat on her head, and flashed her gaze back and forth between the distant Cascade Range and her 140# Aquarelle paper. She was back to work. I fixed lunch, then was content to lie back with arms under my head and watch for eagles or hawks. I dozed.

The afternoon sun took its toll, so we packed up and hiked back down to the car. We parked in Deanna's reserved space near her office at the Capitol. She invited me in. She directed me to a cupboard, and I poured some chocolate-covered peanuts into a dish. I slouched on the sofa and helped myself to the newspaper while she worked.

After moving files from one side of her desk to the other while I read, Deanna turned in her chair and snapped me out of my reverie with her next comment.

"Matt, how bad do you want the money for your theater?"

"What?" I sat up, then stood up. I moderated my voice. "What are you talking about, Deanna? Don't play games with me, please?"

I retraced the legislative history in my head—the language I'd written, the tricky path we'd been down, the waiting game *she* was in charge of.

"So, what the hell are you talking about? What are you thinking, for God's sake?"

"Matt, calm down. I know how big a deal it is."

"Tell me Deanna, why are you asking?" I glared at her. "No, I'll remind you. Remind you of ten million dollars for a developer to leverage his forty million, plus the twenty million match to the city from the Feds. An ornament, by the way in the middle of your district. Centerpiece of the mayor's platform last election. Months of work to get to where we are. And, oh yeah, maybe my job. No biggie, I guess." I stopped to catch my breath. I was overreacting. I waited.

"I was thinking about you and me. How we go back a long way."

What in the world? Deanna Mackenzie eyed me like Sylvester eyeing Tweety Bird. The air in the room had changed. She rose and walked over. I thought for a second she was walking past me, but then there was no space between us. Her face was inches from mine, her hair disheveled and backlit by the window behind her.

"Matt, surely you've wanted ... thought about it." Her voice had dropped half an octave.

"Deanna, please. We can't."

"Mr. Archer, please don't play all reluctant virgin with me." She leaned into me, all that womanliness she'd demonstrated up on the mountain, and I didn't back away. All that hot sun and exercise. The musk of perspiration and faded perfume, her loose hair against my face—I wasn't about to stop.

Deanna lifted her hands to my face and kissed me. I tasted her tongue. The want in her eyes released months of pent-up stress in my body. We stumbled to the sofa. I pulled her T-shirt up over her head. She was all fresh air and warm skin.

I glanced at the door.

"It's locked."

She arched her back and took off her bra. Our hands fumbled at the buttons on her shorts. I tossed her shorts onto the coffee table, knocking over the plate of chocolate-covered peanuts. She wrestled me out of my Levis, knelt, and pulled my shorts down. Her tangled brown hair brushed against my thighs. She stood and pressed full against me as she slid her panties off. We pulled each other down onto the sofa, and she was all over me. And vice versa.

"Oh God, Matt!" was all she said.

Too quickly, we were panting, exhausted on the faux Karastan carpet where we'd ended up, her sweaty head on my shoulder.

I kissed her hair, messy and erotic as hell.

"Sheesh, look at the clock," was all I could think to say, to disengage.

"Matty'd better help Teacher pick up all these clothes. You've been a naughty boy."

She kissed me and I kissed her back. We repaired the damage to our clothes and I let myself out.

What rule? Oh, that.

Walking back to my apartment, when the rush wore off, what I'd done started to sink in. Big time. First, I tried rationalization; I was no stranger to rationalization, it was in my job description. I'm human, and male. Deanna had been lurking in my subconscious, certainly since high school. So sex was bound to happen.

Next I tried blame. What was Deanna thinking? What was the bullshit about how important Church Harbor's project was? Plus, she knew the effect she had on men. I had no choice.

Then guilt came running up and slugged me on the shoulder. Cheating on Ellen who I deeply loved! Get real. Pretty soon, I'd have to get a grip. I didn't have time to figure out the rest of my life. There was still work to do.

19

I lay awake for hours that night and stared into the dark, replaying the tape of what had happened over and over, trying to make it come out with a different ending. No luck. What happened was beyond wrong. Cheating, pure and simple. Betrayal. Of Ellen, for sure, and certainly Allie. But like brazen red lights at a railroad crossing, I couldn't get past images of Deanna's naked and unrestrained body, and mine no less rampant, like starved teenagers climbing all over each other again and again. My besotted brain had been hijacked—by me. How could the comfortable and trusting conjugal marriage bed compete with brand new, out-of-left-field, exhilarating sex?

When finally dawn crept across my room, I resigned myself. It was one time. I'd been beyond helping myself. Once. One time, miles from home, I hadn't been able to resist those damnable urges. It wouldn't happen again. No one would know.

I did the obvious thing. I called Deanna and asked her to meet me for dinner. I'd tell her. That would be that.

The Keg, one of a restaurant chain, had the best steaks in Franklin. Despite its reputation as a watering hole, it offered a modicum of privacy. Deanna was there when I arrived. We paid appropriate obeisance to a handful of legislators and lobbyists in the bar before hunting up the hostess and wending our way to a corner booth. She was hard to ignore, in silk slacks, a pastel tangerine color, and a white blouse, crisp, with the sleeves rolled up and with a pendant lying against her skin where she'd left a button undone. It was orange jade perhaps, an irregular, polished stone enclosed by two tiny gold bands that crossed. The pretty girl from our little town, grown up and now a big shot, was classy.

She ordered a scotch and I asked for tonic water with a lime. We hemmed a bit about what to order, and stayed away from the obvious subject. We pretty much knew the menu.

"You're looking good, Matt."

"You look great," which was not what I'd planned to say. I started again, "Deanna, about what happened …"

"Matt, I know, I know. You're a happily married man and we got carried away. No one needs to know, right?"

Was it going to be this easy?

She brushed away a strand of hair that had the habit of falling across her cheek. "Let's have dinner, not ruin a pleasant evening amid all the craziness of this town."

We ate. She had salmon. I made a show of enjoying prime rib, but in the back of my brain I kept hearing the beep beep of a far-away, runaway car alarm. Where was my resolve? She was right across the table.

The waiter cleared our plates. We declined dessert. Deanna reached across and took my hand. She laid four crimson-polished fingernails on my wrist, turned my hand over and did that very naughty thumb massage thing on my palm. We paid the bill and left.

Back at my place, she went into the bathroom and I heard the shower. She emerged minutes later wearing one of my pajama shirts she'd found hanging behind the door—and nothing else. It fell to her thighs, her hair glistened, and her face shone. I told her that was fucking unfair, so she shrugged the shirt off. The buzzer in my brain kept screaming as down the rabbit hole I went, again. I remembered later it was my birthday. My fortieth.

She let herself out the next morning—I feigned sleep—something about an appointment she absolutely couldn't miss, some contractor down from Church Harbor who built health clubs.

I hauled myself out of bed and made coffee. Hell, going back for seconds (thirds, fourths?) is a cliché, isn't it? That pathetic attempt at justification, that I could make an easy joke about the situation, scared me as much as anything—scared me enough to tell Deanna it was over and mean it. So I promised I would.

Midafternoon, I tracked her down.

"Deanna."

She walked away from one lobbyist and was headed toward another, then spotted me.

She was frowning. "I just spent twenty minutes talking to an idiot, so tell me something I want to hear." Out came the Cheshire Cat grin, or was it Sylvester again?

We stepped away from the congestion. I put on my stern, courtroom face. "Deanna, we can't keep doing what we've been doing."

"Okay," she said, still grinning. "Didn't we have this conversation already?"

"This time I mean it."

She put her hand on my arm and moved closer. Our bodies were almost touching. I pushed her hand away and stepped back.

She reached out again and my evasive action backed me into a pillar. I wriggled away. Pretty soon it'd be a game of tag on a playground—in the jam-packed Capitol rotunda in plain view of maybe a hundred spectators.

"Stop!" I hissed, and she did. We walked around behind the pillar. "Look, you're a wonderful person, and I can't say I haven't …"

"Oh, Christ, Matt. I know, I make my own clothes, love animals, and am a wonderful cook."

"And I'm a weak, horny male who you caught in ..."

"You weren't pushed, cowboy. You jumped! Enthusiastically, I recall. So don't blame me for what happened. We are, as they say, two consenting adults."

"One."

"One, what?"

"Adult."

She took a breath and let it out slowly. She actually looked hurt.

"Matt, we have some time left before we go home."

Wrong word, "home."

"I think about you," she paused, "a lot," looking winsome as a schoolgirl.

I tightened my gut and forged ahead. "Same here, Deanna. I mean, I did. But I can't ... We're not doing this again. Period."

"You've thought this through."

Alarm bell ignored. "Yep."

Her blue eyes went electric. "Whoa! This is different!"

She spat it out. I heard affront. This certainly did not often happen to her, Deanna Mackenzie; disbelief, as in why would a hungry man turn down a free steak dinner; and even hurt, a woman scorned.

"I'm sorry," I said.

"Bullshit!" She spun on her heel and left me standing there. Then she stopped and came back. She reached into a pocket and handed me an envelope. "Here, I guess we won't be needing this."

Off she went, not before firing something back at me I didn't hear. I prayed there'd been no witnesses to our soap opera, but a young page walking past her heard her. He let out a low whistle. I watched Deanna Mackenzie breezily wave across the hall at someone and keep walking. She *was* good at what she did.

I opened the clean white Senate embossed envelope, pulled out an official "State Senator Deanna Mackenzie" note card, and read:

*"You are an animal! And Matt, **Oh my God!***" The script was covered with a messy, full-on lipstick kiss. I shoved the goddamn thing in the pocket of my sports coat instead of tossing it in the trash where it belonged.

Back at the apartment, I retrieved my mail which had languished for three days of misbegotten sexual carnival and trudged up the stairs. I was feeling pretty good about myself, had done the right thing. I'd do my penance in days, maybe weeks, of self-recrimination, work off remorse by going the extra mile for my wife and daughter. That's when I found the birthday card.

Terrific! My birthday! I hadn't phoned, emailed, texted, nothing. I'd had my cell phone off in case Ellen and Allie had tried to call.

Pink lettering said HAPPY BIRTHDAY across the front of the cream-colored card with flowers and little cartoon birds and a picture of a white cake with yellow candles on the front. Inside, the card had one of those shiny little mirrors and below it, the words "Look at the person we love so much." Under that was Ellen's trademark line-drawn heart with an arrow through it, then Allie's careful fifth grade handwriting: "Come home soon, Daddy. We love you." Up in Church Harbor, yellow and blue checkered curtains in a little girl's bedroom waved in a breeze. My daughter in pj's, book in one hand, stuffed gorilla in the other, jumped into bed—her loving mother tucking her in. Or, so I'd imagined nearly each night for weeks.

I collapsed onto a kitchen chair and stared into the card at my miserable, two-timing visage, distorted in the flimsy reflection. The mirror in the card was like a looking glass. Through it I saw my faithful mom and dad eating dinner, Ellen and I struggling to hang wallpaper, me standing by a hospital bed staring down in amazement at the newborn miracle cuddling next to Ellen's happy, tired face. We'd named her Allison, which means "true, noble."

The ache in my stomach was so sharp that I lay down on the sofa. The pain arrowed into my chest. I pulled my knees up and I wrapped my arms around my body into a ball, clutching the card as tears started to come. I cried, then stopped, then started again. I thought I might throw up. I rocked and rocked and rocked, I don't know for how long.

In time, I sat up and wiped my runny nose on my sleeve. It was dark outside. Thank God I'd at least done what I'd done. Ellen would never know. But the suffering, the guilt inside my gut, that was another matter. I managed a peanut butter sandwich and finally got to sleep.

20

Given how much I had on the line, legislatively speaking, I was now a walking, breathing textbook example of violating Rule Number One. There was a good chance I'd undone all my hard work. My prime sponsor was a woman spurned who could fold her cards and walk away. She was the senator; I didn't have a vote.

At first, I stayed out of Deanna's way. If our paths crossed—and it was inevitable in those few, crowded, hectic days—we'd smile like you would at a passing acquaintance, not like someone you've known for years, let alone been intimate with. No knowing wink, no stopping to make small talk, not a hint of what'd happened. Which was okay by me. I had other things to do—shore up a vote here, answer a senator's question there—try to hang onto the support I'd cultivated and make sure of the votes I had when the time came. If the time came. Sooner or later, I'd have to reckon with my senator.

The final hours of the legislative session were moving and picking up speed, and the situation in the Legislature itself did not improve. It got worse. Days continued to warm up, as did temperatures inside the Capitol. The pressure cooker technique of keeping people at their desks and forcing compromises was starting to be counterproductive. Then, just when I thought the dynamics were complicated enough, out of nowhere (in fact, from Salish County) came a problem that was neither meteorological nor culinary.

I was on my way across the rotunda, avoiding the Senate door. Striding toward me, looking confident as a banker, was Salish County Sheriff Lucas Barkley himself, in full dress uniform, tall and impressive. In Franklin, of all places, end of session.

"Sheriff! Welcome to Bedlam."

I hoped I hadn't sounded as surprised as I was. Or alarmed.

"Hey, Matt. Nice to see you."

We shook hands.

Our sheriff always impressed folks. Pushing fifty, with recruiting poster good looks, he had what in high school we'd called "coat-hanger shoulders" and a waist still pretty trim, showing just a hint of time's toll. He always had a slightly amused look in his eyes like he'd just caught you slipping a Milky Way into your pocket on the way out of the store. Fascinating to me (and amusing, I confess) was his totally bald head under the standard issue sheriff's hat. Shiny as a ball bearing, he had to shave it daily, which was more tonsorial effort than I could ever imagine taking time for. I understand some degree of waxing or oiling is even part of the drill. To be fair, I was happy about my fulsome locks, but I had heard that chrome domes make the sort of masculine statement some women are gaga about.

"Luke, didn't you have enough of this place when you worked here?" He'd served a term as a legislator until he realized how much better the pay was as a sheriff.

"No. I come down here only when I can afford enough ChapStick to kiss this much ass."

Crudity and a slam, in one short sentence. He was on his game, the version of Luke Barkley that most people didn't see.

"Yeah, I didn't think that brown on your nose was all tan," I tried to volley. "What brings you down here?"

He dodged. "Har har. Of course, you're here because there's

so much available womankind around. Too bad none of them are worth shacking up with."

I stepped back. The stench was making me nauseous.

"Our local senator excepted, of course," he added.

Segueing, hopefully, "Have you caught up with The Honorable Ms. Mackenzie yet?"

"Yes, indeedy. She and I were just exchanging pleasantries." Luke shifted his feet and his gaze, noticing the look on my face no doubt, and his eyes began searching for an escape route. "Sal!" he yelled over my shoulder, and patted me on my arm before chasing down an imaginary acquaintance.

He knew he'd run into me. That was obvious. So I stepped outside, away from the din, and called Mayor Ev Riley. Five minutes later, my stomach was in a knot. Sure enough, Luke had called him out of the blue and asked if we needed "any help with that theater thing" I'd been working on for the entire session.

"Why do you think ...?"

"It made no sense to me either, Matt. He isn't up for re-election."

True enough. Though maybe he was padding his résumé by giving a helping hand to the biggest city in his county, ours, with its thousands of votes.

I asked, "What'd you tell him?"

"I said we were keeping a low profile, things were on track. He agreed what a financial boon to the community it would be, how great a leader I am, blah, blah, blah."

"He'll screw us if he can, Mayor."

"What was I supposed to tell him, Matt?"

Several answers flooded my brain at once, none of them helpful.

I suggested, "How about 'No thanks, we've got it covered'?"

"Matt, he's the county sheriff. He gets re-elected by eighty percent."

"That's because no one runs against him who can count to ten without notes. He's a fraud!"

"He's a successful fraud."

"Ev. Mayor. He's never supported you in his life. What do you owe him?"

"Why am I explaining entry-level politics to you of all people, Matt? He can hurt me. I need every vote I can get. Plus, he's usually armed."

"Oh, good. I feel much better. Did he say why he picked now to come down here?"

"Nope. Your guess is as good as mine. Our enigmatic sheriff isn't known for his charity."

"Nor is he below taking undeserved credit." I was getting nowhere.

"Listen, Matt," said my mayor, "I've got a hungry group of citizens in the lobby. I don't know what they're hungry for—my guess is money—and I'm late."

I hung up, still angry, but not before putting a little lobbyist salve on the boss's feelings. He did approve my invoice for services every month.

I saw Barkley again in the cafeteria. He was standing with a couple of people who still called him "senator" and yukking it up. Former legislators loved being addressed reflecting the apogee of their careers, and senators outranked sheriffs even if the pay was less. Luke's record in the state legislature had been mixed. During his one term, he was the best Republican that party could have asked for, except that he was a registered Democrat. He would jump back and forth across the aisle with dizzying speed and even more dizzying logic. Behind his back they called him eBay; he'd put his vote up online to the highest bidder.

Luke sat down next to my friend Susan Reddy and I joined them. Susan was the lobbyist for the state Sheriff and Police

Chiefs' Association, so she couldn't get up and leave. She also couldn't stand Luke. As I sat down, Luke was finishing some story or other, hilarious in his mind. Suze laughed politely, then rolled her eyes for my benefit when he looked away.

We both got a reprieve when Luke left to greet yet another former crony. For now, he was staying out of my way, it seemed.

"Did he say what he's up to?" I asked her.

"He says he's here to keep tabs on things. 'Seeing friends.' He's lying," she added.

"How can you tell?" I lobbed the softball to her.

We chorused in unison, "His lips moved."

She continued, "Besides, he has no friends."

Susan was concerned for me. She knew what I'd been working on because we were soul mates. To paraphrase Harry Truman, if you want a friend in Franklin, get a dog. But there were some good friendships made there, and Susan Reddy was one. She also knew how little it took to get things wrapped around the axle and how precious little distance there was left before the finish line we were all racing for.

We drank our coffees and listened to the colorful transit around us of lobbyists, state employees, legislators, and here and there an actual member of the general public—a discordant symphony of china and silverware, food aromas, and assorted babble reminiscent of a train station at five o'clock. Tax dollars at work.

"Hey, could you do me a huge favor?" I batted my eyes at her.

"Nope," she answered. She knew what was coming.

"Honest, Suze. What if you take him somewhere and screw his brains out. Find out what he's up to."

"Pulllease, Matt, I just ate." She got up and left.

Luke came back to retrieve a file he'd left. I motioned for him to sit.

"I'll try again, old buddy. Just for laughs, what does our

county law enforcement majordomo need from his favorite city lobbyist?"

"Matt, okay. I don't like surprises and neither do you. I was looking over your legislative effort, the one that would get state money for the Pine Street Theatre."

I braced myself. Homicide against a law enforcement officer carries extra sanctions, I recalled.

He continued, "How about a teensy language addition? No skin off your nose, just something I think the county will benefit from. I think the good Senator Mackenzie will be amenable to this."

"Like what 'teensy addition'?" He'd said "will"; clearly, he'd already met with Deanna.

"Words to include the county in the mix along with the city."

Luke continued, "We want to be at the table. Plus, if I'm doing the numbers right, the city could also gain by accessing the county's additional tax base."

I took a breath and tried for the civics class approach.

"Luke. As you know, a floor amendment at this point is the only way to get that done. That would send the bill back across the rotunda to the House of Representatives where it would die because there's no time."

I went on, "How about if the mayor agrees to include the county in the deal? Gives the county a role when we're through here and when he starts final negotiations with the private sector money guys? We don't need language in the bill for that."

"That's very generous, Matt. But you know how we all like things in writing."

I didn't respond. The twitch in my right eye did.

He said, "Tell the mayor I'm not saying no. And I promise not to make any moves until you and I talk again."

Coming from him, this was no easier than believing in

the Easter Bunny, but there was no point in arguing further. Luke Barkley's presence in Franklin was as welcome as ants at a picnic. And wasn't I in enough trouble?

21

I stepped outside for some fresh air. The sun was high above, warmth always welcome in our northern clime. Tulips and yellow daffodils had given way to rhododendron, lilac trees, roses, early dahlias, and everywhere it smelled like lawns being mowed. I spotted a port of rescue, I hoped, in the form of Pepper Martin, reporter extraordinaire, covering the legislative session for the hometown rag. He was sitting on a stone wall by the Capitol steps, against a backdrop of an endless row of tour buses. He was reading a book!

I remarked upon this odd fact. Pepper pulled his prescription dark glasses down and peered at me. "Yes, it's a book, Matt. You ought to try one sometime."

He took a sip of an iced beverage, chocolate it had to be, out of one of those tall barista cups with the round clear plastic bubble top. The straw stuck out of the whipped cream trapped inside. It looked delicious.

He was relaxing. Usually the very picture of a newspaper reporter: collar unbuttoned, tie loose, gray fedora tipped back on his head; everything except a cigarette dangling from his lips, since he didn't smoke. That day, Pepper Martin was slumming, without his trusty spiral notebook and a pencil tucked behind his ear.

"How can you be reading a book at a time like this?"

"You mean as opposed to being inside watching paint dry?"

"If I may interrupt your literary pursuits, I need to pick your brain. Guess who showed up in Franklin?"

"Luke Barkley."

I covered my surprise with an "Of course, nothing slips by you."

Pepper said, "Nope."

I filled him in. "Pep, I'm getting blindsided here, I think. Hardly any time left on the clock," (he was a sportswriter at heart) "so I'd love to have some dirt ... uh, some information I could use to throw him off track, distract him, you know."

I told him my concern about Senator Deanna, leaving out certain details. "Pepper, we both know Luke's not as clean as a whistle, despite the press he receives."

Pepper ignored the slam. He closed his book, took another swallow of the beverage that I coveted, and cupped his chin on his palm. I waited.

He said, "Okay, how about this. Rumor stuff, nothing even approaching factual. The word is, he does favors."

"Favors?"

"Think about it. He has power. If you found yourself in a pickle, like on the wrong side of the law and you knew someone who, by the way, was the sheriff? Assuming he was a friend, so I'm speaking hypothetically here. Mightn't you give him a call?"

"Keep going."

"Charges not being pressed, for example. A citation neatly dropped into a special file in his office and not sent to the prosecuting attorney."

"Charges against who?"

"You mean whom."

"Goddamn it, Pepper!"

He told me he'd picked up bits and pieces from time to time. Someone would be boasting over drinks at a bar that he'd gotten nabbed for speeding, had too many drinks, but wink wink, he'd called his good buddy Sheriff Barkley whose personal cell number he had, and poof, there went the citation.

Then, Pepper told me, a note came in over the transom at his office one day. Someone, he guessed a woman because the handwriting was grade-school Peterson perfect, said that she'd been arrested for shoplifting. Not much, under ten dollars or some such story. Seems she'd been "invited" (her word) to go to a certain room at the Aloha, a no-tell motel on the strip, where, lo and behold ... well, she left out the lurid details. She didn't say it was Luke, but the note started with "What kind of a man is our sherrif," misspelled.

"And?"

"No details, no story. I tossed it."

I let that sink in. Folks were passing us, up and down the Capitol steps, in and out, busy with the wheels of lawmaking.

"So how's it end?"

"That's it," said Pepper. "I don't know any more."

"I mean the book."

"Kate Atkinson. You never know till the last couple pages."

"Ditto, in my sorry situation. Do me a favor, please, and see what else you can find out. You seem to have time on your hands."

He stuck a piece of napkin in his book and closed it. He shrugged and gave a sigh. He pulled his cell out of his shirt pocket. "Matt, you do know who Sheriff Luke Barkley is?"

"Yeah, an asshole."

"And ruthless. And would drown me in printer's ink if he could."

"So, be careful. Pep, I'll snoop around, too."

"Meanwhile, Matt, doesn't sound like you've read the morning paper."

"What's that mean?"

"I'll give you a hint. Go read it."

I grabbed a paper, but first I put in a call to Jack Tulio, my golfing buddy. Jack was a talented criminal defense attorney who hated Luke Barkley more than the garden-variety professional dislike all criminal lawyers have for cops, and vice versa. Badges and guns intimidate most people. Criminal defense attorneys aren't intimidated. They get to fight back, inside the ropes. They get to put uniformed officers, the more righteous the better, on a witness stand under oath and make them answer questions.

Jack Tulio, one of the best, was the target of the gut-level enmity that the law enforcement community reserved for the likes of sex predators, a few of whom, to make it worse, Jack had successfully defended. Luke Barkley, as the top law enforcement honcho around, hated Jack. Like middle school kids in the hall, they'd glare at each other if they happened to cross paths.

Jack and I had spent many a beer-besotted afternoon on the fantail of his live-aboard, the *Y-Knot*, solving the world's problems. Jack's aptly named boat would rock gently in her berth, secure in the knowledge that she would not be put through the rigors of having to brave the cold waters of the bay any time soon. The harbormaster, who owed Jack a fee for rescuing his state license, had given him a series of lessons on seamanship, loosely defined. That worthy fellow somehow succeeded in teaching Cap'n Jack the intricacies of backing in and out of a ten-foot wide slot, which questionable feat, accomplished as witnessed by several of us, was thereafter memorialized in waterside taverns throughout town, Coronas all around.

I liked Jack, and he was someone I could trust.

"Hello, Jack! Matthew Archer here. Your good buddy whose golfing losses always find their way into your wallet."

"Buddy, my ass! You better have some good news, to be bargin' in on me. Do you know what a nap is, Matt?"

"Why so grumpy?"

"It started this morning. I came above deck and seagulls had crapped all over the swivel chairs. You know, the ones you guys sit in to fish from. Took me at least fifteen minutes to clean 'em off, and that was before I made coffee."

"Jack, we haven't been fishing in years, at least not off your boat."

"Are you trying to cheer me up?"

"Yes, as it happens. I'm proud of you living aboard. Adds to your, uh, 'mystique.' But promise me you haven't taken her out. Braved the deep and briny."

"You kidding? Unless they widen these berths another five feet or so, the *Y-Knot* is harbor-bound."

"So, Jack, here's why I called."

I told him I'd pay him five dollars to solidify our attorney-client relationship and confidential conversations, then filled him in on what I'd learned.

"What a son of a bitch!"

"We agree," I said. "Hey, I need a favor. Does anyone over at the prosecutor's shop still return your calls?"

"One."

"Good. See if you can find out anything about Luke doing favors, like maybe sitting on citations."

"Will do. Goddamn, I used to love cross-examining that piece of crap. Better than sex."

"Which says volumes about your sex life, Jack."

Back at my apartment, I paced around, washed dishes, and watched the sun try to break through clouds and show me how much my big picture window needed cleaning. Then I remembered to read the morning's hometown paper.

Wow! Click, click went the cogs in my brain. Bold font headlines blared that Superior Court Judge Scott Key, accompanied by his pretty wife Dolores, had been stopped one recent morning for driving under the influence of alcohol and drugs, to wit, marijuana. This was off-the-charts, especially in our small, otherwise quiet community.

It was after two when Jack Tulio called me back. It seemed that one of the worthies in the prosecutor's office already had gotten wind of Luke's shenanigans, one of which was radioactive. No charges against Scott Key had been filed, Jack told me. The bombshell he'd discovered was that this wasn't the first time for His Honor the Judge. There'd been other non-arrests with no charges filed. The Sheriff's Office hadn't bothered to turn the reports over to the prosecutor.

Nothing was official, nothing released to the public by the prosecutor's office yet, Jack said, because they felt they hadn't substantiated enough, and this was incendiary, to say the least. So they were sitting on what they knew. That was their excuse anyway.

"Matt, here's what else he said. Even though Luke probably held onto the prior reports, there's a reason they can't prosecute Scott for them now. The three-year statute of limitations has run on the earlier two."

"So what? Now there's the latest bust."

Jack and I reprised the fact that it was the prosecuting attorney who makes the decision to prosecute, not the sheriff. The sheriff sends the arrest report over, and the rest is up to the prosecuting attorney—charging him or offering a deferred prosecution with conditions. Poor Judge Key might never have to face a jury. There'd be Twelve-step meetings, State Bar probation, community service, et cetera.

"Do you think Luke is pressuring them?"

"I doubt it, Bucko. My contact over there thinks this smacks of misuse of government authority. Or suppression of evidence. Or hell, call it extortion."

"So what'll they do?"

"Nothing, for now, I guess. Whether they press charges

against Scott or don't, my contact thinks a formal investigation by the state is in order."

"What was Luke thinking?"

"My guess is there's a female involved and his trousers have been talking to him. He's not sitting around nights watching bad porn."

I interrupted his fantasy. "Jack, how about if you type this up and fax it to me. Make it appear sort of official. Not an affidavit or anything that heavy. Call it a draft of something."

"Done. Here's another tidbit. How'd the prosecutor's folks learn of the prior incidents, you might ask?"

"I'll bite."

"An anonymous call. A woman's voice."

"You don't say. Jack, you're a gem. What do I owe you?"

"How about a date with that foxy senator lady."

"I thought you enjoyed the peaceful life."

Static broke up his reply. Before I hit end I caught, "Bye, Matt."

Jack's "memo" came across my home fax in half an hour.

I forwarded it to Pepper, who said he'd get on it. But I told him I'd sic Luke on him if he did any more than write up a draft of a story for now, which he did:

SHERIFF SUPRESSES ARRESTS
Superior Court Judge's History of Drugs and DUIs
Pepper Martin

Sheriff Luke Barkley has suppressed prior arrests of County Superior Court Judge Scott Key for driving under the influence of alcohol and possession of marijuana, according to a confidential source and documents now available to this newspaper.

The most recent stop of Judge Key was not his first, nor his second, but his third. Beginning over three years ago, Scott Key has been stopped twice by a sheriff's deputy, been administered field sobriety tests, and should have been subjected to further breathalyzer tests and arrest. He'd been smoking pot, and marijuana was also seized.

Had he been convicted of the earlier infractions, he would have been subjected to State Bar Association sanctions, his driver's license automatically suspended, paid healthy fines, and possibly been incarcerated.

None of this happened because Sheriff Barkley unaccountably, and secretly, held onto the arrest records, allegedly after assuring deputies he'd take care of the matter. He never turned them over to the prosecuting attorney.

Prosecuting Attorney Miles Warren was not available for comment but, my source told me, he could launch a formal criminal investigation into obstruction of justice and possible extortion. He might also refer the matter to the State Bar and to the State Association of Sheriffs and Police Chiefs for possible ethics violations.

As reported previously, Judge Key was arrested in the early morning hours while driving home. According to the arrest report, he was not belligerent with the deputy, but he declined to take a breathalyzer test. That alone will cost him his driver's license for a year. He has promised to cooperate fully on the pending charges. He declined to comment on Sheriff Barkley's motives for not seeing that he was charged for the earlier events. The two earlier arrests are now barred by the three-year statute of limitations.

Judge Key has previously announced his intention to run for re-election this fall, and he has affirmed his decision to do so. He said, "I am embarrassed beyond belief and ashamed of my conduct. I apologize to the citizens of this county. I will face the music and pay the penalty, and I will trust the voters to understand that none of my previous behavior has interfered with my duties as Superior Court judge for the past eight years of which I am very proud."

Sheriff Barkley is out of town and could not be reached for comment.

I wasn't going to extort Luke Barkley. But I could give him something to think about.

22

Back inside the Capitol Building, I took to snooping. On the second floor is a square promenade and a thigh-high railing made of marble that runs around the rotunda from one huge pillar to another. It's impressive. It's also an excellent vantage point from which to watch jumbled meanderings of people below, the madding crowd of lobbyists and citizens outside the House and Senate "working the doors," as it's known. I staked out a spot and lurked. There was one too many cooks in the kitchen.

Luke Barkley showing up, who'd already met with Deanna Mackenzie, who was already pissed at me. Canceling our sexual gymnastics classes was one thing. She'd also made those cryptic comments in her office before all the romping around that sounded like she was already been reconsidering our game plan. It was becoming clear in my erstwhile besotted brain that she attached a lot less significance to what we'd done than I did. Maybe I was projecting, but probably not. And the end-game clock continued ticking.

Earlier that day, after sending Pepper on the hunt and calling Jack Tulio, I'd also phoned Yuri, up in Church Harbor. I told him what I needed.

He said, "Matt, I'm gonna take a pass. I have a high-class clientele now. My days of peeping through the shrubbery are over. Stake out a motel? Really?"

I pleaded.

"Okay, I'm kidding. God, you sound terrible."

"You don't know the half of it. I'll fill you in later."

So, sure I was snooping. It paid off. There came Deanna out of the Senate chamber to meet up with Mr. Law-Abiding himself. I stepped back and watched them stroll, heads together, huddling. She giggled, he laughed, she touched his arm, they stood face to face, still talking. He rested a hand on her shoulder, then her arm. Good old friends. One more little humorous aside between them, another laugh. Then she waggled her bright red fingernails at him and walked back in the doors. I was surprised they hadn't kissed. This was more than the legislator-to-legislator camaraderie—the secret grip and all that.

Susan Reddy walked up. The look on my face was not encouraging. I said, "Any last words for the condemned man?"

"Why are you discouraged? Gotten worse?"

"Suze, you told me how it goes. When it comes down to the wire, we spectators just stand back and watch, like rubber-necking a smash-up on the freeway. The ones with the actual votes are on their own now, and my good senator is fully capable of doing what Luke Barkley wants and amend my idea to death row." I told her what I'd seen. All lovey-dovey. "This will not end well." I was whining.

"Yes, it will."

"How do you know? Inside information? Tea leaves? Pillow talk?"

"Pillow talk with whom, pray tell? Myself, maybe."

Back downstairs, I met up with two comrades-in-arms gathering up papers—bill drafts, position papers, notes of conversations—and shoving them into briefcases. Word had started around that an agreement on the budget and appropriations was imminent. One of my associates, Billy Barnes, represented the state's largest city. None of us envied him; his docket involved dollar figures in the tens of millions and important people to answer to. Compared to him, my piece was chump change, but Billy fought in the same trenches with the rest of us. We city folks helped each other when we could, but today, lucky for him, his work for the year was done. He was going home for time with the wife, another session under his belt, sleeping in and playing Frisbee with the kids.

"Matt, you'll be here till the last dog is hung, huh?"

"Bad choice of words, Billy."

Another of the lucky ones, Barbara Evans, represented a mid-sized city like mine. She gave me a kiss on the cheek. Maybe it was lifeboat mentality, but we were all supportive colleagues.

"You're outta here, too, Barb?"

"Done! With several hours to spare. How's your deal?"

"It'll happen or it won't. The friends aren't friendly at this point, and the rest don't give a good goddamn."

They commiserated. Billy shook my hand and Barb gave me a hug, and off they went. The rotunda, by now, was about half as full as the day before. None of us survivors looked pleased to be there. This end-of-session diaspora was making me sad despite the nail-biting. The "have a great summer" and "we'll get together" were well meant, but the words reminded me of departures after a big family reunion.

The last horseshoe's flung, the clatter of table hockey silenced, and the long walks and gargantuan potlucks done for the year. There's the perfunctory wave goodbye to the cousin who you always understood, again, why you never sought out each other's company. There were Uncle Fred and Aunt Eunice climbing into their rented Dodge Polaris heading to the airport and the continued anonymity of their retirement community outside Fresno. Tossing her suitcase into her little red Miata, long lusted-after Cousin Amanda was still mighty fine for her forty-five years, even after a reportedly vicious divorce from "Kyle" who, naturally, you always hated.

I shook it off. No time for reverie. Finally, Yuri called me back.

"I did go by your sleazy motel. I quizzed the desk clerk whose license to tend bar I'd rescued until, that is, he reoffended. They caught him with a case of whiskey in the backseat and an underage girl in the front. If criminals had brains, the crime rate would be half what it is."

"And you'd be out of business."

"True. Anyway, for a few little green pieces of US government paper with pictures of presidents on them, which you now owe me by the way, he confirmed that Sheriff Do-Right had maybe, sorta, kinda been around from time to time."

"Yes!"

"Hold on for the punch line. I showed him a few pages of photos I carry in that three-ring binder your lovely daughter gave me. He didn't recognize any of them, but he picked up the newspaper lying on the counter and pointed to a look-alike on the front page of the *Harbor Light*."

Dolores Key! That one stopped me cold.

"You are a god!"

"Matt, be careful. And I mean what you do with this. He's not a nice man."

"Message received."

Maybe I'd just drop some hints. Make some inferences. Maybe more. I was desperate. For sure it was interesting how, in our little out-of-the-way town up north, things could be so intertwined.

I've always been a "belt and suspenders" kind of guy, so it was time to make a doctor's appointment. The "doctor" in question was a senator named Randolf "Doc" Hooker, the same fellow Deanna had lampooned while on our hike. He was someone whose help I needed.

In every legislature, as in life, there are concentric circles of those who pull the real levers of power. In Franklin, I'd found, the outer phalanx consisted of run-of-the-mill legislators, either first- or second-termers or the occasional multi-term sycophant from a safe district whose main motivator was risk-aversion. The next loop inward consisted of chairs of committees—satraps and princes who controlled the flow of bills, counted votes, and famously held up someone's bill because he or she hadn't acted on theirs. Sandbox politics.

At the very top of the food chain in Franklin was a small group of four folks. One was the governor. The veto pen is mighty as a sword, if for no other reason than the Legislature was in town for a few months a year while the incumbent chief executive worked the gig year-round. The other three were the Speaker of the House, the Majority Leader of the Senate, and a curmudgeonly icon, and my best hope right then, the Right Honorable Doc Hooker.

Hailing from the prairie land east of the mountains, Senator Hooker did his constituents proud, for which they'd returned him to the Legislature seemingly since statehood. A veterinarian by training, Doc had found that extracting legislation from a balky legislature was less taxing than extracting buckshot from a wounded hound.

Not an imposing man despite a mane of wavy white hair that made him seem taller with each passing session, Hooker was nonetheless, well, imposing. His defense of agricultural priorities on behalf of the folks back home more than compensated for his liberal apostasy on social issues. It also helped that the logistics of having to campaign in five large, sparsely populated counties fended off would-be challengers. In Franklin, he wielded his power quietly but surely, his only remarked-upon flaw being his less than politically correct attention to members of the opposite sex, as remarked upon by Senator Mackenzie.

Doc and I had struck up an acquaintance at a fund-raiser I'd had the foresight to attend before the session started. He was impressed that I'd taken the time to venture into the hinterlands to see him in his district. I was impressed that a Democrat could survive in the rural, largely Republican eastern half of the state. Over office visits and a couple of meals we'd come to know each other better, in that careful way of lobbyist and legislator.

Doc Hooker hung out in spacious corner digs on the third floor of the Capitol, prime seniority real estate. Passage into his inner sanctum was zealously guarded by, first, his scheduler Miranda and second, by The Lady Elizabeth, his executive assistant.

Elizabeth (God help us, never "Liz") was a challenge due to a personality with all the warmth of a buzz saw. She was a she-wolf and guarded her lair like one. It never failed that when I'd go by to ask for an appointment to see the Great Man, I'd get the same routine. Without looking up from her computer, she'd reach in and adjust a strap, hold out her hand and inspect her manicure in the time-honored way, and tell me he was busy. I pointed out that I hadn't yet said when I wanted to see him. It reminded me of the time I tried to ask a girl out in college. "Sorry, I'm busy." "All the time?" "In your case, yes."

Despite, or perhaps because of, my friendship with her boss, her truculence continued. This was unusual because of my otherwise winning ways, which included interested inquiries about her vacation, and little boxes of Cadbury chocolates I'd scattered liberally around Capitol Hill on Valentine's Day.

Access to Doc Hooker got easier, however, after I'd gotten the receptionist Miranda her job as a favor to her dad, who'd grown weary of paying for half a dozen years of college.

Miranda flashed me a conspiratorial look. "Wait a sec, I'll see if he's with anyone."

She sashayed past the she-wolf's desk, tapped on the oak door, and stuck her head in.

"Send that peckerneck in!" came a yell.

I tried my best to sashay, too, but I hit my hip on the

corner of a desk and limped in. Doc stood and waved his hand at a chair.

"Matthew, please sit."

The first thing any lobbyist in Hooker's office saw facing him as he sat down was a rectangular block of dark wood of the sort that carries a name plate. This one was embossed in gold Gothic script and placed slightly off-center at the leading edge of his massive desk. It read: YOUR BILL IS DEAD! Intended as a joke, Hooker's beatific face as he watched you read it obligated you to laugh lightly, like you used to when you asked dad for the car keys the day after the report card arrived home. You had to laugh; otherwise you'd cry. Doc could deep-six any legislation he chose.

I explained my plight: the amendment I needed, the end-of-session bell looming, his senatorial colleague Deanna Mackenzie's sudden reluctance (details omitted), and my county sheriff in town messing around. I blurted this out and sat back.

Doctor Hooker pondered a minute or two, forefingers at his chin. His response didn't take long. He leaned forward and slid the sign on the desk in my direction.

"But Senator …," I started.

"Don't 'senator' me, Matt. We've both been around the barn. Who do you propose I roll here? The good Senator Mackenzie is *your* senator, she's sponsoring *your* little amendment, she's a respected member of my party, this is a messy little scuffle outta *your* neck of the woods. In addition, I've got a problem of my own. There's a little matter of a canola tax credit bill for the folks back home and I'm two bricks shy of a load. I'm facing the same deadline in the session that you are."

Each second-person pronoun was a hammer blow on a different nail in my coffin. Begging was unseemly. So were tears. Homicide would sort of defeat the purpose. A quick mental inventory of my checkbook took bribery off the table.

"But," the Senator added as my stomach continued to churn, "I'll give it some thought." His eyes twinkled. "After all, Matthew, what's the use of having power if you don't use it? Give the amendment language you need to my staff. I'll watch for it."

I beat feet out of there in a flash. At least now I had a Plan B.

23

I did as Doc suggested, found his aide, gave her the language I'd worked on, then went for a stroll around the capitol grounds. It was midafternoon, warm, with the unmistakable tang of spring. Birds twittered in the cedar branches above me, singing about how little my human drama signified. Way up north in Church Harbor was where I belonged, now for more reasons than ever. This place was toxic.

Before my calamitous misstep, I missed Ellen—everyday after-work conversations, doing dishes together, cuddling on the sofa. She'd have been the first person I would've called about the legislative predicament I was in—to whine and get sympathy, of course, but also to get her clear-headed advice. She'd always been there—eleven years of "there." Now, of course, she was the last person I could call.

And I was missing the quotidian events of raising Allie— what cereal to choose, who got in trouble in class, which school pals were important in her life, where'd the missing sock go—the soil out of which children grow. Every phone call with her, the more of a real person she was becoming, the more her opinions stood on their own, the more lovely she became, the longer the lump in my throat lasted after hanging up.

When I walked back into the capitol rotunda, the ambience

had changed. I was met by worried faces. Shelf ice was beginning to crack and ominous rumbles resounded through the hollow building. Word sped through the crowd that a deal had been struck on the operating budget. "All but cooked," said a colleague. The pace was picking up, a palpable hurry-up that put waxlike gazes on some faces, an attempt at bemused stoicism on others, and simple fear on many.

I flagged down Doc Hooker's staffer to whom I'd given my deathless prose. She dashed into the Senate wings. "No time to talk, Matt. Can't stop. One maybe two sticking points left," she yelled back over her shoulder.

A buddy of mine, a capitol security guard at the Senate door, yelled my name across the din. "Matt, they're moving bills." He handed me a status sheet. There it was, the operating budget; it was now or never.

I sent in a note and Deanna came out. She gave me a curt nod of her head and we went outside. She tapped out a cigarette and lit it, tossing the match against a pillar. "What is it? I should be back in there." She was scowling.

"This will only take a minute. I know you've talked to Luke and I know what he wants. You gonna help him or me?"

She looked tired and stressed, and every bit her age. The soft glow of our days of lust was replaced by today's sunlight glancing off granite and glaring in her face. This was more than an up-or-down call for her. There were several moving parts and they were all personal.

"I haven't made up my mind."

"Then before you do, Senator, here are some interesting tidbits that came my way." I told her about Luke, and doing favors, and sitting on tickets, and motels, and a woman who was a dead-ringer for the one on the front page of the hometown paper these days. I didn't say the words, "Dolores Key." I didn't have to.

If I'd expected an "Oh my gosh, Matt, thanks for telling

me, I'm with you on this one," I'd have been mistaken. The remarkable blue eyes didn't betray her, but I knew calculations had to be racing like strobe lights through her head. One corner of her mouth twitched and she couldn't stop it. Expert as Deanna was in the art of seeming unfazed, an elected official's first response to unexpected information, she failed the test this time. I handed her the memo Jack had sent me and Pepper's draft newspaper article. She read them, then handed them back. I told her to keep them, and please don't show them to Luke. The Br'er Rabbit approach.

She flicked the ash off her cigarette and said, "So fucking what?"

It was my turn to scramble. "So, let's say Scott Key's going down. And let's also say a judgeship pays more than a senate salary." I was making this up as I went along. "Who's a candidate who might choose to run for an open superior court judge's seat with help from the local sheriff?"

Senator Deanna Mackenzie, one-time friend whom I'd helped get elected in the first place and with whom I'd broken Rule Number One, took another drag on her cigarette, then ground it out with a twist of a well-turned ankle.

"Matt, you better keep this ugly and unsubstantiated bullshit to yourself."

God knows, I was far from the last person to know what a rejected lover looked like, but I was sure I was staring into the eyes of one. Of course. It made sense, Deanna and Luke. How well *did* they know each other, both public figures in our town, and attractive?

"My, my, Senator, I seem to have struck a nerve." I should have shut up but my troubled male ego wouldn't let me. I asked, "How well do you know Luke?"

"Fuck you, Matt!" She was seething. She turned and started to walk away, then pivoted. "Know what, Matt? Luke's serious eye-candy. And by the way, single adults do have sex with one another."

The emphasis was heavy on "single."

"I guess I'm surprised at how hard-up you are," I said, in my sleep-deprived state. So she slapped me. Hard. Thank God we were outdoors; no one seemed to have seen us.

"And further, Mr. Brilliant Lobbyist, I don't have to run a sword through your precious proposal. I can play it both ways—put the language Luke wants in it *and* yours."

"My goodness, Senator, you certainly have me over a barrel. Har, har." I didn't even try sheepish. Two could play this game. It was her turn to look disconcerted. She tried to recover some ground.

"Matt, think of it this way. Luke wants a favor. Scott's a jerk. That's a no-brainer for me."

"And I'm road-kill."

"Did our sexcapades mean we're engaged? Grow up, Matt."

That did hurt, but I remained composed. "Of course, Senator. Good advice. And as for my, that is our, theater amendment, let your conscience be your guide."

"Thanks for that, Mr. Boy Scout."

Was that sulfur I smelled? My turn to walk away. She reached for my arm. I let her hand miss.

With no choice but to follow through, I dragged myself up the marble steps and into the Senate gallery. I thought of Sidney Carton and a guillotine. Bad analogy; at least he was doing something noble. From the gallery, I'd watch the final act in the drama I'd been acting in all session.

What happened next became lore in the annals of the state legislature, folks swearing they were there whether they were or not.

Like its counterpart in the House of Representatives across the rotunda, the Senate chamber was intended to inspire visitors and the senators themselves with the *gravitas* expected for the important work undertaken there. The disconnect between such lofty sentiments and reality from time to time only proved that everybody's human. Meanwhile, the décor, the high arched ceiling and enormous chandelier, the hushed echo of voices, the very tang of laws being enacted, never failed to impress me.

Forty-nine simple wooden desks, *escritoires*, each with its own laptop, were aligned facing a raised podium. An wide aisle ran between them separating the political parties and to a lesser extent their ideologies. The carpet was heavy but not gaudy—ash gray in color and textured with pink and maroon florets on pale green stems. To the right and left, under the overhanging galleries, were the wings. Each wing was a hallway, the modern equivalent of the "lobby," for which my profession was named back in the day, and lined with crackled, over-stuffed leather sofas.

High above the Senate floor, a ceiling arched; from it hung a dozen bronze-barred art deco lamps decorated with three-dimensional rosettes. A bas-relief pastel fresco the size of a small town depicted historic days of our state. It wasn't the Sistine Chapel, but it worked.

The raised podium in the front of the chamber consisted of two levels where sat clerks and the sergeant-at-arms. Behind them was the outsized, elaborate chair of Lieutenant Governor John Britton, who presided over the Senate. Like his counterpart at the federal level, the President of the Senate could not vote except to break ties. His primary role was to call up bills, rule on motions, recognize individual senators to speak, gavel the congregation to order, and try to keep a straight face for the entire sixteen weeks of the session. He was ably assisted by an attorney whose knowledge of rules of order would put Robert himself to shame.

The visitors' gallery where I sat ran the length of the chamber, above the Senate floor on either side. Each gallery consisted of three ascending rows of polished wooden benches like pews, but lacking hymnals and the little holders for pad and pencil my mother used to hand me during the sermon to stop me from squirming. Stepped aisles between the pews descended to a knee-wall in front of the first row on which a round brass railing ran along from one end to the other. Benches were roped off by thick, wine-red velvet ropes with polished brass cuffs and hooks at the end.

From this vantage point, curious spectators watched, down on the coliseum floor, not Christians and lions but latter-day gladiators pressing every advantage, but without the blood. They spoke on every subject like it was Lincoln versus Douglas, especially during the last weeks and days, and certainly this final afternoon.

I took a seat in the front row. Up on the reader board, there it was in glowing red letters: Bill Number 2225, third one down and counting, the huge State appropriations budget, nestled inside of which would be Church Harbor's money if I was lucky. How would Church Harbor's distinguished senator Deanna Mackenzie play this?

Susan Reddy slid in beside me and bumped her shoulder into mine in support. "Let the play begin," I muttered.

24

Lieutenant Governor Britton, dapper in a dark suit and rep tie, distinguished dark hair perfectly coifed, rapped his gavel once and called for the vote on an earlier bill under consideration.

The Chief Clerk began calling the roll: "Allen ... 'aye' ... Bishop ... 'aye' ..." and so on to "Thurman ... 'nay' ... Tomsen ... 'aye' ... Underwood ... 'nay' ... and so on until a bill designating the Pacific tree frog the Official State Amphibian was voted on.

"Mr. President, thirty-five ayes, thirteen nays, one excused."

"Having received a Constitutional majority, Bill Number 1367 is declared passed."

Lieutenant Governor Britton: "Next up, Bill Number 1507 naming the State Route 424 Interstate overpass after our sadly departed colleague, Senator William 'Willy' Williams."

The scattering of refugees in the gallery dared not giggle. Debate on a bill of this magnitude required every legislator from each party to rise and extol the virtues of the late Senator Williams, several of whom hated his guts. The bill, in memory of a true public servant now smiling down from the Big Gallery in the Sky, passed unanimously by voice vote.

The good Senator Deanna Mackenzie came in from the wings and took her seat. She knew I'd be a spectator, but decorum forbade waves, nods, any sign of acknowledgement to or from the *hoi polloi* up in the cheap seats.

Next was the final bill, Number 2225, the state budget. I was as nervous as I could ever remember being. All ten of my chewed cuticles agreed. Then, while the sound of the clerk's voice still echoed in the chamber, the place exploded!

With a football stadium roar, "You son of a bitch!" Sheriff Luke Barkley in full regalia came barreling in the door and launched himself down the steps toward me. It was clear Deanna'd told him what I'd asked her not to. Shoving people aside, he clambered over one bench, a security guard on his tail, and elbowed aside another unfortunate onlooker. As he closed in on me, waving a handful of familiar papers, the noise and commotion stopped everything cold on the Senate floor. Sixty-plus pairs of eyes stared up at the melee. A stunned Lieutenant Governor Britton's gavel was suspended in midair.

I dodged away, sliding out the other end of the pew as Luke cleared the last bench. Susan, of all people, stood up and blocked him, pushing him back and almost over the red velvet restraining rope. By this time, presiding officer Britton had recovered enough to bang and bang his gavel, and the septuagenarian security guard chasing Luke had called for back-up. I had no time to look down to see the expression on Deanna Mackenzie's face. I was preoccupied with avoiding damage to my own.

Luke regained his balance and, gentleman as always, shoved Susan out of the way. She tumbled back over a bench and others caught her.

"You chicken shit ... " was the last the shocked assembly heard as four security guards trapped and escorted a struggling, enraged human out of the chamber before he could finish the outburst.

Wrestlemania now outside, a sturdy guard on either side held Luke. I went out and we faced each other like a couple of drivers after a rush-hour fender-bender.

His face was red but his breathing was slowing down.

"Okay, okay, you can let me go."

Nobody budged.

"I mean it, I'm okay."

"I believe him," I said. "Right, Luke?"

The guards let go but stayed where they were. Luke's hands were shaking, paper rustling. A crowd had gathered. This was high theater.

"Think this one through, Big Fella." I was surprisingly lucid. "Take your injured ego back to Church Harbor. Maybe none of this gets out of Franklin."

"Fuck you, Archer. You're toast."

"Don't threaten me, Sheriff. All I want is what I came down here for. You were messing with me." Where this bravado came from, I didn't know. "I told you-know-who that she needed to make the right call here. It's called politics."

"We'll see," he growled, throwing the papers at me, and stomped away. The hall was quiet except for the echoing of his boots.

"God, I love this work," said one witness.

"You guys know he carries a gun," said another.

"Okay, ladies and gents, party's over," announced yours truly. And it was.

Except for the little matter of my nineteen-word amendment, my city's money, the whole reason I was there, that my own senator would likely sabotage. Susan and I returned to the Senate gallery and sat down. People's heads turned to watch us, then it was back to business.

Deanna obviously knew that the outburst in the gallery was about our little three-part *ménage à legislatif*. She didn't need the details; she proceeded to do me in.

"Before us," intoned the President of the Senate, "is the final reading of the State budget. First amendment thereto,

Amendment Number 324, Senator Mackenzie, this is your amendment. The clerk will read."

The Clerk did so. The language was the original I'd given Deanna.

Deanna rose. "Mr. President, I have handed up to the Clerk a six-word change I'd ask be included in the language in Amendment Number 324. I believe it has been passed out to the members."

A shuffling of papers.

"Very well, Senator, proceed."

"Mr. President, I urge the members' support of this amendment. It lets counties, not just cities, to make use of the public facilities district statute for purposes of restoring historic structures. After the words 'or for improvements to a building or other structure' add the words 'in a city or a county.'"

Thud!

There it was. Luke had won.

"Is there any discussion?"

There was none. My heart pounded while the clerk called the roll. Forty-eight to zero, one excused. Amendment as amended, adopted.

"Any other amendments? Yes, Senator Hooker?"

"I offer Amendment Number 325."

Deanna jerked her head around to stare at Hooker.

"The clerk will read."

The clerk did. "After the words in the previously adopted amendment, Number 324, after the word 'county' add the words 'provided the city in a county where such historic structure is located consents to such county participation.'"

I almost wet my pants. Susan and I stared at a stunned Senator Mackenzie. I could have written those words. In fact I had.

Lieutenant Governor Britton: "Is there any discussion?"

Senator Hooker: "Mr. President, I've studied the matter very carefully, and it seems fair that a city that undertakes the burden of improvements to property within the city limits should be allowed to determine how and with whom to arrange financing and such like."

Up jumped Senator Mackenzie: "Mr. President, may I have a moment?"

She walked over to my new best friend Hooker. She stood very close to him. She leaned forward and whispered very animatedly into his ear. Hooker was very intent, said very little in reply, and Deanna went back to her seat and slumped down.

"Any discussion of Senator Hooker's amendment." The Lieutenant Governor surveyed the assemblage. "Seeing none, Clerk, please call the roll."

The vote was unanimous. Deanna couldn't possibly have voted against it. If she'd chosen to break a rule and look to see if I was in the gallery, it was too late. I'd left in a hurry.

Susan and I raced downstairs. I sent in a note to Senator Hooker. He wasted no time.

"Thank you, thank you, Senator," I gushed. "So please tell us what she said."

We waited. Hooker was straight-faced.

"No, I won't, son. Let's just say I'm too old to have an affair. Don't think I could hold my stomach in that long, for one thing. She pushed those pretty titties of hers at me, and like an old guy in a canvas chair at the beach, I enjoyed the view."

Even Susan laughed.

Not quite "Ask not what your country can do for you," et cetera, but I'd love to have found a wall to inscribe that one on. We didn't wait around for Deanna.

I didn't stay for the victorious endgame. Back over to the House of Representatives the appropriations bill would go, where it'd pass with the blink of an eye so exhausted people could go home. Then on to the Governor's desk for signature, and into state law.

I jammed my suitcase full of dirty clothes, bundled up a box of legal files, locked the apartment door, and hit the road … exhausted, and relieved for more than one reason. Victory, but at no small cost.

25

A glimpse of my marital undoing took place the first night I was home. I put an excited and sugared-up Allie to bed after chocolate cupcakes she'd made herself. Ellen and I kicked back in the living room.

"Oh, this came," she said and slid a manila envelope over toward me with the Governor's office return address on it. I'd already told her I was done with lobbying, despite the success. She was happy. Big hug. "Probably a certificate of excellence," she said. I slit the envelope open with my thumb and pulled out two 8x11 photos from the Governor's Ball. In glowing color. Uh-oh!

"Just clowning around," was the best I could muster on short notice. However, my tongue got caught somewhere between the first two consonants and the diphthong of "clown" so it came out as a kind of stutter. A long look from Ellen, but maybe I was out of the woods. Hah!

"My, she looks fabulous," said Ellen taking them from me. "Hasn't lost a step. Some figure she's got."

There was no safe reply I could make to that statement, so I said something like, "Didn't I look okay?" and "It was a fun event. Both hometown folks, she could go as my date and kid around."

Bullet dodged. We watched some TV. I did say I was still too pumped up to go to bed right away, which meant no love-making that night, even to celebrate the hero's return. Ellen said she understood. As soon as she left the room, I slid the photos back in the envelope, closed it, and planned to bury it in a dumpster.

The next day I went by City Hall to pay an obligatory visit to the mayor. What a waste of time that turned out to be.

I'd emailed him part of the final budget, the pages I knew he'd be interested in.

"Excellent work, Matt," he said, motioning to one of two comfy chairs and resuming his seat behind his large, uncluttered desk. Everett Riley was right at home, and, sure enough, much better dressed than the fashion disaster he used to be on the golf course.

"Thanks, boss." He wasn't technically my boss, since I was on a contract, not an employee, but he liked the reference. "There were a few surprises at the end when ..."

"And you'll tell me all about them, those lobbyist tricks you pulled out of a hat. But not right now, Matt. I'm swamped. Do tell me first before you go, how do you think the Judge Key thing's going to play out?"

I told him it was too early and I'd been little preoccupied working his vineyard. "Maybe Scott will be okay—Twelve-step meetings, Rotary, Kiwanis, et cetera. People are pretty forgiving."

I changed the subject. "Let me fill you in on our so-called ally, Senator Mackenzie. She tried to kill ..."

"I've got about two minutes, Matt. Sorry, then I have to run."

"All right, but know this, Mayor. When, and I don't think if, she takes a run at Scott Key's judgeship, her hands ..."

"So, what happened with the sheriff? Did he cause problems?"

I was too tired to go into the whole who-struck-John, and I was clearly wasting Mayor Riley's precious time. I threw him a bone: "He'll have his hands full, starting with the prosecutor." Which sailed right past him. He didn't ask why, just said, "Ah, local politics at its finest. Meanwhile, the streets need paving, I'm on the police union's you-know-what list, and it's my wife's and my wedding anniversary tomorrow. Gotta run. Thanks again, Matt. Fine job."

He stood up. So did I. A little celebration at least would have been welcome. A handshake? I wanted to push his smug self back into his chair. After all, I knew him when.

"This will only take a couple minutes, Your Honor," I began as he escorted me to the door. The honorific usually worked. Not today.

"Matt, no time to chitchat. Sorry. I've got a meeting due in here with some loyal citizens who want the city to sign onto a petition to save polar bears or some damn thing."

"You gonna do it?"

"One of the guys is a neighbor."

"The one with the boa constrictor?"

"The very same."

"You wouldn't want to hear how a few million dollars got into the budget by the skin of its teeth when polar bears are at stake."

"Don't get snarky, Matt. Trust me, you don't want my job."

He was right, I didn't want his job. His salary, maybe.

"Correct, boss. One more thing. Do you know Dolores Key?"

"Not well. Why?"

"Tell you why later. For now, don't believe a word she says."

I left and wended my way through a crowd of earnest environmentalists in the reception area. Was I cynical? Yes. Even winning has a brief half-life. Was I angry? Not really. I'd made my decision. I'd tell Everett Riley I was no longer working for him. No more lobbyist, no more Franklin, no more politicians. That'd get his attention.

The minute I got home and saw Ellen's face my stomach

plummeted to somewhere near my knees. What happened in Vegas hadn't stayed there. I knew it, even before she threw the torn note card at me and screamed.

"You asshole! God damn you!" She slumped down on the sofa, face in her hands and her body shaking.

What now? What does an asshole do about a smoking gun, a torn-in-half note card emblazoned with lipstick and pornographic script lying on the living room rug?

"Ellen, I …" but no more words came out. What on earth would they be? It happened once, that's all? It was an awful mistake? I was lonely? Hell no!

She choked and sat up, narrowed eyes shooting lasers. "Matt," she snapped, "Allie—your daughter and mine—won't be home for an hour. So get out of this house. Go away and don't come back!"

"Can I please tell you …"

"No fucking way!" This, from a woman whose use of profanity was tentative at best. "Get the hell out. I'm going to start screaming and won't give you the pleasure of watching."

"Ellen, I love you! A stupid flirtation got out of hand. I can't tell you how sorry I am. A horrible betrayal …"

She glared at me. She covered her ears. I bent to pick up the torn card and she yelled, "No, you leave that piece-of-shit note right there. I'm going to need it."

I backed out of the room and closed the door with a quiet snick before I heard her in hysterics.

I checked into a motel, with the clothes on my back. Why didn't that clothing include the goddamn sport coat with the card I'd forgotten all about, and instead leaving it for Ellen to take to the dry cleaners?

Next morning there was a message on my cell saying she'd dumped some of my belongings in the garage and I was to pick it up and not under any circumstances go in the house. She'd told Allie I was taking a vacation. "You don't deserve that, but she does. And oh yeah, screw you." Click.

Welcome home, Asshole.

Needless to say, my friendship with Yuri Brodsky was put to the ultimate test. I told him what had happened and he went ballistic. After chewing me up one side and down the other, which lasted most of a day, he calmed down and tried to be rational about an irrational situation. He'd advised, no ordered, me to get the hell out of town, as much as anything to give Ellen room to figure out how to handle any spreading news, not to mention protecting Allie.

26

took Yuri's advice. I packed up the truck and drove south the next day, then east over the mountains into the empty expanses of the Great Basin desert. Just kept staring at the road, driving. I stopped at an IHOP and nursed a bad cup of coffee sitting in the parking lot. It was cold. The sky was gray. The wind didn't help. The branches on a row of fruit trees were bare and whipped around in the gusts. There was a storm coming in.

I tried calling Ellen. No answer.

I had not a clue what to do next. Terra incognita, like it said on old maps. "Terra-fied" was more like it. I sat forever with my forehead against the steering wheel. I cried. Beat the dashboard with my fist and cried some more. At some point, I put the truck in reverse, backed out, and went in search of a campsite. I found a spot and pitched the tent. Dinner was a sandwich. The night was fitful and the wind picked up. The trees gave some protection but they amplified the sound.

In the morning I went into a little bump in the road called Emery, population 103, to get provisions and take them back to camp. My mood, if not clarity about my situation, improved a little after a few days. Forays into the black nights to relieve myself were a pain. It was as chilly inside the tent as out. I had dreams I couldn't shake that repeated themselves like a film loop. There'd be a pretty woman, then two, and I'd try to get away. My dad would take my truck, and I'd watch it fly off a cliff—again and again, sail into empty air. I was alone. Absolutely, helplessly alone. Some shrink might diagnose that a pernicious worm had made its way past my always faulty conscience and slid into my reptilian brain. It found my oh-so-mortal heart. And ate it. Thanks for the help, Dr. Shrink.

And Ellen forget? Impossible. Forgive? Unlikely. Imagine Matt, if the situation was reversed. How many years of atonement would be called for? Lots and lots of it.

One morning before dawn, I gave up trying to sleep. I splashed water on my face and then on dead campfire coals. Cereal, a banana, and leftover coffee from the thermos would do. I broke camp.

I hit the road and crested a pass at around six thousand feet. In front of me was an emerald meadow sparkling with purple wildflowers. A marsh hawk skimmed the sage and willow shrubs on her morning rounds. Clouds were high and thin and the day was already warming up. A panorama of basin and range country stretched ahead as far as I could see—an open tableland of stubbly grass, hilltops in muted grays and blacks and browns mottled by passing cloud shadows. Tan bluffs, once ancient seamounts and ridges, now planed smooth by mile-thick Ice Age glaciers, had calved russet and black boulders at their base. Turkey vultures surfed the updrafts.

I passed stacked rock cairns that anchored lengths of barbed wire. Center-pivot ag sprinklers with booms a thousand feet long worked their slow way along rutted tracks. Their spray threw rainbows into the air. Like messengers from the cosmos, two bald eagles circled out of the cottonwoods and sailed into the sky.

This was "fault and block" country, I'd learned back in geology class, formed by the tipping of massive sections of the earth's crust into ranges miles long and thousands of feet high, the way an iceberg tilts if its center of gravity changes.

Inconceivable to humans trapped in minuscule lifetimes measured in decades, the planet's mantle moved and roiled and faulted for thousands of millennia.

The parallel was not lost on me: fault and block. Whose fault, Blockhead!

I circled back to the grocery in Emery. The bell over the door rang when I walked in. At the cash register, a woman, trim and maybe in her thirties, wore a heavy, plaid wool shirt tucked in. Her hair was light chestnut brown and pulled back. Her nametag said Deanna.

Were the gods futzing with me? I paid and got out of there. At an untended park with a picnic table, I cut up the apple and started in on a ham and cheese sandwich.

"Mister, can you help us out?" The voice was of a teenage girl standing with her boyfriend behind her. A pale arm stuck out of a worn blue sweater with the sleeves rolled up. On the front of the sweater was a white poodle. The boy kept a respectful distance. They'd worked this gig before.

"Our car's out of gas."

Running out of gas in this tiny town in the middle of nowhere was a ruse. They were broke and hitting on me. I attracted people like that like a magnet.

"Sure," I said, and handed her a twenty.

"Thank you," she said, and they walked off. The girl glanced back at me before they rounded the curve in the highway. I must have looked pitiful.

I sat and munched. The tules were alive with birds. Beyond in a marsh pond was an ibis, a group of teal, and a solitary pelican. There were blackbirds with yellow heads, a pair of white egrets, and swallows flitting in the sky. Nestled in a sunlit depression by the dike was a white-tailed deer, antlers shabby, taking his leisure protected by the tall grass.

Ma Nature, a restorative. A tiny dose of perspective, anyway. The isolation and the uncertainty got to me.

I backtracked through Emery. It was deserted except for a shirtless nonresident squatting beside his backpack with a desultory thumb in the air. The store was locked up tight and dark as a schoolhouse in summer. No one stirred at the highway maintenance yard up the way, nor in its rutted field of derelict backhoes, a trencher, a couple of tractors, part of a grader, and pieces of rusted implements. A metal building like an outsized meat locker, and its neighbor with a ghost-image of a Flying A logo on its side and a solitary gasoline pump out front—that was it. A pair of power lines disappeared into the distance. So did I. After a week, I turned back for Church Harbor. I found a house and rented it.

Going downtown even on rare occasions was a mistake. Church Harbor wasn't that small a town, but it sure felt like the sordid story had gotten around—hopefully the expurgated version. Sure I was paranoid, but every whispered conversation had to be about me and Ellen. Every second look at me was a double-take. I thought people crossed the street to avoid me. Not everyone, but enough: friends, acquaintances who counted.

I took to wearing a hoodie, maybe a mistake. I didn't shave, not so much because I didn't give a shit as that I hated the sight of my face. I used a grocery store on the edge of town. If I did go out, I went after dark. I was clear that the first priority was to somehow arrange a truce with Ellen.

The first break in my social quarantine occurred when Yuri called and ordered me to have lunch with him. The anticipated verbal onslaught didn't happen. He'd visited Ellen and told her he was going to check in on me. She said that would be a good idea. I made sandwiches and he and I ate at my place.

"Got any plans?" he asked. "Beyond drinking hemlock?"

"I'm examining my life. Even your buddy Socrates would suggest it."

Yuri was single, and resolutely so, he'd say. That was by

choice, given his notable prowess with women. He'd have one or two prospects at close range for a while, but they didn't go anywhere, it seemed. As for monogamy, however, he cut me no slack. But after his first blow-up, he'd let that go.

"You know, Matt, virtue is its own reward, or so I've heard."

"You're going into the ministry?"

"No. I subscribe to the corollary: 'Vice is its own hell.'"

"Ah, I see. Adultery is a vice. Who knew?"

"You don't have to wear it like a scarlet A."

"Is this where I tell you to go pound sand?"

"Nope. I'm not going anywhere. And you're not buff enough to make me. My plan, which will now be your plan, is to help you get out of hell. Free."

I drained my Coke, ice cubes against my scruffy upper lip, and looked out the window. I wiped my cheek with the back of my hand facing away from him. I started to cry, my shoulders shaking under Yuri's hand. He waited until I stopped, then got a paper towel.

The path back to Ellen was like bushwhacking through a thicket, but there began to be patches of open terrain ahead, starting with counseling. I was not misled by the polite greetings in the waiting room, nor her civil demeanor when I was finally allowed to pick up Allie from school. I knew Ellen too well. But she'd be damned if her actual feelings left a mark on Allie. Disgust with me, anger at going through the motions of single parenthood, crying—these were reserved for when Allie wasn't there. Not once, according to Ellen, did she vent about the slimeball I was.

At counseling, I was careful and cautious. I paid close attention. Sessions consisted of me nodding my head and agreeing to everything that was said. I forced down the awful tasting medicine. I was a ventriloquist's dummy with the shrink's hand up my back. I'd sneak peeks at Ellen, lips pursed, back straight, hair perfect. I'd watch her walk out and I'd stare at the door closing behind her, until the counselor would say, "Matt, find someone to talk to. Not a friend. A professional."

"I will, I promise," I lied.

The months that followed my return had their ups and downs, the former gradually beginning to outweigh the latter, if not by much. I set about remaking a law practice: found office space, tossed the old business cards and printed up new ones, went to bar association meetings. The first few clients dribbled in, including a motorcycle gangster named Gunk which brought me a good-sized fee. The major downer was that visit of two look-alike biker thugs—not friends of Gunk's, as he'd assured me—who invaded my home and roughed me up a bit. My pride and my prowess, primarily.

Part Three

Imari

Fall, continued

27

I spent the day after the slugfest at home, nursing various body parts. The hits I'd taken from Biker Goons One and Two just plain hurt, plus a shoulder I'd thrown out when I clobbered Gunk. I slept until ten, thanks to a handful of ibuprofen. It hurt to stand over the sink, but I managed to shave, gingerly. I forced down a piece of toast and peanut butter and went to the office. Thankfully, I wasn't expecting company.

I dragged myself up the stairs and found three messages on the little pink slips pinned to my door. Gunk wanted to talk to me, maybe more salve for my wounds. Ms. Murray, the Public Defender, wanted to compare notes, and Yuri Brodsky wanted to know when I was coming to the gym, or was he going to have to recruit someone else to spot him lifting weights? It hurt to think about lifting anything heavier than a donut.

Trying to get my law practice off the ground was one thing; running interference for an outlaw biker, quite another. I wanted to believe Gunk that he was clueless about the attack on me, but how would I know? Biker World was a strange place. Regardless, the three phone calls could wait. I went back home and slept.

On Friday, Yuri came first and we met at a city park where by midmorning the sun was back out and it was quiet. He took one look at me and winced. I told him about my attempt at fisticuffs. He didn't say anything right away, but the blood vessels at his temples gave him away. The Allie part.

I said, "I want to hire you. Or find a hit man."

"Forget it. Neither. This is now personal. Besides, you can't afford me."

"I'm ready to bail on this case."

"Hold on. What do we have? Two thugs, perhaps from across the border, who mess with you. A phone you found at the scene. A client who sounds like a reformed drunk. Four other bad bikers who look like a cartoon. A mystery member of the gang who speaks sophisticated English but who missed out on the fun."

"Like I said, I'm going to quit. I didn't sign up for this."

"They give boxing lessons at the club. I'll sign you up for them." Neither of us fell for the light-hearted approach.

"Matt, give me a couple hours. See what I can find out."

I agreed. I rubbed my jaw with my good arm. He winced again.

Back at the office, I shoved files around on my desk but I couldn't concentrate. Yuri called in twenty minutes.

"That was quick."

"Today-Only Special for you, Counselor."

He told me to meet him at a place called The Palms, a biker bar north of town.

There hadn't been palm trees in our neck of the woods since the Cretaceous Period, yet on the roof of a scruffy stucco building stood a pair of crossed palm trees, paint peeling off the metal and generally the worse for wear. They leaned precariously over a green and yellow neon sign reading THE PALMS in four-foot cursive. At night, the lurid glow from the rooftop could be seen a mile away. I'd driven past but never been inside.

Uninviting as the venue was—ominous was more like it—I

parked the truck and got out. A phalanx of buffed-up two-cylindered machinery, angle-parked and arrayed like a row of pricey dominos, led the way to the entrance. The high-barred and raked monsters took up most of the parking lot. They were black, some dark blue or red, one yellow, and each one had signature fat rear tires, glistening metal-worked footpads, and sissy bars. The scene screamed "bad biker bar." Did "bad" modify the biker or the bar? I decided both.

I pulled open the door and sent a glare of sunlight into the murk. The place stank of stale beer and cigarettes. When my eyes adjusted, the patrons looked like you could have assembled them for a fashion shoot of street criminals, to coin an oxymoron. Long, wild manes, dirty denims and greasy leather vests adorned with patches accessorized long-sleeved shirts and big arms sleeved out with tattoos. The word "gearhead" crossed my mind. So did "ex-con," "PTSD Vietnam vet," and "violent sociopath." Of course I was projecting, but who wouldn't after the previous night? The music was deafening. Pink Floyd or Santana—no way to tell at eardrum-damaging level—pounded away along with loud whoops and laughter.

Some of the habitués looked up when I walked in, then went back to darts or shuffleboard or telling lies. From a corner in the gloom, I saw Yuri call and wave me over. Adding some swagger, I took my conspicuously ordinary-citizen self over. Next to Yuri, two other hulks stood up. One was Mongo.

"I gather you two have met," said Yuri.

We shook hands. Once again, I marveled at the size of the man. His hand was the size of a catcher's mitt.

"So, you know each other?" I looked at Yuri.

"God, Matt, who could forget this freak of nature?" I trusted he was making this up on the fly.

"Matt," said Mongo, "This is my associate, Freight Train."

Freight Train had a menacing face like the guy you'd see driving a black muscle car in the lane next to you at a stoplight daring you to race. He reached out a hand and said "hello," flashing a gold-plated front tooth. Once again, Mongo using the word "associate" didn't sound like standard biker lexicon.

The two of them reminded me of pictures I'd seen of a pair of Norse giants in a cartoon, enormous towers of muscled flesh adorned with biker regalia. Impressive biker regalia, I had to say, unlike the scruffy ambience in the rest of the place. Yet these two seemed tame by comparison, despite their size. Maybe I could take them to Allie's fifth grade class for show-and-tell.

"We've been talking," said Yuri. "Let's go outside where we can hear ourselves think."

We did, and found a table with a view of the bay. The sky to the west was clear. To the east in the distance, the Cascade mountain peaks were white-tipped and backlit by high clouds. Off to the north in Canada, the range of mountains was also snow-capped. Trees around us were losing their leaves but still flush enough to shade our table. Mongo and Freight Train sat across from Yuri and me.

Mongo started. "First off, Matt, I'm very, very sorry about last night."

I turned and got up to leave. Yuri grabbed my arm.

"Sit back down, Matt. Hear him out."

"Like I said, I am very sorry, and you deserve to be outraged." He seemed sincere. "Those guys will not bother you again. Or go near your little girl. Nor will anyone else."

"And what possible authority do you have for that, before I have you busted for being an accessory?"

Freight Train chimed in. "We know who they are and they have been, um, reprimanded." He turned to Mongo.

"Reprimand" in biker lingo, I knew, meant anything from patches being torn off or bikes confiscated or very gruesome corporal punishment.

I said, "Suppose you fill me in."

"Not going to, Matt," said Mongo. "Not necessary. I will say that they decided to take certain matters into their own hands, matters that were under control."

"Matters having to do with my seeking extenuating circumstances to get your runnin' buddy Gunk a better deal?"

"Sort of."

"Sort of what?" I growled.

Yuri looked at me.

"Matt, you can trust these guys. I don't have the details either, and I don't want to know and I don't think you do either. I will say this." Yuri searched for a word. "Mongo's connections with the Bandoleros and their sometime rivals north of the border make him dependable."

"The rivals with red and white patches, I assume. I saw a flash of red and white on a patch when those psychopaths left."

"Let's move on to more constructive conversation," said Mongo.

"No, wait," I said. "The one guy—not the talker, the ape with him with the trapdoor for a mouth—who was he? He was lit up and buzzing like a neon light."

"It won't help you to…" began Mongo.

"One or both of them are in that dump over there, aren't they?" I nodded at The Palms. "I saw the bike with the red cross on the tank."

Mongo, looking sincere despite the goldilocks and his almost comic book mien, put his size twelve hand tight on my arm.

"I'm going to do what I can, Matt, to keep you out of harm's way. And that includes keeping you from going in there."

I removed his hand. "I happen to have a length of good chain in the truck bed. I'll wrap it around the back wheel of that piece of shit and drag it to Canada."

They laughed. Even Freight Train chuckled. And he was the stoic one of the pair.

"Matt," said Yuri, "you will succeed in stripping your clutch and trashing the transmission. Then they will take you on a trip down the road with your chain around your ankles. Those guys have little to lose."

Mongo resumed, "I am aware that you have stumbled onto some evidence that you gave to Yuri here who subsequently gave it to the police. That is quite proper. I take it your two visitors didn't mention that."

"Correct. Why?"

"It further demonstrates their stupidity and rash behavior. Perhaps, it even opens up a valuable stratagem for Gunk's defense."

"Mongo, I'm trying hard to believe you. For now, I'll buy Yuri's faith in you. But tell me, where'd you learn to speak like a Harvard prof?"

"I read a lot."

Mongo reminded me of a Dickens character: his appearance, the literate jargon from a gang biker outside a squalid biker hangout filled with hoodlums and raucous behavior. More Magwitch than Miss Havisham, to be sure.

I let it go. We stood. Mongo shook my hand like we'd made a deal. I returned the effort because what did I have to lose? It was trust him or … or what? I did not need to decipher his mysterious hocus-pocus right then.

He and Freight Train said so long, and Yuri and I sat back down.

He said, "Have I got some interesting news for you. Number one, Mongo the Bandolero? He used to be a Hells Angel. Down in Texas. Maybe still is."

"What? How'd you find that out?"

"Not saying. Someone I know. I believe Detective Mick Malone is following up."

Yuri went on, "I don't know what Mongo's up to, but he has great cover or great street cred, and he's pulling it off. Whatever it is."

"What else?"

"Here's what I found on the cellphone sim card before I turned it over to Mick. It's a one-off phone, first of all. Meant to be used once, then tossed. I think one call was to the mule who humped the pot into the States. It's a B.C. area code. Another was to the local DEA office. So far, no surprises. Consistent with what we know. But here is a surprise. One of the calls I traced was to none other than Mongo."

"You don't say."

"Wait. There's a fourth call. To the North County Credit Union in Church Harbor."

"What's that about?"

"Not a clue." Yuri took his time. Then, "I ran the phone under my ultraviolet light. No fingerprints. None."

"Somebody scrubbed it good."

"Or think, Matt. What are the chances of you finding this, all by yourself and after you've been hired on this case, and after a thorough search at the scene by a platoon of law enforcement officers?"

"It was planted."

"I wouldn't rule it out."

"So what do you make of the credit union number?"

"It's an account access number. It asks for a PIN."

We sat there across from each other. We could have been playing checkers. I wished we were.

So I said, "Have I hired you yet?"

"I guess so. Same low, low rates."

"Tired old videos at your place. Take-out Chinese?"

"Uh-huh. And hoops with Miss Allie."

We got up. Yuri swatted me on the back like a coach sending a player into the game, got on his machine, and rode off.

Next on my list, Mick Malone.

28

M ichael "Mick" Malone was a donut shop cop. Old school through and through. He'd moved along with the times—mandatory college education for new recruits (he had one, regardless), women in the ranks, detachable state-of-the-art laptops in the patrol car—but he refused to let go of his street-wise, cop-on-the-beat persona. The new PC term was "community policing." "The policeman is your friend" mantra, lampooned by student activists decades before, was now dressed up in New Age jargon.

Mick Malone's detective skills were formidable and acknowledged. He'd been the lead officer awhile back, tracking down a sensational serial killer who'd terrorized the country and ended up in Church Harbor's backyard. They'd nabbed the guy by surprise in a downtown biker bar. Where else?

My friend on the force and I had known each other forever and had interacted professionally both on the same side of a case and opposite one another. I'd tell him some other time, however, about my adventure with the goons. If I'd told him then, as law enforcement he'd have to take a statement, do a report, et cetera. That could wait. If he asked about the bruise on my cheek, I'd make the usual excuse about the cabinet door in my kitchen that refused to stay shut.

I walked into Station One. Behind the waiting room glass sat Norma Dyrland, the receptionist, who always reminded me of Dame Judi Dench. Norma had been holding down her unenviable job as long as anyone could remember. Time after time, she'd turned down what others might consider career advancement. I think she enjoyed being the first line of defense against the incredible flotsam that washed up daily in a police station.

"Hey, Matt! Come to turn yourself in?"

"I'm innocent, damn it, I'm innocent."

"They all say that."

"Know a good lawyer?"

"Just you, Blue Eyes."

"Aw. How are you, beautiful?"

"Livin' the dream, Matt, livin' the dream."

"I'd expect nothing less. Hey, is Mick around?"

"I'll see." She pushed a couple of buttons.

"He's on his way. Watch out. He hasn't had lunch."

We walked downtown. Mick being a detective meant a suit and tie, not a uniform. He wasn't a big man, and his once-red hair, cut short and cop-like, had gone to gray. He tended toward "round" but kept fit. I didn't kid him about a donut shop.

Anonymous he was not. People said hi, block after block, even if Church Harbor was not the small town it used to be. Mick and I remembered the old days. If you saw both patrol cars (as in the two) in the parking lot behind City Hall at night, you pretty much had a license to steal, or drag race, or get into whatever mischief you cared to. Small town, small force, small incidence of crime. Times had changed.

We walked to the default Lunch Bucket. Attorneys, accountants, stockbrokers, realtors, and those who paid them crowded the joint. I got a table by the wall; I didn't want to be overheard. Mick ordered clam chowder. I guilted myself into a house salad, dressing on the side.

"How's Pamela?" I asked.

"Perfect, as usual."

"Yes, she is. The only woman courageous enough to deal with you for what, fifteen years?"

"Seventeen."

I'd pulled Pamela Malone's (née Albright's) pigtails one time in third grade and she whacked me. Thus began my lifelong *suavité* with women, I suppose. I had a crush on her all through grade school.

"She said she saw you the other day, but didn't have time to chat."

"True. We waved."

Lunch came. Mick said, "And Pamela will ask me how you're doing, how's Allie, how's Ellen, if that's something you want to talk about."

"Allie is amazing, of course. Ellen and I are okay given the circumstances. Things are up in the air. I'm glad I'm home and can work on what I'm supposed to work on."

"I'll tell Pam you gave me a rain check on the personal front. What's up, Counselor?"

"I'm representing one of the Bandoleros in the bust up by the border."

"I know. And you're asking me, Enforcer of the Law, to help get the guy off."

"I don't think acquittal is in the cards, but a couple things aren't adding up. I think I'm in over my head, Mick. I expected this to be a guilty plea, caught dead to rights, extenuation, reduced sentence, go home. Slam dunk."

"So?"

I told him about my conversations with Gunk, and about Yuri and meeting with Leonard "Mongo" Smart. He nodded.

"Ever heard of this guy, Mongo?"

"Nope. But we're looking."

"So, tell me about the Bandoleros."

"This will cost you."

"I realize that."

I flipped to a clean page of my legal pad. Mick tucked a

napkin into his shirt collar and motioned for us to eat. Half a bowl of clam chowder disposed of, along with a chunk of corn bread, he took a breath followed by a swallow of soda, wiped his chin, leaned back, and started to talk.

He told me that back in the day, the Bandoleros were like one of the Big Five bad motorcycle clubs. They even called themselves the "One-Percenters" like the others, referring to a comment once upon a time by the president of the American Motorcyclists Association. He'd said that 99 percent of motorcyclists were law-abiding citizens and the remaining 1 percent were outlaws. This became a badge of honor, kind of like getting your book banned in Boston.

"It is a badge of sorts," said Mick, "a patch sewn on their cut saying so."

"On their what?"

"Their cut. It's the cut-off vest they wear. Denim or leather. On the back is the club name and the state they're from, and a patch saying 'One Percent.' Pagans, Outlaws, Mongols, and of course the Hells Angels have their distinctive colors."

"Like sports teams."

"Hardly. All that code of honor, club and colors malarkey, it's all illusion and delusion. They betray each other at the drop of a helmet, and over some of the pettiest stuff. Insults, girlfriends, violating pecking order. Plenty of it's serious, sure, usually drugs and guns. The results are killings, kidnapping, gunfights, stabbings."

I had trouble squaring this with the motley crew I'd seen at Gunk's arraignment. I told Mick so.

"Don't be fooled, Matt."

Mick said that all over the United States and in Canada and places worldwide, they're dangerous as hell. In LA, the Mongols have chapters of vicious Latino outlaws. In Denmark, of all places, a Bandido gang launched rocket-propelled grenades at the home of a Hells Angel.

He continued, "They're as organized as the Mafia. But unlike the Cosa Nostra, which values secrecy, these ding-dongs pride themselves on being out there and bad. They want you to know who they are and be afraid."

And I'd let my little girl ride with one.

"But not so much around here, right?" I put a forkful of salad in my mouth.

"Yes and no. A while back, the Bandoleros were falling behind. Turf fights, drugs. Then along came a new guy who took over. Get this, born and raised right here in Salish County. He cleaned house."

"Here?"

"Yep. And nationally. He pulled the Bandoleros away from their roots in New Mexico and moved their HQ right here. To his hangout in Church Harbor, a bike repair shop."

I stopped eating. I pushed my salad around on the plate separating out the sliced beets. I can't do beets. It's less the texture than the blood red color that seeps around on the plate.

"I don't make this stuff up, Matt."

Mick took another bite of Lunch Bucket signature corn bread and went on. He said that the new guy used his considerable management skills to try and reform the membership. No drugs, no guns, less humiliating initiations, even spiffed-up uniforms and patches.

"How'd that go over?"

"In fact, the organizational part worked. The Bandoleros were back. They were the biggest and baddest club in the universe, so they said."

I asked him what didn't work. Seems in 1985 a Seattle grand jury indicted fourteen of them. Part of an eight-state sweep in which more than ninety people were arrested on racketeering, kidnapping, assault, and drug and firearms violations.

"So, bye-bye bad guys?"

"Nope. Wrist-slap. Eighteen months and early release."

"Back up, Mick. I'm still having trouble getting my head around a group of desperados in a club named after a bad Dean Martin movie."

"You're forgetting Raquel Welch."

"Oh."

"Matt, I warn you that dissing these clowns, as an outsider, could get you maimed for life. By a member of another club, it might get you dead."

"So the locals here got the message."

"Surely they did not. In 2005, some of the very same suspects were paraded into court, nabbed in a nineteen-count indictment. The head guy and twenty-seven other Bandoleros and associates. All of 'em got plea deals."

"Again."

"You know how it goes down. In the first place, it's hard to make racketeering charges stick. Getting witnesses to come forward is another problem. Snitches don't have a lot of protection since an accused has the right to be confronted by witnesses against him, and law enforcement resists giving up an insider who's been helpful."

He went on, "Matt, back at the office I have photos. Bad, bad outlaws, bearded and balding, some in their sixties. One media scribe said, 'They look like a bunch of ol' grandpas'."

I hadn't even been scribbling to try to catch all this. Mick paused for a breath. My appetite was gone. Gunk. Mongo. Allie! I motioned for the check. Mick wasn't done.

"The craze started in 1947 when GIs who'd learned to ride bikes in the war were home, out of work, and amped up. A few of them crashed a legitimate motorcycle event in the town of Hollister in California. The damage they did was minor compared to the notoriety. Nationwide, the press grabbed it. 'Havoc in Hollister.' 'Terrorism!' Laughable now. After that came Brando and *The Wild One* and a mystique was born, later embraced by angry Vietnam vets and the bully element that's always been around."

"I really liked *Easy Rider.* Peter Fonda on Captain America. Who was the other dude?"

"Dennis Hopper."

"That's right. And in *Blue Velvet.*"

"With Isabella Rossellini!"

We both lost track of where we were for a second. God, we were old. Neither of us said anything.

"Another tidbit," Mick continued. "This isn't fiction. The reality is that murder in interclub rivalry is widespread. In 2008, in Ontario, Canada, eight members of a Bandidos chapter were massacred. They say it took hours for them, one by one, to watch the others get killed. It was said to be the largest mass murder in Ontario since the French and Indian War, but I can't vouch for that."

"What was it about?"

"The French and Indian War?"

"No, Mick, the murder."

"Seems the international headquarters in the United States didn't approve of Canadians using the name and patches without official sanction. Stupidity, pride, drugs, and nutcases did the rest."

"So, we're talking Canada."

"Matt, the largest concentration of Hells Angels today is a little more than twenty miles north of where we're sitting."

"Vancouver?"

"Lower mainland British Columbia. They control pot and meth distribution into the United States. They run subsidiary legitimate businesses up there for cover and revenue."

Some of this was making sense, but for one glaring disconnect. Who were Gunk and his friends? Murderers? I couldn't see it. For that matter, why would the characters I'd seen in court ever try to challenge the big, bad dogs up north? I asked Mick.

"Your Bandoleros, Matt, are not your father's Bandoleros. At least not in our county. The 1985 and 2005 busts took the sauce out of their tacos. I think I'd know if it were otherwise." Mick laughed at his own humor and wiped his mouth with his napkin.

"So why were these yoyos set up? Why launch all the law enforcement against five guys in the woods?"

"You're a smart guy, Counselor. You're getting paid to find that out."

I picked up the tab and we left. I should have eaten more. I knew Mick well enough to know he'd gone overboard on purpose, to make me get real about my once-upon-a-time nickel-and-dime drug case. On the walk back to the station, we didn't say much. He did tell me he'd sent the cell phone I'd found to the lab for testing and would get back to me. We said goodbye. I said, "I'm gonna download *Blue Velvet*."

"Horndog!" he shot back. I went to my office. I was due in court.

Mick's information was chilling. I might have gotten myself mixed up with psychotic outlaws; putting Allie in harm's way was totally not okay. That Ellen knew nothing about it wasn't okay either, and the uphill climb back into her good graces hadn't gotten any easier. Weeks still felt like an eternity. No more impulsive suggestions that the three of us get together as a "family." That agenda was up to Ellen.

My agenda, on the other hand, was Allie—not least given Mick Malone's Biker History Lesson. Whose word did I have that she'd be safe? Leonard "Mongo" Smart? Oh, good.

I called and left a message with Ellen to be sure Allie and I were going camping the next day.

I checked in the mirror before leaving the office. The whupping I'd enjoyed the night before hadn't done much damage to speak of … physiognomically, that is. My ego was another story, but happily that would get some rehab over the next couple of hours. Off to the courthouse I went.

29

L ike most lawyers, I tried to avoid Friday afternoon court calendars. They involved time-consuming, inside baseball skirmishes like motions to compel answers to interrogatories, challenges to evidence that will be offered at a trial, and other detritus that falls into the legal machinery. These are not unimportant matters, but why would a sane person want to hang out in a musty courtroom wearing a suit and tie on an otherwise pleasant afternoon? Better to be heading home for a well-deserved nap or a quick nine holes if the weather cooperated.

An exception to the never-on-Friday rule, and one in which I was honored to participate, was finalizing an adoption—-the one legal proceeding where all parties enjoy themselves and leave the courtroom happy.

Eliza McCoy and her partner of eight years, now her spouse, Sandra Weeks, had decided to adopt a child. The Children's Home Society had done the required processing, and the couple was approved. Both in their thirties, Eliza did intakes at a residence for at-risk children and Sandra taught at the university. They'd agreed to accept a newborn right from the hospital, boy or girl. Weeks of waiting and nail-biting followed. Eliza, who I'd known since childhood, had called me soon after I returned to Church Harbor and re-opened my practice; she asked me if I would represent them. I said I'd be thrilled.

She told me they were on the home stretch. There was a false start at first, not that unusual, when the CHS caseworker decided that the young mother who was about to give birth was uncertain enough that they shouldn't risk placement. This was a prudent decision. Uncertain or unwilling moms, or dads for that matter, can result in legal entanglements that last for years.

A few weeks later, however, the couple had gotten a green light. Another newborn, a boy, whose arrival on the planet was imminent. They'd held off decorating the baby's room until they got the news, then scampered out to buy blue furnishings instead of pink. Consent was not going to be an issue this time.

The big day arrived. I hugged my clients; just two of them. The third was not to be disturbed inside his comfy cocoon. I shook hands with Sandra's father. Juvenile Court Judge Andrea Martin called us into her chambers. This was the usual practice; it lent itself both to privacy and to intimacy. The court reporter followed us in with her stenotype machine and the clerk closed the door. In contrast to the dark, open expanse of the courtroom, Judge Martin's chambers were roomy and pleasant. Her drapes were drawn back and we could see out over the city. A vase of yellow chrysanthemums sat on the windowsill.

In Eliza's arms, "Baby Robert" seemed tinier than the court reporter's stenotype machine. He was swaddled in powder blue, in the tiniest article of clothing I'd ever seen. Witnesses to the event included a representative from Children's Home, Sandra's father, the guardian ad litem, and me.

Oaths were taken, questions were asked and answered, and Judge Martin next recited important words from the state statute about promising to care for Baby Robert. I teared up— for obvious reasons. The court reporter, a veteran, had trouble hitting the keys. Robert slept.

The judge signed the order of adoption, then said,

"Welcome to your family, Robert Weeks-McCoy." By this time, the Children's Home lady and the guardian ad litem were also crying. The new moms grinned from ear to ear. Granddad took the baby and looked like he wasn't going to give him back. Everyone shook hands, along with hugs, including Judge Martin. Off we went for cake and ice cream at Dessert Delish where I inhaled a piece of coconut cake with butter cream frosting. So much for my fitness resolve. With rock-solid logic, I reasoned that a celebratory post-adoption snack didn't count.

Strolling back to the office, I kicked at small stones in my way, sending them into the gutter or onto the damp grass next to the sidewalk. They ricocheted hither and thither like the shards of my own life.

My route back took me by City Hall. Out in front was a crowd of people carrying signs and listening to a speaker on the steps. It was the middle of October and election day was coming up. The crowd yelled and bounced signs up and down like campaign rallies everywhere in the Land of the Free. What caught me up short was when I noticed who the candidate was.

Sure enough, Deanna Mackenzie wasn't wasting any time running for superior court judge, as I'd predicted she would. Our paths had not crossed since I'd been home, which was good. But this was too much. She was running against Judge Scott Key before the ink was dry, or whatever metaphor to use for sheer *gaucherie* and shameless opportunism.

Scott was working hard to rehabilitate himself, I'd heard. Deanna's "blameless" character (and her allure, it must be said) compared to Scott's predicament didn't make it a fair fight. Add to this her gender. Salish County's "first woman superior court judge" was a powerful slogan. Kicking Scott while he was down suited her fine, come to think of it. Right in character.

Deanna spotted me across the sea of eager heads and waved. I did not wave back. I put my head down and kept walking.

I drove home. I needn't have worried about dinner. That's why God created peanut butter and jelly … and the coma I fell into on my sofa. It'd been some week.

30

It was a Saturday. The day before had threatened rain, but that morning the sun was back. Allie and I were going camping, come hell or high weather. Early fall often brought temperatures in the high seventies, even low eighties, which constituted a heat wave in the Pacific Northwest.

I drove to Ellen's house to pick up Allie. I was giddy and nervous at the same time. She and I had spent a day together here and there—not least involving an ill-advised motorcycle ride on Gunk's machine—but this felt different.

Ellen and I were back on tense good terms; always if Allie was in earshot.

"She's pretty excited."

"What do you think? So am I."

"Coffee?"

"No, thanks."

Ellen seemed cheerier than usual, which I took as a good sign. I was happy to settle for cheery.

"Challenging case you picked up, I gather from the paper. Biker gang?" she asked, closing the door.

Here's when I was supposed to tell her, after Allie disappeared down the hall, about getting beat up, the veiled threats involving our daughter, taking her to a crime scene, and while I was at it, a ride on a gangster's motorcycle. I chickened out. Would it have helped? She'd have gone ballistic. I told myself things were under control. Yuri and Mick Malone were on the case. And what could go wrong on a camping trip? I'd fill her in another time.

"Yeah. Weird case. My guy and his pals were busted in full moonlight so I probably won't have to break a sweat." Sheesh, what bullshit I was capable of!

"My money's on you, Counselor."

That quip also qualified as cheery.

"So where'd the little rascal disappear to?"

"Down the hall. She wants to show you her room. New bunk bed."

"Bunk bed? You expecting?"

"Very funny. Not. No, for kids to sleep over."

We walked down the hall. Allie was on the floor stuffing her suitcase—pink, of course. She'd changed into flowered pants, pink tennis shoes, and a T-shirt with a puppy on the front. Ellen and I looked at each other. This was not a subtle child.

"What do you think, Daddy?"

"Wow, what a cool room. And a bunk bed."

"Yep, and the bedspread matches the muslim curtains."

"Honey, I think they're called 'muslin' curtains."

Behind me, Ellen suppressed a giggle.

"Well, whatever. We're learning about Muslims in class, is all."

"Which bunk is yours?"

"The upper one, of course."

"Why 'of course'?"

"Because it's the coolest. Up on top of the world."

"Of course. You ready?"

"Yep, everything."

Allie hefted her pack over a shoulder and started down the hall pulling a very important-looking roller bag behind her, a stuffed gorilla under one arm. I picked up her pink sleeping bag with cavorting reindeer on it, and Ellen and I exchanged time-honored glances, again friendly, I decided, and followed.

"You're going to the coast, and you'll call me when you get there."

"Absolutely. The weather should hold. I'll call."

I thought Ellen's voice checked a bit when she bent to hug Allie. "You sure you've got everything, sweetheart?"

"Sure, Mom. I'm not a baby."

She kissed her mom goodbye and ran to the truck. I didn't dare try a hug with Ellen and a handshake would have been strange. Instead, I rested my hand on her upper arm for a tiny instant. I looked her in the eye and said thank you.

We left the freeway and hit the open road as soon as we could. Like the lady said in the song, "Freedom's just another word for nothing left to lose." I felt freer than I had in months. I'd traded in slings and arrows and adversaries for camping trips, sausage-making in the legislature for kid's room decor, birthday parties, hoops in the driveway—the magic of childhood. No-brainer.

I glanced over at my young companion. Behind the seat was the pink suitcase and sleeping bag ensemble. I slipped a disc into the CD player. Allie listened a bit, then looked at me.

"That's a very silly song, Daddy."

"Yeah, sorta."

"Who's singing?"

"They're called The Wailers."

She pulled her yellow dark glasses down on her nose, the ones with the daisies on the temples.

"Whalers? Like orcas?"

"No, honey. 'Wailers.' Bob Marley and the Wailers. They were real popular a long, long time ago."

She continued to stare, the look every parent knows whereby one's IQ diminishes by the second. Good sport that she was, Allie reached over and turned up the volume. We bounced along the road in glorious sunshine and sang as loud as we could, "I shot the sherifffffff, but I didn't shoot no deputeee ..."

∾

I glanced at the rearview mirror and my stomach flipped. Two motorcycles, black as night, were tailing us. They followed us for too long. They could have overtaken us if they chose, so I slowed down. So did they. I sped back up and they did too.

I was jumping to conclusions. We were on a state highway, in broad daylight, not much traffic, but oncoming cars every so often. Trying not to alarm Allie, I tried to make out the riders in the mirror, but that didn't help. Sure, lots of bikers wear black half-helmets out of a WWII movie, like Nazis, with goggles to match. I slowed down again looking for a pull-out. If Allie asked, I'd say I wanted to change out of my jacket.

Finally, they passed, riding Honda Gold Wings for Christ's sake! The front guy yelled "license plate" and gestured with his thumb toward the truck bed. Then he waved and sped by. So did his wife. My heart rate crept back toward normal, or as close to normal as the events of the past week permitted. I pulled over and checked. Sure enough, a screw had come loose and the plate was flapping around like a loose tooth. I fixed it and we motored on.

We reached our campground and were in luck. The weather was downright balmy. As far as I could tell, we had the place to ourselves. After calling Ellen to check in, we set up camp in a sheltering grove of madrone trees with a view of the water. I sat on a driftwood log, elbows on my knees, and watched my daughter skip stones across a flat lagoon, a valuable skill taught her by her dad. She ran this way and that with the boundless energy my out-of-shape self envied. Eventually, she collapsed onto the log beside me, and we listened to light waves lap the rocky beach. Allie said she was hungry.

My camping skills allowed for browning pork chops in a large saucepan that doubled as a Dutch oven. I layered the meat with green beans, carrots, and red potatoes and covered it all with onion soup mix and half a cup of water. Simmer for thirty minutes. Dessert was brownies Ellen had made. Food eaten out of doors tastes best.

After dinner, we found a rock by a creek that fed the lagoon and washed the pot and utensils with sand. No detergent, of course. A water ouzel bobbed and weaved across the way. The breeze picked up. Darkness would come soon and it was getting chilly. We cuddled by the campfire. Allie's hair was saltwater perfume with a leftover hint of shampoo. Away, over the water, we watched stars twinkle on and begin their slow pivot across the sky. Later, the moon rose. We were light-years away from everything. This was where I belonged.

The shiver in my soul was not due to the chill.

"You cold, Daddy?"

"No, honey. Just happy."

Happy didn't begin to describe it.

31

On the drive over to the coast, as once or twice before, I'd dreaded *the* question-and-answer session with Allie. I'd been understandably cautious (read, totally silent) about bringing up you-know-what and interfering with whatever progress she and Ellen and the counselor had made. I hadn't been excluded from the sessions; I'd taken part often. But here we were, alone, the two of us, and away from home. How was I to account to my daughter for me?

"Daddy ..." Allie had changed into her pj's, slippers, and hoodie, and stashed the rest of her gear in our tent. I was moving other paraphernalia back and forth to the truck. She plopped herself down very importantly in a camp chair.

"Can I ask you a question?"

Uh-oh. Here it would come. Judge, jury, eye-witness, injured party, prosecutor, and ten-year-old inquisitor rolled into one. "Up against the wall, Mr. Archer. Hands behind your back please. Blindfold or no blindfold?" This conversation had to happen sooner or later.

I unfolded the other camp chair and sat down. It was dark enough that she couldn't see that the blood had drained from my face.

"Sure, sweetheart. What's up?" I think I kept my voice level.

"Tell me again about how you and Mom met. That's so romantic."

Maybe Allie wasn't setting me up. On the other hand, what choice did I have? It was a plain enough request. Yeah, right. Smoke drifted into the trees. The fire had dimmed to orange coals peeping out of gray ash.

I took a shot at changing the subject. Allie'd gotten her hair cut. The ponytail was gone. Wisps poked out from underneath her baseball cap.

"You cut off your ponytail."

She shook her head. "I didn't, Daddy. The hairdresser did."

Hairdresser. Good grief.

"Why? It was cute."

"That was before. This makes me look more grown-up."

Grow up? Not if I can help it, I thought.

"Why's it longer in the front than in the back?"

Patient sigh. "It's supposed to be. It's called an A-line."

"Oh."

She was persistent. "You and Mommy. How you met?"

"Okay. Once upon a time, a very pretty girl walked past me …"

I told her the story she'd heard most of before.

We sipped our hot chocolate. There was rustling in the underbrush back in the woods. An owl hooted. It was so quiet we could hear the click-click of a sea otter cracking open a shell on its chest—a mussel I'd guess—and the soft lapping of tiny waves.

"Keep going, Daddy."

"We waited to get married until after I took the bar exam. Your mom's idea."

"Yep. She always makes me wait when I want to do some things. Wants me to think it over, whether it's a good idea or not," is what came out of the mouth of my child.

More silence. Her wide-eyed and innocent face stared

across the cast iron fire ring at me. "She was so pretty, you were so handsome."

"Were?" We laughed.

"Allie, my perfectly amazing Allie." I shook my head. "She is beautiful. She's the best. And I would give anything to not hurt her. Or you. But sometimes I don't think things through like I should." I had no idea how much she'd been told, so I didn't risk an explanation.

Allie gave me that serious look she has, like when she's beating me at Hearts. This was different, though. She pulled her chair around beside mine. There were tears on her cheeks. I put my arm around her and kissed the top of her head.

"I'm not going anywhere. I'm here to stay. With you. And Mom."

With the fire out, it was now definitely cold. Allie sniffled and wiped her nose with the sleeve of her pajamas.

It was my turn to pry. "Is Mom, um, seeing anyone?"

Allie didn't hesitate. "Just Arthur." She drawled the first syllable, "Aarrthur." She didn't say "yuck" but she might as well have.

"Arthur?"

"Yeah. He has a car that the top goes down. He's an SPA, she says, or something."

"CPA?"

"That's it." She looked at the fire, then gave up trying to weigh her words. She said, "I hate him!"

"Allie, you don't hate him."

"Yes, I do. He sends her these cards and writes poetry in them. I call him 'Author.'"

I grabbed my cocoa mug with both hands to keep it from spilling.

"Mommy hates that."

I loved her loyalty, so I went ahead and asked how old he was.

"Old. Really old!"

"Uh, does he spend the night?"

"Daddy! Gross!"

I backed off. Allie changed the subject, too.

"Hey, Daddy, tomorrow I want to go find those goats we saw. They are so weird. Is it true that goats will eat anything?"

"That's true. Anything. Even cafeteria food."

We settled in the tent, snug as bugs, and Allie was out in seconds in her reindeer bag. I snorfled a few times, then joined her in the Land of Nod.

SNAP! A crack like a bullwhip shot me up and out of a solid sleep! Heart-monitor time. I strained to listen. Nothing. Then murmurs; and a cur-rrack! I slithered out of my sleeping bag fast, careful not to waken Allie. I reached and found the heaviest object I could find, my crummy heavy-duty camping flashlight that might have weighed all of three pounds—the weapon of choice against marauding bad guys. Damn, I'd left the hatchet out by the campfire.

In flannel pajamas and wool-lined moccasins, I would open the tent fly and flash blinding light at the intruders. A force of nature, with surprise and rage on my side, I'd, I'd scare the hell out of … the stately three-point buck browsing by the fire pit, two of his harem nibbling on low tree twigs. What's up with you, human? he might have asked before wandering away.

Allie slept through it all. I stayed awake a long time, lying on my back staring at the dark tent roof, heart thumping in my chest. Who could find us here? Who even knew we were here?

Anybody, who wanted to bad enough.

Allie and I got back to Church Harbor Sunday evening near dusk. I gave her a colossal hug before surrendering her to her mom, standing in the porch light on the front steps.

"I think I survived," I joked. Ellen did me the favor of

smiling before she thanked me, and they went inside. Allie waved before the door shut. I was sad and happy at the same time, like it said on a Chinese fortune cookie somewhere. I'd take the euphoria while it lasted.

32

Monday morning, an inventory of my kitchen revealed that I was out of the basics: shredded wheat, orange juice, milk, mixed berry yogurt, eggs. I might cut the mold off the bar of cheddar cheese, but I didn't even take the lid off a Tupperware container of uncertain provenance; I thought about taking it to the hazardous waste dump out in the county. A bag of coffee in the freezer looked okay. In my cupboard were some crackers with a use-by date in the last century and two cans of mushroom soup I'd take a chance on. Make that, we. Maybe I should stock up on real food with some nutritional value necessary for a growing daughter. Meat, vegetables, fruit, that sort of thing. Wouldn't hurt my tenuous resolve to exercise more and eat better either. I set off for the grocery store.

I was walking through the parking lot, when what should I see but an all-too-familiar green Jaguar. I skidded to a stop a few feet away and watched as Luke Barkley and Deanna Mackenzie, all casual as hell, hefted bags of groceries into the trunk. They finished, and Luke walked Deanna around to the driver's side, opened the door for her, and gave her a kiss. A real one.

Sonofabitch.

I strode over, all John Wayne, and interrupted the romantic interlude.

"Luke, good to see you," hand out to shake his. "I had no idea bag boys were so chummy with customers."

He was startled, but recovered quickly.

"Matt, are you ever without a smartass comment? Deanna, let's go."

He walked around to the passenger side. I planted myself on the driver's side and leaned against the door.

"Hello, Matt," she said, lots of teeth, bright lipstick, but wary eyes. "A belated welcome home."

"I'm going to guess, Deanna, you're not just giving this guy a ride to his house."

"No, I'm not. Luke put his condo on the market a month ago. We bought a place."

"We? A month?"

"Yes. You're a smart man. Can you connect the dots?"

"So you two were playing games with me."

"Yes, we were. Would it have helped or hurt for you to know?"

Luke leaned over from the passenger seat. "Listen, Matt. We'd love to chat, honest. Deanna, honey, let's go."

She pushed him back to his side.

"Matt, you got the result you wanted."

"No help from your passenger. Next I'm going to hear that Lover Boy over there actually helped the cause."

She didn't reply.

I said, "He was Raging Bull up there in that gallery. You saw how much he added to Capitol City Days of Yore. They'll be re-running that tape for years."

Deanna started the car. She took a final swipe. "Know what, Matt," she said, "You're plain old green-eyed jealous."

Even Luke took pity. "Deanna, enough. He gets it."

I couldn't let that charitable gesture go unrewarded.

"Gee, Luke. I thought I was talking to Deanna. By the way, how are the anger management classes going?"

"Matt, give it up," Deanna said.

"Yeah, I do get it." I stepped back from the car door. "I was confused there for a while, Deanna, thinking there was such a thing as honor among, um ... friends. Friends that share a history."

"That's the point. History. The past versus the present."

Of course, she was right.

"Believe what you want, Matt. Tell yourself any story, but think it through later. And don't confuse thinking with your testosterone level."

"Testosterone? Hey, Luke, how's Dolores?"

He jerked up the passenger side door handle.

"Matt," Deanna held onto his arm, "you might have one of your sleuths do a little digging into Mrs. Scott Key. Just a suggestion."

She waved me away. "Here is the truth, Matt. Luke and I are together now. We like it. It feels right. P.S. Why don't you worry more about your own domestic situation."

Bitch! But I couldn't argue with that either.

"I don't want us hating each other," she said. "We both live here. Things worked out for you." She added, "Legislatively."

I took a step back, unable to think of a good parting shot as they drove off.

I went in the store. The congestion of ordinary people wheeling grocery carts and herding kids, busy clerks hustling around, and aisle after aisle of canned tomatoes and jars of olives, green heaping bunches of celery and parsley, endless varieties of cereal, milk, butter, frozen meals, and eggs, apples and bananas, paper towels—calmed me down. I even bought an over-priced bouquet of flowers.

The day that hadn't started out so well didn't improve.

An attorney's overhead is not overwhelming compared

to other professions—say, a doctor's—but even minimal furnishings and a rented copy machine, heat and light, legal periodicals, case law updates, and supplies add up. That Monday afternoon, it was brought home again that practicing law is, in the end, about the clients, whoever they are—angry landlords, check kiters, credit card maximizers, shoplifters, juvenile delinquents, their parents, con scheme victims, to give a few examples.

Warm and fuzzy adoptions were the exception. On the other hand, taking whatever washed up on the beach as a client was what to expect. Later on, I might get to be choosy: bustling business plans, optimistic incorporations, knotty probates, not to mention grisly but lucrative personal injury cases with lots of insurance. The economy was in a slump, which didn't help, and even more established offices than mine were doing workouts with banks, meetings of creditors, lease restructurings. Into the office would walk the apocryphal, but too often true, story of the anxious couple for whom the best and honest advice was to not throw good money after bad and "buy" themselves a job. The deserted downtown corner was not the place to open a cozy bistro, no matter how good a cook mom was. Do not listen to the brother-in-law whose racquetball partner had stumbled on the Best Kitchen Utensil marketing opportunity since Cutco knives.

And the flotsam and jetsam syndrome was never more on display than at my court appearance that Monday afternoon. Most lawyers try to avoid "dissolutions" (the technical euphemism for a divorce) for good reason. They're like an afternoon soap opera, more often than not.

Four of us sat in a stale conference room across the hall from Salish County Superior Courtroom Department Number Three. Our case would be heard in twenty minutes. We were squeezed around a table: my client, a dentist; his soon-to-be-ex spouse; her lawyer Al Sobjack; and me. There were no windows or pictures on the wall, not even a Walmart knockoff of a snow-capped mountain. Ventilation was terrible and there was less and less oxygen in the room as the meeting went on.

Incredibly, the wife had had the audacity to show up that day accompanied by her new "friend." That bungler had the further audacity to requisition an extra chair from the hallway and try to join us in the conference room. Attorney Sobjack quashed that and shut the door on him.

My client was a hard-working guy in his thirties. The wife had put him through dental school, but she'd been laid off from the bookstore where she worked. She hadn't found a job in months, which she blamed, with pursed lips and a frown, on "the stupid competition," whatever than meant. The sordid details of the disintegration of their once idyllic marriage followed the textbook account of student and supportive spouse, studying late but still time for exhausted sex, finals, state boards, delayed honeymoon in Hawaii, then real life. It was a common scenario in the era of serial marriages. Thankfully, there'd been no kids.

The veil of their marital bliss had become more of a curtain behind which to rehearse recriminations and entertain fantasies. His fantasies centered on scrounging for patients; hers, I argued, didn't include scrounging hard enough to find another job, any job. His fantasies were more of a fiscal kind, while hers were fantasies born of trade paperbacks and assorted bodice-rippers hanging on racks at the big national chain store where she had worked. She'd decided she'd be a writer. Anyone could do that.

She joined a writing group, a member of which just happened to be the next Ernest Hemingway, the guy waiting out in the hall. Who knew! "Hem" was tall and fit, going to gray, and had crinkly brown eyes bespeaking too many days marlin fishing in the Caribbean, no doubt. He was tan; he was not from around Church Harbor, that was clear. He could be confided in. Trusted. Supportive. She needed that.

Their domestic crisis was not unique. Life imitated art, in fact not fiction, as my client found out when the missus didn't come home one night. So he sued for divorce. There wasn't much property to divide in our community property state. The good news was that Mrs. Dentist had hired an attorney who was an old pro in the divorce game. He, Al Sobjack, Esq., was my age, a little more in need of physical exercise; his signature tortoiseshell half-glasses made you smile. He had long ago learned that the more time a divorce takes, the worse things get. Hopefully to be avoided was the agony of endless depositions, of putting witnesses on the stand and extracting shaded versions of the truth under the guise of swearing to tell nothing but, all fodder for years and years of bitterness afterward. Better to be candid with one's client about the reality of property division and alimony, to settle the case in a timely fashion, and get on with life.

About divorce lawyers, specialists in "domestic relations" (of which I was not one), the good ones are worth every penny they charge. They are not the bottom feeders as often portrayed. Sure, the sensational headline grabber in Tinsel Town is the public's all-too-familiar model. But in real life, non-flashy stalwarts like Al Sobjack perform an essential service for troubled people and practice a type of law other lawyers run from.

It is also true that a court of law is like a blunt instrument when it comes to domestic relations. Take the most intimate of human relations, a marriage, and expose each party's worst peccadilloes to the searing light of day—make a public record of it, and have it all boil down to a fifteen-minute ruling by a judge. Five-year marriage or twenty, it's the same fifteen minutes. Case closed.

Al Sobjack and I were both the cordial, non-confrontational

sort, and we had litigated together before I moved home. So it was that after a few meetings, each with our own clients then with each other, Counselor Sobjack and I had hammered out an agreement. Our clients had grudgingly come to accept the middle ground. The wife had agreed to less, and temporary, alimony. Under the circumstances, she should have. Judges are human beings, after all. There was no real property; they leased. So the property to be divided consisted of a savings account, personal effects, household furnishings, and a pair of cars.

We shuffled papers back and forth and read them. Everything was resolved, or so it seemed.

Al Sobjack said, "Matt, my client has mentioned one item that is missing from Exhibit A to the Settlement Agreement."

"Sure. What's that?"

"Uh, it's a jar of sand."

"Excuse me?"

"She has noticed it's gone from the mantel in their home where it used to be."

"A jar of, what, ordinary sand?"

"It's not ordinary sand," she exclaimed.

I looked at my guy. He looked unperturbed.

"What is it, then?"

"It's sand we collected on our honeymoon and brought back. It's a keepsake," she said, firing the words like pistol shots.

Her lips were trembling. She glared at her husband.

I asked him, "Can you help out here?"

"I took it. It is not from our honeymoon. It's from a trip I took with some buddies when we went clam digging over at the coast. We used to kid about it."

"He's lying!" She was livid.

"The hell I am."

"Al, tell me we're not going to screw up … er, not resolve

this and have to postpone the hearing, which now starts in, let me see, ten minutes."

Al looked at me and didn't blink.

"Matt, my client is insistent. He returns the jar of sand or the deal's off."

"Okay, okay. I'll talk to him."

They went out, she into "Hem's" consoling arms where she began to sob. It was beyond ridiculous for the jackass to be anywhere near the premises under the circumstances. My otherwise mild-mannered client witnessed this through the open door and tried to chase out after them until I pulled him back into the room. We sat back down.

"So what's up with this?" I asked.

"It's like I said. I took it."

"What's it like?"

"It's an ordinary Mason jar. With a lid. Couple of seashells, and sand."

"Clam-digging?" I asked.

He was staring up at the ceiling, not at me. I asked him again.

"All right. It was from our honeymoon. Jesus Christ, she wants a memento of our *honeymoon*? That takes the freakin' cake."

Yes, divorce proceedings and falsehoods. I gave the wife some credit. This was a very tense time, and none more so than this day of reckoning. Her emotions were at flood stage. My client, by contrast, had been pretty stoic about the whole thing. Heck, he delivered pain for a living. The presence of Mr. Wonderful out in the hall had him dug in. What to do?

I let the silence do its thing. When you're in a hole, you're not supposed to keep digging, so they say. The minute hand on the ancient clock on the wall crept past eleven. There was a quiet knock on the door and Al stuck his head in.

"A couple more minutes. Could you please tell the judge we need a teensy bit more time? Maybe he wants to take a break anyway."

The door closed.

"It's up to you. Go or no-go?"

"Shit."

"I agree. But let me try this on you. A year from now when today has become a distant memory, and Hemingway out there has found other fish to catch, you'll be taking a week off to go play golf in Palm Springs."

He sighed. "I have it out in the car."

"Good boy. I'll tell Mr. Sobjack."

Justice was served yet again. Al Sobjack and I owed each other a drink.

33

I could no longer put off calling Gunk. I'd stalled as long as I had because I still had no news, good or otherwise. For starters, there were a lot of loose ends: angry bikers from BC, a blinking cell phone, no hint of who the informant might be, if there was one. The enigmatic Mongo—from Texas? And Gunk wasn't going to want to take the government's offer anyway, whatever it was. I hadn't heard from Lem Fish—which was okay, since I had nothing extenuating, not to mention exculpating, to offer him. If we ended up going to court to cop a plea, we needed something to work with. Make that I had to do something to earn the money I was being paid.

Unrelated, but nonetheless hanging around in the back of my brain were Dolores and Scott Key. And our stalwart sheriff. Seamy stuff, to be sure, but I still wasn't entirely buying her excuse for calling me to ask for help.

I punched in Gunk's number, but no one answered. Turned out he was on his way to my place.

I drove to Allie's school to pick her up. She was spending the night; Ellen had a meeting at work. That was good, because Allie and I had a very important task ahead of us: assembly of a basketball hoop. Was it just my imagination that I heard Ellen suppress a snicker over the phone at the thought of Mr. All-Thumbs with tools in his hand?

On the way to pick Allie up, I'd passed a boarded-up storefront where a bunch of teenagers and other out-of-the-mainstream losers were hanging out exclaiming this, gesticulating that, and smoking pot. Public opinion ran the gamut about the state's recent legalization of marijuana. I understood the dollars and cents argument about law enforcement needing scarce resources for dangerous crimes versus busting pot users. But I couldn't get past the idea of the waste, the waste of human resources squandering whatever little cash these streetside yo-yos might have to spend it on marijuana, and scrambling their brains in the process. Maybe it was the mood I was in.

"Vaping" is what these lost souls were doing—some not much older than Allie. "Vape" was a word I'd made up as a verb, combining "vapid" and "gape": to wit, staring stoned at nothing, or dope-flashing on profound subjects like teaching a pit bull to fetch or a pig to fly. Couldn't these kids find a job; stay clear of the tall dude with the do-rag and calf-length, shiny black overcoat holding forth, arms waving, his obligatory pit bull chained to a meter? I told myself to quit being preachy—preachy, meaning O.L.D.

Promptly at 3:30 p.m., I pulled up in front of Allie's school and parked across from the yellow buses queued up in their designated lane. At 3:31, Allie walked out of the building chatting with friends—all girls, I was happy to note. She saw the truck, said goodbye, and started to run my way—then caught herself and lapsed into a nonchalant saunter, a sophisticated pre-teen saunter. She tossed her parka and backpack behind the seat, and I got a quick smooch. She glanced back to be sure none of her group were watching, which they were because the truck was not a vehicle they recognized.

"Who were those girls?" Oops, Dad, don't start off asking questions.

"Friends."

I wasn't doing the inquisition thing. I was just making conversation, but that's not the way kids see it. Still new at this, I was learning to negotiate the thin line between caring too much, wanting to know everything, and trying to simply be a chum. Every parent knows this conundrum. The conversation might resume if I shut up and let her take the lead. Sometimes she'd jabber on like I put a nickel in.

There was also the time I made a pb&j for her lunch plus an apple and some Oreos. When she went to brush her teeth, I wrote "U da best!" with a magic marker on the paper napkin I put in. She was mortified, but hey, I was getting the dad-groove back and couldn't help myself.

We pulled out past a row of buses, and I did a double-take. Across the street were two motorcycles, parked. They weren't Hondas or Suzukis. They were lowered choppers, both ebony black, high bars and all. I hit the brake and Allie braced herself with a hand on the dash. I didn't see any riders, but what in the hell were they doing across the street from an elementary school?

"What happened, Daddy?" I'd scared her.

I slowed down and looked again. I wasn't going to stop and get out, but I thought I'd seen part of a gang decal. I tried telling myself that bikers, even those I might not want to invite to dinner, had kids. Maybe they were at a teacher's conference, maybe visiting someone who lived on the block. But two of them?

I moved on. I told Allie I was sorry. That because of Gunk's case, I might have recognized one of the motorcycles. Just curious, honey.

But it shook me up, was not okay, despite Mongo's blithe assurances. That they were parked in a No Parking zone and angled side by side kept my stomach churning all the way to my place. Maybe I was overreacting, but I would call Yuri and Mick and let them know. Trust *Mongo*?

It was still light enough to start assembling a youth-sized

basketball standard, a challenge I looked forward to with the enthusiasm of ridding a nest of spiders. "Easy assembly— needs no special tools" for me always meant "this will take the better part of a day, and you'll make at least two trips to the hardware store and utter naughty words." My tool chest, if it could be called that, consisted of a tack hammer, a wobbly pair of pliers, and a bent flat-blade screwdriver, all of which rattled around in the back of a kitchen drawer.

Manning up, and determined to prove my mettle, I opened the large box in the driveway. Allie's job was to keep the instructions from blowing away. A bewildering assortment of parts lay strewn around. It was cold, and we were bundled up, but she was ready. She wore jeans and a powder blue fleece vest over a long-sleeved black T-shirt, and black, Vibram-soled knock-around boots to match, with red shoelaces. My sole addition to her wardrobe was a Chicago Cubs cap, which she wore backward. This had nothing to do with Abner Doubleday's game; she thought cubs were cute.

I was dressed more appropriately: three layers, not two, which included a down parka, thick socks, and a green knit ski hat pulled down over my ears. It had a tip on the top like a condom, which I'd never say to her. I looked ridiculous, but "Northwest." Allie looked adorable and Northwest.

"Instructions, Page One: First, remove contents from box." Who did they think we were? How'd we get to the instructions otherwise? We managed that one okay. "Read all instructions before starting assembly." Right. Book-length. Who had time?

"Dad, I think it'd be a good idea."

"'Dad'? What happened to 'Daddy'?"

"That was when I was a little girl. Now I'm ten."

"How does Mom feel about that?"

"Mommy likes 'Mommy' best."

"Let me think about it."

Allie retrieved the booklet from under my foot, so I read it.

Next page: "Place all contents on a flat surface and make sure all pieces are included." We complied, per the admonition of my assistant. There were lots of metal and plastic pieces, a wooden backboard painted white with black trim, and the basketball hoop and net. Allie was getting excited. I was getting worried. The apparatus supposed to anchor this contraption to the ground was like something from the French Revolution. As promised, there were nuts, bolts, and screws for "non-special" tools, namely, ones I owned.

At this moment, Fortune smiled and Yuri Brodsky rode up. He was impressive—glistening bike, rakish helmet, handsome face, and mustache.

Allie cried, "Uncle Yuri!" and ran to get a hug.

Yuri kissed her on the cheek, then shook his head at the mess in front of us.

"Yuri, please help my dad put this thing together."

"Sure, sweetie, but your dad doesn't need any help."

Noble of him.

"Yes, he does. He has that look on his face."

"What look would that be, my little princess," said I, as sarcastically as possible.

"The way you look when you can't find something."

Yuri ignored her. My phone rang. It was Gunk. Chipper as a chipmunk, I said, "Yo, Gunk. Nice to hear from you. How've you been?"

"Matt. I'm in town. I hoped it might be okay to come by."

I told him how to get to my place and went inside to make coffee. I left Yuri and Allie poring over the instructions and starting to assemble parts.

34

I came back out as Gunk rode up, but he was not alone. He dismounted as did a slight, tousle-headed boy of about eight, wearing coveralls, a plaid shirt, and a gray fleece vest unbuttoned. Like his dad.

"Matt, this is Gordon, my son."

Like Pete and re-Pete, they hooked their helmets on Gunk's bike. The boy and I shook hands. His grip was confident, though his face betrayed some understandable wariness when Allie and Yuri walked over. I made introductions, Yuri meeting the eponymous Gunk for the first time. The big boys compared their two-wheeled toys for a few minutes. Allie and Gordon watched; he was just a little shorter than she was.

The backboard was completed and they were ready to put the standard into place. It had taken them minutes. Yuri defused any awkwardness. "Gordon, you play basketball?"

Allie said, "Yeah, give us a hand, okay?" like she'd known him for years. My daughter, Ms. Hospitality.

The three of them went back to work. Gunk took it all in. I shrugged my shoulders and we went inside. I took coffee back out for Yuri and hot chocolate for the kids.

Back inside, I said, "Good-looking young man, Gunk."

"Takes after his mother."

"Not going to argue with you there." Levity, before I had to level with him.

"Hey, how come he's in the US?"

"He's here till the weekend. I told you. We make it work. Less said the better."

We sat across from each other and I put on my game face.

"Let me get right to the point, Gunk. Who ratted you guys out?"

"Why are you so sure someone did?"

I shook my head. "We've talked about this. What are the chances a bunch of DEA guys and some local cops are driving around aimlessly in the middle of the night and happen to stumble on you boys beneath the full moon partying with a freshly delivered stash of pot?"

Before, Gunk had been all helpful and earnest and polite. Now, he was defensive, not that I could blame him.

"Let's do it this way." I started to list names. "Stan Stanley."

"Stinky? He's a county farm boy. Works at his dad's dairy."

"Could he have been the guy? Any trouble with the law? Does he owe somebody money?"

"I doubt it. I don't know about scrapes with the law. If he owed money, it'd be for gambling at the casino, but he's not smart enough. Besides, he's getting married to a Dutch Reformed girl."

"Prescott Endicott?"

"Pissy runs a business, like I told you. He's educated. I don't think he'd play footsie with the DEA."

"Gunk, he's from Back East where big-time crime happens."

"Matt, Pissy's a nice guy. Loaned me money back when I started out. I repaid him. He's good people."

This was going nowhere. From outside, I heard the whap whap whap of a basketball on the pavement, the clunk of it hitting the backboard, a yaaay when someone made a basket. A shout or two from Yuri.

"Daniel Higginbotham. 'Butthead.' The 'ipso facto' guy. That was funny."

Gunk didn't smile. "I'd be very surprised," he said.

He took a sip of coffee and inspected my kitchen. Dirty dishes were on the counter, towels in a clump.

"Nice place, Matt." Of course, I'd seen his living arrangement.

"Let's get back to the possible culprit. Tell me about Mitchell Scruggs. You told me you don't hang out with him other than to ride."

"That's true. Sheila doesn't like him. Says he's trashy, for starters, and chain-smokes."

"Rebecca Murray would agree, in case you didn't see her body language in court."

"The public defender gal?"

I nodded. Yuri and Allie came in, trailed by Gordon, all breathless and wanting a drink of water. Gordon leaned against his dad, face flushed and panting. Allie mimicked him against me. Two tableaux. A glance by Yuri at Gunk and me, he shooed them back outside.

"So, Scruggs. Could he have been the snitch?"

"Can't say, Matt."

Couldn't or wouldn't, I wasn't going to push it. Instead, I suggested it might be someone who wasn't there that night. Mongo, for instance.

He shrugged it off. "We kept it to ourselves, the arrangement. Pot smokers are not known for extra generosity, as you might have heard. Dividing the stash among twenty or so was not in the cards."

"I see."

"Matt, remember I told you. We're a group of guys who do tame drugs once in a while and party at somebody's place out in the county. We do group up and act like we're bad sometimes, but it's the high. You get pumped up. Doesn't everybody do something stupid sometimes?"

I had no reply to that. But I didn't think Lem Fish, or a federal judge, would be forgiving of these carefree, just-for-fun Bandoleros, so I kept on drilling about how they happened to get caught. I repeated the suspicion about Mongo. No answer.

"All right, Gunk." I put the picture of him and son Gordon out of my mind. "Let me tell you something about your Mongo." I stared at him. "He's a patched Hells Angel from Texas."

I did not get the reaction I expected.

"Was," said Gunk.

From out front, whap, whap, whap, clunk. I switched from wannabe confidant to hard-ass lawyer.

"Gunk, you clearly know more about this than I do, or than you're telling me."

"Matt, I'd stake my life that Mongo did not turn us in."

"I hope you're right. You may be staking your freedom on it, too. Here's what I think the US Attorney will be willing to do."

I told him what I thought Lem might offer, minimal time probably served in the local lockup. Gunk got up, jammed his hands into his pockets, and walked into the living room. He stood there watching the basketball game outside. He didn't return to the kitchen. I went to him.

"So?"

"So, fuck!"

"Fuck is right, Gunk. Do we go to trial?"

"I'll think about it. You and that prosecutor guy seem like pals …"

"Oh no, no, no, Mr. Carlyle. Don't even go there. Don't even start to think it."

I was pissed off, but he was angrier.

"Cool off, Gunk. It's a shitty deal, but you did the crime …"

"So, I'll do the time. Right? Meanwhile, you'll go shoot hoops with your daughter."

It was time for the conversation to end. Of course he was

angry. Reality will have its way with each of us, creeping in at its own pace and on its own time. Most of our perceptions each day that we patrol the planet are through clouds of how we hope things are, from little things like signals changing from red to green on time, to bigger matters like, oh, affairs being worth trashing marriages.

Gunk didn't say goodbye—to me, anyway. I followed him out. He and Yuri did that biker hug thing while Gordon shuffled his feet and grown-up Allie gave him a little wave. I started to reach for Gunk's hand to shake it, when Allie dashed off across the lawn. Her mother drove up.

Uh-oh. What had I forgotten? What new transgression had befallen me? My guess was she wasn't bringing me a winning lottery ticket.

But Ellen had a pleasant look on her face, followed by her pretty smile as she walked toward Yuri. They had a full-on hug. She handed Allie the white parka she'd forgotten, the one with the elephant on it. Then, my oh my, yours truly got a squeeze.

Chivalrous as always, Yuri introduced Ellen to Gunk and Gordon.

"So this is the famous biker friend of my daughter's," she said, shaking Gunk's hand. "And your boy."

"A pleasure, ma'am." He put his arm on Gordon's shoulder. "I hope Miss Allie hasn't been filling your head with made-up exploits."

Exploits? Right out of the Mongo lexicon.

"No, actually it's her father's expl …" She caught herself before her quick wit got the better of her.

Yuri cleared his throat. We all looked like the freeze-frame in a car commercial or something. I came to, and tossed the basketball to Allie. She threw it to Gordon and they went back to hoops. The four adults decided to watch the round-ballers chase rebounds before attempting more conversation.

The brief silence was followed by a comment on the weather, then small talk and polite conversation resumed. Ellen asked Yuri what his adventurous mom was up to. Just back from a trip to Vegas, it turned out. Ellen shook her head. She asked Gunk how business was and if it was too soon to put in bulbs. No, anytime before the ground gets frozen. Gunk asked Ellen about work. She'd just come across a new line of holiday cards and the print run was underway.

The three of them looked at me. I was dumbstruck by the scene, like something I'd made up in my fondest daydreams. I had the presence of mind to close my open mouth. I'd thought of six or seven brilliant ways to enter the conversation, but was too baffled to interrupt. "Stunned" wasn't too strong a word. And, after Ellen's near faux pas, almost giddy.

Whap whap whap went the basketball.

The wind was picking up. I recovered enough to invite everyone inside. Gunk said no thanks, favoring me with a smile that looked a bit forced; I wasn't to forget he was angry at me. He hollered to Gordon. In their look-alike duds, the father and son "outlaws" looked like they were off to a Dad's Day field trip to the zoo.

"Nice to meet you, Allie's mom," said Gordon.

"Likewise," said his dad.

Then, helmets strapped on, they were off.

Ellen said, "Matt, I'm sorry about the sarcasm."

"It was okay," I fudged. "I'm just happy you came by."

"Watching the kids, meeting Gunk, I …" She stopped and looked away. "I mean, I see what you're up against. You know how I'm too quick to judge."

Yuri took the opportunity to chase Allie across the lawn.

"I think you have every right …" but before we could wade any further into maudlin, Ellen held up her hand. She called to Allie, hugged her goodbye, then said a cheery toodle-oo, and left.

Yuri punched me on the shoulder. I winced.

Despite my offer to cook dinner, he took a pass. Allie wanted Mexican so we ordered in. After dinner she did homework— in fifth grade, for heaven's sake—while I worked on some files I'd brought home. Before bed we watched *The Sound of Music*, which I liked a lot.

Next morning, during cereal, orange juice, and a banana, I absently paged through the newspaper, sports page primarily. Allie was unusually quiet for a change.

She set down her glass. "Daddy, do you think there's a chance that you and Mom ...?"

Silence. Another spoonful of Cheerios. Head down. I summoned courage. "Sweetie, I don't know if your mom will ever ..."

How often people communicate with unfinished sentences.

"Yeah. She was pretty mad."

"Uh-huh." Brilliant reply. Where was the handbook on this?

"How about this?" I tried, "I won't rule anything out, okay? I've been back in town for, let's see, a couple of months."

We both slurped the last of our Cheerios.

"And another thing," said my daughter for whom no advantage would be missed.

"Yes, sweetie," I said, bracing myself.

"About a dog."

"That might be easier than your mom."

35

I took Allie to school and went in to work. Rebecca Murray had called again. I called her back. I owed her a report, defense counsel to defense counsel, on what I'd learned—and vice versa. She had come to town the night before and was staying at the rather upscale bayside hotel on the water I couldn't have afforded in good times. The federal government's fiscal situation apparently wasn't as bad as the state's.

She was dressed that day not in full armor, courtroom style, but in a khaki skirt and white blouse. A fleece vest hung on the back of a chair. Two files, a legal pad, a cup of coffee, and a half-eaten scone were on the table. She didn't stand when I got there but extended a hand for a businesslike handshake.

"Good afternoon, Mr. Archer. Please sit down. I need to finish a note to myself here before I lose my train of thought."

Outside, seagulls swooped past the window of the hotel restaurant. It was clouding up and promised rain. The bay was battleship gray with tiny dots of white icing on swells far out where the channel came our way from open water to the south. Side-glancing at Rebecca, I noticed what I hadn't seen before, a slight tremor in her right hand beside her cup of coffee while she wrote on a legal pad with the other. Nerves. Jitters. An occupational hazard of daily trial work that increases with age, and I guessed she wasn't much older than me.

Ms. Murray's nerves betrayed her studied calm and took some of the shine off her otherwise professional façade. Attracting qualified candidates to the Federal Public Defender's office, or assistant US Attorney's, for that matter, wasn't difficult. Competition for well-paying jobs was fierce. The problem was retaining people. Big law firms swam the waters in courtrooms like sharks after prey, not to eat, but to lure attorneys into high-paying jobs. Good trial lawyers were a scarce commodity. Smarts and quick thinking are a given. Reacting in a flash to high inside fastballs or change-ups thrown by lying witnesses, opposing counsel objections, questions out of the blue from a judge, is a skill that can't be taught. It took its toll, however, at the same time experience was accumulated.

Not that I was passing judgment. I knew the drill and I sympathized. I'd handled my share of criminal defendants and they were a sad lot. It was often said that if stupidity was a crime, they couldn't build enough jails. Stupidity coupled with difficult economic straits swelled the criminal ranks. Representing that element of society on a regular basis had made the hands of more than one attractive, intelligent defense attorney shake.

"All right. Finished. Good day again, Mr. Archer."

"Matt, please."

"Matt. And I'm Rebecca, but you know that."

"Yes. You got the information I emailed you, I hope." I was referring to a summary of my work I was glad I'd sent her, including what Yuri had learned.

"Yes. What luck, you finding a critical piece of evidence the Feds missed. Any word back from our associate Mr. Fish? Or has the DEA contacted you directly?"

"No to both."

"You found four calls on the cell phone. Anything more about them?"

"Not yet." I switched subjects. "Have you decided which client to keep?"

Ethics rules required that an attorney not be allowed to represent more than one party in a case, and this was definitely true in a criminal matter. There were always conflicting objectives and degrees of involvement on the part of defendants.

"Amusing name, I agree. I farmed out the other three to colleagues we have on contract."

"Can you tell me about him?"

"Sure. Not much to hide. He is what he appears to be. He's cooperating and realizes that there's not much downside to pleading guilty to either a lesser offense or less time locked up."

"How's Mr. Fish with this?"

"Don't know. I haven't spoken with him. I wanted to check signals with you first."

"I'm in the same boat with Mr. Carlyle. Gunk."

She did that pretend amused thing and shook her head. "Butthead doesn't have the same poetic opportunity, sad to say."

Ms. Murray—Rebecca—slid her chair back and yawned politely behind her hand. She apologized, then said, "Here is one thing I found out about Mr. Higginbotham. He's probably in the country illegally."

"He's a Canadian citizen who got in trouble up there awhile back. Somehow he got into the US. I don't know how. It was ten years ago and the Mounties have stopped looking for him."

I wasn't surprised. People got into the country illegally in a number of ways. Over-staying visas, which I doubted in his case. Sometimes getting waved through by border agents without being questioned. There's often a random sort of quota system going on at a crossing; if he'd answered questions respectfully, he might not attract suspicion.

"Why wouldn't his tricked-out bike have put them on notice?" she asked.

"Maybe he used another one, or bought a gang bike down here."

The lady did look tired. Like Lem Fish on the other side of the case, the size of her caseload was prodigious. No amount of comfy beds in hotels with a view changed the grind of travel and diligent trial prep.

"How'd you find out about his status?" it occurred to me to ask.

"A friend of yours, Leonard Smart, told me."

"What? Mongo, a friend of mine?"

"Yes, I do believe that's his gang name."

"When did you see him?"

"Last night. He bought me a drink."

I tried to think of something to say. I went with, "He's a large fellow, wouldn't you say?"

"Very large. And very polite. He called me a week ago and said he'd like to chat."

"Where'd this take place, if I may ask?"

"Right here, in the lounge."

"I imagine he hung his cut up over there on the coat rack?"

"His what?"

"His cut. His motorcycle vest with the patches on the back and front. It's an advertisement that he's a dangerous man, with notches in his belt."

"Matt, I know he's a Bandolero. He told me so. I gather evidence where I can."

"Let me guess. He ordered a tasty little chardonnay and some *foie gras*. You shared experiences with vineyards in the south of France."

"You sound sort of ... um ... envious. Which is absurd under the circumstances."

"Of course it is, but you have to admit ..."

"He didn't hit on me, if that's what you're wondering."

"Maybe he's gay."

"Yeah, right. And so's Bill Clinton."

That was funny enough to get me to laugh. I did notice for the first time that she wasn't wearing a wedding ring. I lingered a moment over the image of clean, appropriate, five-foot-nothing Rebecca Murray in a tete-a-tete with enormous Leonard Smart, laughing and chatting like longtime acquaintances.

Rebecca said, "He told me he'd met with you and your client. And asked why you or I hadn't spent time trying to find out who the snitch was. Did I know anyone who that might have been?"

"Rebecca, let me tell you a bit about our Mr. Smart. He is, or was, a fully-patched member of the Hells Angels. Do you know what 'fully-patched' means?"

"Tell me."

So I did. Then I added, "The Hells Angels' original base of operations was Texas. Still is, to some extent. Today, there's quite a large contingent of them in British Columbia. They are still bad bikers. Law enforcement here is curious why, out of nowhere, Leonard Smart shows up in Salish County, now a member of the Bandoleros."

I enjoyed the turquoise eyes staring at me.

"Add to this the Hells Angels presence a few miles north of here, period. Your and my Bandoleros are like grade-schoolers hanging out with an inner city street gang."

"So, why did our Mr. Smart want to talk to me?"

"Excellent question. My guess, asking you whether you might have an idea of who our snitch was."

"So he'd know I'm clueless."

She nibbled the rest of her scone and took a last sip of coffee.

"I don't know about you," I said, "but I'm not going to call Lem Fish until I have more to work with. Not to mention, finding a heart-warming personal interest story to tell about my client."

"I agree. Me, either. It's the plea deal path for, um, Butthead."

We thanked each other for the conversation and I left.

36

Next on my list was Assistant US Attorney Lem Fish. What I'd told Rebecca about not talking to Lem Fish before I learned more turned out to be half true. I hadn't called him. He'd called me the day before and said he'd be in town tomorrow—as in, today. His message meant he'd be pushing for a court date. There was often a backlog in court and I wanted more time, because I needed some extenuating circumstances, or anything, to negotiate a plea deal for Gunk. So far, I hadn't a dime's worth.

I met Lem at the courthouse in the offices of Salish County prosecuting attorney, Miles Warren. Ever the team player, Mr. Warren would let his federal counterparts use a conference room on the fourth floor. Lem and I sat in a large room, open and airy with a decent view despite the brooding weather outside. There were comfortable chairs and a mahogany table. A sobering addition to the decor was a row of black-and-white 10x12s on one wall, photos of Mr. Warren Esquire's stern predecessors reaching back to statehood. A state flag and copy of the "Star-Spangled Banner" on imitation vellum flanked the photos.

I liked Lemuel Fish. I honestly did. We'd known each other a long time. Lawyers owed each other honest communication, and more so when they practiced law in the same locale. No one likes surprises. Yet there's a fine line between being truthful and doing the best for one's client—not to lie or intentionally mislead, but to decide how much and what to divulge.

For example, I wasn't going to share with Lem what I'd learned from Mick, Yuri, Rebecca, or, for certain, Mongo. He, I'm sure, had information up his sleeve, too. There was a heavy mandate imposed by case law on a prosecutor to disclose information to a defendant's lawyer, including exonerating information. Hide-the-ball was not okay. The same rule applied to me, but Lem's breaking it might result in cases getting dismissed. My indiscretion would usually merit only a reprimand by a judge.

Lem was tall and wiry. He had deep brown eyes and black hair cut short to disguise early-onset male-pattern balding, one of the traits of aging I'd managed to avoid so far. He sported a tasteful gold ring in a pierced ear. My, how times had changed. Lem hailed from the East Coast. He was the first person I'd ever met who not only knew what lacrosse was, but had played it. He even started a pick-up league in law school and tried to teach us philistines the game. The result in my case was a fetching splinter of a scar an inch long on my cheekbone. As they say, though, you shoulda seen the other guy.

That day in Miles Warren's conference room, we were adversaries, warily circling around each other, each knowing more than we'd reveal.

I jumped right in. "Tell me about the informant."

He shook his head like I didn't know any better. "I'll give up his name when you file a formal request with reasons why it's important for preparing your defense."

We sparred a bit about the law on that point. I pointed out the fact, not the law, that he was protecting a name he wasn't going to divulge unless he was forced to.

"How does it help your case?" he asked, looking outside, not at me. Raindrops had started spattering against the window.

"I don't have to tell you. It might, it might not."

"Your guy did the crime. The bust was textbook. We're not really going to trial on this, are we?"

"I haven't decided."

"Oh, give me a break, Matt."

"I haven't heard about any break the government's giving me. The snitch, Lem. Who is he?"

Lem leaned on an elbow and rubbed his other hand back and forth across his forehead like he might be able to erase the last ten minutes.

He said, "Okay, Matt, I'll reduce the jail time. In light of your client's sterling reputation in the community and this being his first offense. Eighteen months."

"How much suspended?"

"Six. With that, he won't do hard time. They're full to the brim at the federal pen down in Morton anyway, so twelve months means county jail. He'd be home, here in Salish. With good time off, he'll do, what, eight months? Some of it work release."

This was a good offer under the circumstances.

"What about a fine?" I asked.

"Find out what he makes a year."

"I'll ask, but you can guess he's not Bill Gates. Would you like his tax return?"

"Don't tempt me. You don't want the IRS in on this. Just let me know what he tells you. I'll make my own guess about how much is hidden in the mattress."

"I'm curious, Lem, what's the situation with the other guys?"

"Rebecca and I haven't discussed Higginbotham yet. Stanley Stanley, I gave a break to. Seems his Dutch Reformed Church community here has confiscated his bike, and his mom and dad made him stand up and witness, I think is the word, in front of the congregation about his sins in the eyes of a vengeful God. He's to do hard labor around the church grounds for a year."

"Hey, I told you Gunk could teach Sunday School."

"Nice try. No deal. We pled out Mitchell Scruggs. Hard time, due to several priors. And get this, Prescott Earl Endicott showed up on a warrant from Illinois for non-payment of a ton of child support. He's awaiting extradition."

"There goes the hair-care neighborhood. I wonder if the place is for sale."

"Ask your man Gunk. He's tight with the local business community, I'd bet."

"Very funny. Lem, you are a fine American. And you love your job." I wasn't being sarcastic. To lighten things up, I asked, "So how's it going with you otherwise?"

"I've been in a relationship for a while. You could call it long-term, almost two years now. Her name is Amber. She's not a lawyer."

"Good for you. On all counts."

"She's a pediatrician. Doing her residency at Sister Agony."

We laughed at the nickname for the big city's largest and best hospital, Sister Agnes.

"We have an apartment on South Hill."

"And work?"

"Good, as a matter of fact. Riding this circuit keeps it interesting. How many motorcycle gangsters do you meet in a lifetime?"

"One, if I have a vote." I must have grimaced.

"That bad?"

"Not really. But restarting practice … it's been a slog."

I was glad he didn't reciprocate and ask about Ellen and me. He knew about my stint in Franklin but not about its painful conclusion.

I did say, "Legal work has challenges, but it's no harder

than tap dancing through a legislative session; trying to convince a wobbly legislator to hold the line when the end is in sight. Especially if she's got stars in her eyes and a possible new campaign target back home."

"Anyone I might know?"

"Send me an affidavit explaining why you need to know."

"Touché."

"In a way it's a paradox, Lem. There are many more rules to follow in legal work, for sure. So you know where you stand most of the time. There are a lot fewer constraints in lobbying and the result is shifting sands, possible shipwrecks, and playing whack-a-mole, to mix metaphors. I'm ready for fewer surprises."

"I'm glad you're around again, Matt. We had some good times."

We finished up. Lem checked his watch. I looked at my own timepiece, the one on the wall behind him.

"Matt, let me know what your client says. Oh, and by the way, I called the court. We can finish this up pretty much any time—even later this week if that's not too soon. The trial calendar is clogged, but she—it'll be Judge Stone—might be able to take a plea in the afternoon."

"That might work. I'll get back to you."

Lem unfolded his tall frame and patted me on the shoulder as I picked up my file to leave. We shook hands and I was out the door.

37

I drove to the post office to buy stamps and mail an oversized envelope. I parked the truck, fished for coins out of the ashtray, and retrieved a manila envelope from the front seat. I walked around the front of the truck to the meter when I happened to glance across the street. There, at a window table inside Johnny Fong's Chinese restaurant, sat my wife and some guy I'd never seen before. I stood there like a dope; couldn't help myself. Big mistake.

They paid the bill and came out. Ellen turned her cheek and the guy gave her a peck, whereupon she did a double-take and steamed across the street straight at me. There I stood, envelope in one hand, two quarters in the other.

"Did you put enough money in the meter to stay long enough to stalk me?"

"Ellen, honest, I wasn't ..." How often I didn't get to finish sentences with her these days.

Here's the thing about marriage breakups. They're awful. Your former best friend is now your enemy. You trusted each other, know every nuance—facial expression, hand gesture, posture, sarcasm, inside jokes, bathroom etiquette—all the endearing, and sometimes not so, characteristics that make marriage work. Until it doesn't.

Eleven years of marriage, thirteen years of love, cohabiting, cooperating twenty-four/seven—together forever. Yet there I was, face to face on a public street with someone from another reality. Who was this new, but not new, person? How do I act? What do I do with my hands? How close is too close? Are people watching?

As if on cue, someone drove by and gave a couple of beeps. Ellen waved.

"Who was that?"

"Matt! Stop! How stupid do we look standing here, in the street. Half the freakin' town knows what's going on."

We moved onto the sidewalk.

"I'll save you having to hire a private investigator. That was Arthur, a friend. He's the shop's accountant."

I had seen a "Arthur Hunnicutt - CPA" listed in the local business rag. No way would I blow Allie's cover about "Author." (Old joke: Know what an actuary is? A guy without even enough personality to be a CPA.)

"And, since our daughter likes to chatter, yes, Arthur and I have gotten together a couple of times. All on the up-and-up. He's very kind to her."

Talk about steaming! Heat was rising through my chest and into my head. Somehow, I stayed calm.

"I'm sure he's a nice fellow." To myself: If you're into perfectly groomed, slim and in-shape bean counters on the other side of fifty.

"He's divorced. Has a pilot's license, how about that! He flies."

Big deal, so does Dumbo.

I said, "And I bet he wants to give my daughter a ride." Was the fire in my brain making my eyeballs as red as they felt?

"*Our* daughter. Yes, he wants to take us up flying."

"Oh?"

"I'm sure he's careful."

"So was Amelia Earhart."

That made her laugh, an actual funny-joke laugh.

Ellen looked gorgeous standing there. Perfectly gorgeous. White turtleneck, tan slacks, no lipstick, the fall sun peeking through clouds and carelessly glancing off her light brown hair. Her earrings were shiny gold hoops. There was no tennis racket in its cover by her side, but could have been. Still no wedding ring, either. Standing in her own self-assured but not showy way, she was close enough I could smell her perfume. She knew how attractive she was.

I was consumed, and tongue-tied, remembering how she breathes, how she runs her fingers through her hair and gnaws on a ballpoint when she's stumped by the crossword, runs her fingers through my hair before we drift off to sleep.

"Ellen, I love you!"

"Well, I love you, too, Matt. I just haven't figured out what to do about that. Meanwhile, if a man I like wants to take me to lunch, I'll accept. Now, if you'll excuse me, I have to get back to work. And please stop following me around!"

"I wasn't, honest. And by the way, since when do you like Chinese?"

"I don't," she shot back, and I watched her walk away and turn the corner.

I took stock. My biker client was PO'd at me. Who could blame him? And he didn't know the worst. The plea deal Prosecutor Lem Fish had offered Gunk's crackerjack counsel was what I'd predicted—to wit, a stay in the local jailhouse. The fiasco with Luke and Deanna in the grocery store parking lot had been embarrassing. Super interpersonal skills!

And now Ellen. Wasn't it enough that she'd stomped on my offer of dinner as a family a week before? Today she confirmed Allie's intel about "Author." A lunch date.

Loving me, as she'd said, or not, and looking like a million bucks, no wedding ring, she was okay with a rendezvous in plain sight with a well-groomed male who flies his own plane. How nice for her.

So why should I eschew company of the opposite sex? All on the up-and-up, end quote. Did doing my level best to resuscitate my marriage, including a Scout's Honor promise to Allie, mean I couldn't enjoy the harmless society of a female person? Ellen with some wannabe suitor, and I'm supposed to scourge myself like a repentant friar?

My stomach was growling. It may have been still-simmering acid, but on the other hand I hadn't eaten anything but a stale power bar since breakfast. Blame it, then, on my insistent abdomen that I took a chance and drove out to Betsy's Breakfast eatery—and to Megan (last name Janssen), a friendly face. She and I had settled into a sort of rapport, flavored with flirtation. I pulled in, went in, and took a seat at the counter.

"Hey, Matt!"

Her trademark zillion-watt smile felt like she'd been saving it up for me. She came toward me untying her apron and looping the neck strap over her head.

"Quittin' time, and look who showed up."

I looked around pretending to see who she meant—pinching myself—looked back and said, "Hey! What's up? How's your day been?" More skillful repartee.

"Sort of slow. Now it's off to laundry, groceries, vacuuming. Doesn't get any better than this." She sat on the stool next to me. "How about you?"

"My day's been, oh, interesting."

I kept my hands in my lap because they were shaking. Megan's blue eyes were unnerving. Why did I feel like a teenage kid asking a girl out on a date? Adolescent imprinting, I suppose. I was tongue-tied.

"Matt, you still there?"

"Sorry, yeah, I'm here."

"This girl can put off domestic chores if a nice guy wanted to hang out a bit."

"Uh, sure. Say, can the guy back there fix me a sandwich?"

Megan called in the order and went in back to change.

I sucked in my paunch, and we walked down the street to a park by the river, grilled cheese sandwich and a package of chips in my hands. Two tall Pepsis in hers.

She looked really good. Gone were the waitressy pants and shirt and apron. Sitting across from me at a picnic table under the trees with the music of the river behind us, she had on black jeans tucked into boots and a purple v-neck sweater. Her reddish-brown hair, instead of being pinned up for work, was down, parted on one side. I guessed she was in her twenties, and the age gap felt huge.

"I'm sorry if I eat in front of you. I'm starved."

"Wow, Matt. A gentleman. People of your generation know how to be polite."

My generation! Uh-oh. I think she recognized her faux pas because her cheeks turned pink.

We filled in some blanks. She was from Albuquerque, born there, the older of two kids. Her dad was in the navy, a flier, so they moved around. One posting was Adak, Alaska, where she and her mother worked with Inuit children.

Later, in Sacramento, she found a boyfriend and they moved to Church Harbor. I told her she'd chosen a great place to live and bragged a little about my work here and in the state capital. She asked questions, like the difference between practicing law and legislators making the laws.

We found things in common. Megan loved animals. I said I did, too. She volunteered at the Humane Society. She'd taken over Betsy's with a loan from her dad, but hoped to get admitted to veterinary school.

She hated shopping, loved hiking, hated closed-minded people, and loved ice cream. She read books and the newspaper. I succeeded in not dwelling on how much younger she was despite, somewhere along the way, doing the math. She was twenty-three. About midway between Allie and me.

"How old are you, Matt?"

Pause. "Forty. Just." I bit the bullet and told her about my marital situation. She didn't comment, just snagged another potato chip. I segued to Allie and her lobbying me to get a dog.

"Relationships are hard. Sometimes separations are a good thing. Hurdles. Growing pains."

This from a twenty-three-year-old. And she seemed entirely unawed by my profession. She did ask about what kind of cases I was working on. I gave her a sketchy account of Gunk and the facts, tossing some biker lore her way.

"I've never rode a motorcycle. They scare me just listening to them."

Never rode. This jarred me, but I wasn't that concerned. I'd heard legislators in Franklin, in floor speeches of all things, misuse past participles. "I have came here today …" and so on. A woman I knew once was dating a guy who she drooled over. He worked construction, shirtless most often. When I pointed out the difference in education level between her and Mr. Beefcake, she replied, "Complete sentences are optional."

The conversation lagged. I was trying to be upbeat, but she must have noticed.

"Say, Matt." She hesitated, then said, "I have just the thing to top off that amazing grilled cheese you devoured. Would you think I was being out of line if I invited you back to my place? All on the up-and-up, of course, you being married and all. I've got ice cream. And cookies."

"Dessert? It's still afternoon." A bracket of sunlight, lower to be sure, dappled the picnic table.

"Is there a law, Counselor, about eating ice cream in the afternoon?"

I'd like to report that it was the offer of chocolate chip ice cream, chocolate syrup, and vanilla wafers that prompted me to agree. I'd also like to report that two plus two is five.

38

I followed her to her place. Megan's house was small and log cabin-ish, with an oversized yard that backed onto the river. There was no funny business in the kitchen dishing up dessert. I was certain there wouldn't be, and so, it seemed, was she. She even digressed at one point about a girlfriend who'd gotten involved with "Mr. Married" and what a disaster that was. She scooped, I drizzled chocolate.

The only place to sit comfortably in her living room was a sofa, so we both sat there and dug into the ice cream. Megan finished hers first. Out of the blue, she said, "Matt, why don't you tell me more about the motorcycle case you've got?"

"Okay. How come?"

"I dunno. I meet a lot of people. Who knows? Besides, it sounds like a TV show."

"Hardly that, but here goes."

I gave her the abridged version, leaving out the fisticuffs. I told her I had reached a dead end. "I know someone set these guys up, but I haven't a clue which one, or why."

"Maybe I can help," she said. She got up and fetched a piece of notepaper and a pencil. She drew a line down the middle of the page.

"Tell me their names again and something about each one."

"Excluding my guy, Gunk?"

"Nope. All five."

I ran down the list.

Willard Carlyle, "Gunk," florist, middle-aged, lady friend in Canada with their son.

Prescott Endicott, "Pissy," hair-cutter, well dressed, good-looking.

Stanley Stanley, "Stinky," young, no smarts, farm boy.

Daniel Higginbotham, "Butthead," nothing to go on. Gunk had said he was an auto mechanic.

Mitchell Scruggs, no gang name needed, grubby, smelled bad, unemployed, was my bet.

"You're not making these guys up, are you?"

"Not a chance. Who'd believe me?"

Megan huddled over the paper and made notes on the other side of the line down the paper.

"Describe them again, physically."

I did my best. She made some more scratches on the paper.

Finally she said, "Here's your guy." She circled one of the names.

"How do you know?"

"I just do. Wanna bet?"

"At this point, how can I argue? Do you read palms? Tea leaves?"

"Nope. In my biz, sizing up people helps. That and growing up lots of places. I do card tricks, too."

I laughed. Her sense of humor was a good tonic.

Megan sat back with a grin and kicked off her boots. She leaned back and stretched. I didn't think she was being seductive, just relaxed and comfortable, but I was getting nervous. Her head lay against the top edge of the sofa. My arm was there, and her hair rested against my forearm.

It was getting warmer. I was getting alarmed, her disclaimers notwithstanding. My brain and my body started sending conflicting messages. An attractive woman, young and put-together and interesting, lounged next to me on her sofa. The two of us. Was she waiting for me to make a move? She smelled faintly of chocolate syrup. Her auburn hair was slightly in disarray. She wasn't flashy, but she sparkled. I was enjoying her, the person, a lot more than I'd expected to.

Megan turned her head toward me. I moved my arm away. She was no fool.

"Matt, you're uncomfortable, aren't you?"

She sat up and turned and faced me, one knee tucked under the other.

"Uh-huh. But it's got nothing to do with you."

"Of course it does." Her eyes twinkled. "Let me be frank, here, Mr. Lawyer. You're really okay, Matt, and nice to look at. But excuse me for saying it, you're lonely. Maybe if not lonely, out of practice. You're also married."

"I wouldn't say…"

"No offense intended. In fact, I'm actually glad you didn't come here trying to jump my bones. I'm flattered."

"Flattered?"

"Yeah. Plenty of girls I know sleep with customers right off the bat. It's pretty common these days. Hooking up. It's totally the thing."

I felt as out of my depth as a toddler in the deep end of the pool. I couldn't think of anything to say. She was so earnest and so, well, young, and way ahead of me.

"Matt?"

"What?"

"We're not going to ruin our afternoon. I want you as a friend. If you're too bothered, we'll just say goodbye and you can leave. We'll see each other whenever you come in for breakfast, like always."

I shook my head. Didn't that beat all! She took my hand and returned it to the back of the sofa and sat up.

"Say, would you think it was weird if we watched a movie?

In the afternoon!" She did that cute giggle again. "Only don't just leave, okay? That'd be a first."

"I feel like a dolt, Megan."

"Let me decide that." She slid over and gave me a kiss on the cheek.

"Have I told you that your boyfriend must have been a total jerk?"

"Can't argue with that. What would you like to watch?"

I racked my jumbled brain. No doubt channeling my daughter, I said, "Do you have *Princess Bride*?"

"I love *Princess Bride*."

She even gave me the remote. A guy thing, she said.

Right after the part where the little guy drinks the poison, she told me to hit pause.

"I just remembered. In a couple weeks, there's an open house at the Humane Society. Maybe you and Allie should come by."

I said we'd try.

It was twilight by the time the movie was over. Megan walked me to the truck and gave me a full-on hug and another chaste kiss on the cheek.

All the way home, I couldn't get that movie's sappy theme song out of my head. The hug had felt really good, but I congratulated myself on the "up-and-up" bit. I showered, raided the fridge, turned in early, and slept the sleep of the just.

39

woke up at a reasonable hour and was knotting my tie when the doorbell rang. Unfortunately, I answered it. My oh my, look who wasn't wasting any time.

"Come in, Senator."

Deanna was dressed in running shorts, a long-sleeved T-shirt, and tennis shoes. Her hair was pulled back in jogging mode and she was perspiring. She looked healthy as ever. Perhaps she wanted to clear the air after our parking lot dustup. We had been in public, after all.

"Please, Matt, we're home now. You can drop the 'senator.' Oh wait, you're being sarcastic."

She walked past me and took in my humble surroundings.

"May I offer you coffee or a soft drink? A peanut butter sandwich?" I nodded toward the *cordon bleu* peanut butter and mayo sandwich on a plate on the kitchen table. She grimaced and said she'd take coffee. I found a clean cup and poured her some out of a thermos.

I brushed crumbs off the kitchen chair and we sat down. She wore a pleasure-to-meet-you, politician smile tight on her face. I was in no mood to be charitable but wasn't going to throw her out.

"By the way, I've not congratulated you on the good work with Senator Hooker. I did not see that coming. I know when to admit I was outflanked." Her painted-on smile belied the fingers of her hands winding around each other. She caught me noticing, and stopped. I had to give her credit, coming by and all, and bringing up the details of our spectacular legislative denouement.

"You gave me little choice."

"I suppose." She paused. "And like I said the other day, you won that round."

What was this, confession good for her soul? I knew her better than that.

"You're good at what you do, Matt Archer. Always have been."

Was that a wink she gave me? The lady was irrepressible. Maybe an eyelash got stuck.

I recalled the oddball goodbye right after the excitement at the end of the session. I was walking back to my apartment when she swung her Jag around blocking me and parked in a space that said "Reserved for Capitol Police." On the passenger side was a well-fed, middle-aged guy in an open-necked shirt and gold necklace. The Jag's top was down and the fellow's bad comb-over was fighting a losing battle with the breeze.

"Matt, meet Rob Roman."

Rob Roman? This was a name? Sounded more like Visigoths at the gates of the Eternal City. The fellow reached out a hand with the Hope Diamond on his middle finger and we shook.

"Pleased to meet you, Rob."

"He builds health clubs."

"But hasn't seen the inside of one in a while," I thought but didn't say.

Unfazed as ever and wearing sparkly ruby stud earrings I recognized, Deanna gave me a thumbs-up behind the fellow's back that meant "m-o-n-e-y." Back on the campaign trail so soon? Had recent events, all of them, been erased from her cerebral cortex that fast? What a feat of recuperative power!

She'd just gotten blindsided, and in front of a roomful of colleagues, and now was back on her feet. Money is the mother's milk of politics, so flaunting Rob the Roman at me made sense. Off they sped, with a wave.

Now, across from me in my kitchen, I said, "It feels like there's something more you're going to say, Deanna?"

"Okay, I meant what I said the other day. No hard feelings, please. I hope you're not going to be angry with me forever, because I'm here to ask for your help." I waited for the punch line. "As you know, I'm running for superior court judge."

She had to be kidding. "You want my help, Deanna? Scott Key's body's still warm! I checked. Come to find out, he isn't even dead yet."

"This is politics, Matthew. I don't need to remind you, Scott's ... um ... misfortune is of his own doing."

"Don't you think you might be miscalculating by not waiting at least a respectable period of time? That surprises me, even from you."

She glanced away for a second, like maybe that registered.

She said, "Don't go all shocked citizen on me. You know this racket. You and I have a history. We even ... come to think of it, you were there."

"Yes, I certainly was there on that thrill ride with you. It was nice. You're also good at what you do, Deanna. You've always gotten it—usually men—your way. Lots of practice, it appears. Too bad there's no center to you, nothing but your how-can-I-use-him mentality." I stopped before naming names.

"Oh goodie, a sermon from Doctor Freud, or am I hearing post-coital guilt? I ate too much candy at the fair, Mom. Now I have a stomachache. Don't blame me for your fall from grace, Preacher. I'm not the one who's married."

"Subtlety has never been your long suit, Deanna, has it? But since you dropped by, what makes you think I'd want to support you as a judge?"

She sat up straight.

"I'm qualified."

"Spare me the campaign speech."

"Maybe you'll come around, Matt."

I shook my head. "Okay, I'll give you my take on this. No charge." I leaned toward her, my palms flat on the table. "Scott will rehabilitate himself. He's good with people. Plus, he is the incumbent. Smoking pot probably doesn't even get you thrown off the church board of deacons these days."

She parried, "On the other hand, he's got his hands full staying married. I understand that Little Miss Loyal Wife hasn't exactly leveled with …"

"How would I know?" I said.

"Bullshit."

How come attractive women can say that and still be sexy?

"Know what, 'Senator,' I'll give you three reasons why I'm going nowhere near your judgeship run."

"And they are?"

"One, you tried to screw me last session. Metaphorically, of course. Second, you're stomping on Scott Key while he's down, and way too quickly. That's over the top, Deanna."

I stopped for effect.

"That's only two."

"Number Three. You'll have to give up your senate seat to do this, so I don't have to be fucking nice to you anymore." I didn't bother to tell her I wasn't doing the lobbyist shtick either.

She spat, "You didn't seem to mind being fucking nice to me down in Franklin."

"Don't be so sure."

She got up and set her cup on the counter. She walked past me and let herself out without a word. She was good at entrances and exits. Plus, entertaining Deanna Mackenzie in her running togs, all hot and bothered, revived memories I had no business having. Those safely banished, I finished knotting my tie and took a moment to look at my face in the hallway mirror.

I was surprised by how I felt when I heard the door close behind her. For the first time since I'd gotten home, the word "normal" actually popped into my head. Maybe hopeful electrons had decided to join the party, to swim along with the red corpuscles coursing through my veins. I didn't think it was adrenalin—having sent Deanna packing—but maybe I'd gotten some purchase, a handhold on the edge of the hole I'd dug myself into. I felt okay about my life that morning.

Sure, there was a long way to go on the Ellen front. But Allie and I were back into a rhythm. My conversation with Gunk had sobered me, particularly with son Gordon there. A break in his case was overdue. Otherwise, Willard Carlyle, a human being, not a nickname, was headed to jail.

My truck even started with only a polite cough, and I set off for the office.

40

As if on cue, around noon my phone beeped. Mick Malone was calling.

"Top of the day to ye, Officer."

"You sound chipper. Don't tell me why, I don't want to know."

"I eat right, get exercise."

He ignored that. He sounded upbeat himself.

"Hey, Matt, want some interesting news?"

"Can it wait till I finish my sandwich?"

"The peanut butter and mayo?" We had known each other a long time.

"Yep."

"Please. Don't bring it here. It'll be quarantined as hazardous waste. Bring me a double tall latté, non-fat, instead. I earned it." He hung up.

After a nod to Norma behind her window at the cop shop—my hands were full—she buzzed me through. I rapped on Mick's door and went in. He pulled his coffee out of the biodegradable tray I was carrying and sat back down behind his desk. He motioned to the chair in front of it. He had his standard-issue detective eyeballs on me.

"Are you taping this?" I asked.

"Of course not, Counselor. See both my hands here on the desk."

"Read me my rights anyway."

"You've been incriminating yourself as long as I've known you. Why is today any different?"

We laughed at our poor attempts at being hip and witty. Detective Malone began, "This won't take long. I did some electronic research on Mr. Mongo, alias Leonard Smart. I found out more than that he was a Hells Angel down in Texas."

"He played defensive tackle for the Cowboys."

"Close, but don't get ahead of me here. I hacked ... make that researched further into court records. Come to find out he did graduate from the University of Texas in Austin. The court record I found was for assault. Beat up a roommate over a girl, it seems, but the charges were dropped."

"A college grad-you-ate! I knew it."

"More, Matt. He spent a year at UT law school."

"Whoa! But that fits, oddly enough. Then what?"

"Nothing. The trail peters out. Until he shows up here and interacts with your Bandolero boys."

"He switched teams, Angels to Bandoleros? How does that happen with these guys? Isn't there awful and terrible retribution?"

"If they find out."

"Huh?"

"Want my theory?" Without waiting, Mick continued, "Let's say the granddaddy club in The Lone Star State hears of some unrest or breaking of rules in far-off Canada. Intra-club squabbles. They dispatch trusted emissary Mongo the Smart up our way to check into it."

"There's precedent for this. You told me about the Ontario incident."

"Yep. Whatever the unpleasantness Mongo encounters north of the border, he learns about another concern, that some yay-hoos down here in the States might be poaching on the Angels' exclusive B.C. weed operation. Insignificant and paltry as your Bandoleros are, maybe they needed to be taught a lesson."

I chimed in. "So somehow Mongo joins the Bandoleros. He's got the attitude and the size and the bike, and drops some names. My poor guys, thinking back to the Golden Days, buy it."

"Hook, line, and rollbar," said Mick. "Then he sets them up. Engineers a drug bust with enough bells and whistles to involve the DEA."

"After talking one of them into narking them out. Is there no shame in setting up these poor schlubs for criminal convictions?"

"He probably figures they won't do much time. Maybe less than a year, which means they'll be housed locally. At our expense, by the way, not the Feds."

"Dishonor among thieves, criminal and otherwise."

"Did I not tell you?"

Mick reached under his desk and pretended to turn off a tape recorder. I think.

I returned to the truck and the overtime parking ticket in the window. Hadn't I been on official city business? I filed the citation in its allotted place along with others in my glove compartment and went home for a run. I had to get in shape, take exercise seriously for a change.

Despite my sunnier mood, the weather was cloudy and ominous, typical for fall, but the rain held off. Padding along a coastal trail beneath Douglas fir and mountain hemlock and past rhododendron and late-blooming hydrangeas gave me time to examine Gunk's situation, this time from his standpoint, not mine. Lem Fish's offer of a guilty plea, a fine, and a few months in the slammer? While I'd be back on the golf course.

First off, Willard Carlyle and I had stood by my driveway watching young Gordon playing hoops with Allie and Yuri. Then yesterday, driving to the store, I'd spotted the boy again, dressed in the same Levi coveralls and plaid shirt, a little guy racing to catch up with his dad on the sidewalk. He put his hand in Gunk's and Gunk sort of swung him along, happy as any dad and son could be. When I caught up, it wasn't them after all. Nonetheless ...

Second, there'd be jail time, a first for him, no matter in the local slammer rather than the penitentiary. And, unless I missed my bet, he'd been set up. Pot busts were federal offenses, but minor ones. Under our state law, he wouldn't have gone to jail at all; he'd pay a fine and do community service. But incarceration would mean that visitation with his border-jumping son would be on hold for months. His business would go defunct. All on top of the general disgrace and misery of jail.

What nagged at me most was what his sentence would do to his chances of working things out so that Gordon and his mom could come back to the States legally and not have to risk playing hide-and-seek with the Border Patrol. Getting caught would torpedo their chances permanently.

I stopped jogging, hands on my knees, and caught my breath before turning back. Given the minimal—to date nonexistent—chances of getting him off, how did I deserve the money he was paying me? Child support money, on top of that.

Perhaps Matt Archer, Esquire, could do better.

Back home, I hauled my achy self into the shower. Sudsing up, I tried to track down a nagging thought I'd had earlier on my run—one of those phantom wisps I couldn't corral—a word, a coincidence, a connection hiding somewhere in a corner of my brain? Maybe it'd come to me if I stopped trying to nail it down.

As it happened, my as-yet unidentified insight could wait.

The break in Gunk's case showed up, and from an entirely unexpected source. That very day.

41

Few things are as unwelcome as seeing flashing red and blue lights in the rearview mirror, and it's clear who they're for. Damn! I was on my way back to the office. I slowed down and found a safe spot to pull over. There I sat, cursing my fate, blinding flashers visible all the way to Mars continuing to advertise my plight while the curious, the self-righteous, and the law-abiding paraded by.

I cycled through Ms. Kübler-Ross's approved stages of grief: denial, anger, and acceptance. Then I remembered bargain. That's what lawyers do, right? Depression could come later. The vehicle behind me was of the heavy, law-enforcement variety with a sleek light bar, more like an anti-terrorist SUV, with a collection of whip antennas roof, side and back.

A glance at the speedometer showed I hadn't been speeding, much. Maybe a taillight was out. I rolled down my window preparing to plead my case. I watched the officer in the mirror—full khaki uniform, side-arm and bullet belt, regulation hat and dark aviator glasses—walk up and around behind the truck bed. Then he pivoted to the right, came up beside the vehicle on the passenger side, bent, and tapped on the window.

Luke Barkley! Didn't that beat all.

I reached across, opened the door, and he slid in, smiling like a gremlin.

"I hope I didn't scare you, Matt," he said, knowing full well he had.

Arguing with a lawman is fruitless in most all cases, and the fiery confrontation I'd had with Luke in the Senate gallery had been as adversarial as I wanted to get, not to mention the day before yesterday in the grocery store parking lot.

"Of course not, Officer," I lied. "Am I under arrest?"

"I can arrange that. But you being a weasely mouthpiece, you'd just get off on a technicality."

"So is this a cordial visit, Luke, or are you amusing yourself on a slow day?"

He shifted in his seat so his back was braced against the door. He took off his hat and glasses and set them on the dash. He looked like he was settling in for a spell. I turned off the truck and waited.

"Matt, what say we call a truce? At least a temporary one."

"Do I have a choice?"

"Maybe you could stop acting like a spurned lover, which of course you are."

If that was his reality, so be it.

"Luke, I'm kinda busy today. I'd like to be on my way."

He didn't budge. "Matt, I'm here on a mission of mercy courtesy of Miz Deanna Mackenzie."

Mercy was not an characteristic I attributed to Deanna. Yet here was Salish County's numero uno law enforcement officer taking up temporary residence in my truck, so I was intrigued.

"She told me about the little unpleasantness at your place. She wants to forgive and forget, as they say, so I suggested an olive branch."

I doubted it was her conscience. She was running for office and didn't need any more enemies.

"Okay, Luke, show me some mercy."

"It's about your Bandolero case."

Now he had my attention.

"Did you ever question how a superior court judge would get a steady supply of marijuana? Who on earth would sell him dope? How would he go about having the nerve to ask someone?"

"He grows it?"

"Nope, but you're getting warm."

"You're going to tell me why."

"Not exactly, because I'm not sure of this myself. But, how well do you know Dolores Key?"

That was a jump-shift!

"Not as well as you do."

He ignored the slam. I guessed that he and Deanna had rehearsed this conversation.

"Let me tell you the truth about Dolores and me. The sad truth. I understand she talked to you. When she told you her side of it, did she cry? Was she good at it?"

"It wasn't Dr. Phil, but close."

"Yes, I followed them home one night—after the first time Scott called me, back when, not the most recent time. I sent my deputy home and handled it myself. Scott was loaded and stumbled off to bed. Dolores followed him and then came back in a skimpy little bathrobe. She is hot, Matt. I'm sure you've noticed the bodacious set on that girl."

Same old Luke. "Go on."

"I'm solo. She's ready. She's mad at Scott. Cleavage calling my name, so yes, we did the deed. She told me later that Scott came to and found her AFO right after I left."

"AFO?"

"All fucked out."

I made a mental note: he and Deanna deserved each other.

"Luke, is this True Confessions? Bandoleros, remember."

"Matt, I swear it was that one time. One-night stand,

period. I had to change my cell number. She called and called. Wouldn't let up. She's pathetic. Voracious. An animal."

"Luke, given all the good times and intimacy you and I have shared over the years, why should I believe you?"

"Don't have to. I'm trying to do you a favor, Matt, because Deanna asked me to. You and I aren't going to be fast friends and go bowling or anything."

"You were going to tell me why you followed them home."

"I followed them home because he's a judge and I didn't want there to be an accident. What I want to tell you is why I didn't arrest him."

I waited. He was enjoying spinning this tale.

"A day or two later, I got a call. Somehow DEA had gotten word of the stop. A guy I'd worked with before told me to just file the arrest report away somewhere."

"They were already onto Scott and the drugs."

"Maybe, but not entirely. He mentioned a guy I'd heard of before. A Leonard Smart. You've met him, I understand."

What a small world.

"What else did the DEA say?"

"I can't tell you much more. I know only what I just told you. I'm dropping bread crumbs here and thinking you might be able to follow them."

"The Sheriff's Office isn't interested in following them?"

"Nope. It's the US government's case. I'll help DEA if they ask. So far they haven't."

"Weren't your guys in on the Bandolero bust?"

"Backup. A couple cars. Nothing else."

"Tell me something, Luke, since we're now friends, and since you expect me to trust you rather than Dolores Key, how'd you end up in law enforcement in the first place?"

He relaxed and seemed glad I'd asked. The stiffness went out of his shoulders and he got his glasses off the dashboard and wiped them on his tie. Maybe he wanted to establish his bona fides and maybe mend fences with me after all. He started in.

He'd grown up in midwestern farming country. His dad had been a cop, and you know how it is being a cop's son. Or a principal's or a preacher's. He got in trouble a lot, usually on purpose to spite his law-abiding folks. He had a temper, too, and got into fights. He was a big boy, but sports were too mainstream for him. When he went away to state college, he found himself in a place where nobody gave a damn whether he was being good or bad, and habits die hard.

So did an acquaintance of his—die, that is. He got loaded one night and took a dive off the dorm roof. Luke was one of the first to get to the kid and it scared him. Then he fell for a girl who made him go to church with her. The two events tamed his cavalier life, as he described it, meaning his wildness generally and also the wild oats variety. They got married before they graduated.

It wasn't a good idea. They had to fend for themselves and get jobs. Each set of parents wanted to teach the kids a lesson and withdrew financial support. Stress took its toll and bickering got out of hand. Luke was still an angry guy. He put his fist through a wall one night and took apart half their kitchen.

He went to anger management classes and marital counseling to stay out of jail. The counselor patched things up enough that he and the wife graduated. A wise mentor at college suggested a law enforcement academy, which made a lot of sense.

He was a good student, graduated, and sent out applications. The Salish County Sheriff's Office hired him, so the couple moved west. There were no further domestic violence incidents, but underlying damage had been done— not unusual for college age marriages, such as those held together by hay-bailing wire and wishful thinking. Luke started playing around and he wasn't subtle about it. The wife found out, left for home, filed for divorce, and that was that.

"Luke, I'm sorry."

"Things turned out okay. I moved up through the ranks, then jumped at a chance to run for the legislature. One term was all. I bet you understand that."

He went on, "Matt, funny that Deanna put me up to this visit with you. I still do go to anger management by the way. I wanted to take your head off when you set me off that time down south. And the other day."

"Luke, for what it's worth I have been known to sing your praises—stand-up guy, professional, the way you do your job." The conversation was getting close to weepy. Would a man-hug be next?

"Thanks. The fine citizens of this county have been good to me for sure. My dad, who's still living, doesn't believe I'm *the* sheriff. So I send him newspaper clippings."

We stared ahead at sun-dappled trees. With a back-to-work sigh, he clapped his hat on his head and squinted through his glasses before putting them in his vest pocket. He stuck out his hand and we shook.

"Thanks. And thank Deanna for me." I meant it.

"She says to be careful."

"Tell her I already am."

The shiny sheriff's car backed away. It sped around me with a wave from its driver.

It was time for a chat with Judge Scott Key.

42

I turned the truck around and headed out into the county where Scott and Dolores lived. I admired again the raspberry hoops tied up tight for the winter, fields stretching for acres and acres in both directions. Ahead of me was our distinctive mountain, lowering clouds obscuring the peak, white snow even on lower elevations.

I found the address. There was a rustic sign next to the road with Key in raised wood on a plank that was the size of a canoe paddle blade, shaped as a key of course. I turned into the driveway which disappeared into the trees, and Scott himself came walking up. He had on a blue watch cap, sweats to match, and an orange scarf around this neck. He was going for a run.

I invited him into the truck. He said the jog could wait and jumped in. It was a cold day and I'd given him an excuse to skip it. I parked at a circular roundabout in front of the house and we got out.

"Want coffee?" he asked.

"If it's not a bother."

"Not at all. Dolores is out somewhere and court finished early today."

It had to be a challenge hearing cases and running for office, but it was the best thing for him to do. He was complying with the State Judicial Council's disciplinary process, going to AA meetings, and, he said, not drinking or smoking. But, there were circles under his eyes, and he looked like he'd lost weight—not entirely from jogging, I assumed.

He started a coffee machine. I stood with my back to the fireplace warming myself and admiring a Japanese-y vase on the mantle, a pretty, white one with red flowers. I might have seen one like it before, but couldn't place where. I remembered Scott saying Dolores was into pottery and had a studio. Outside, protected from the wind, it wasn't that cold so we sat on the deck on Adirondack chairs with cushions. Shiny cedar logs supported an overhanging roof. Rustic limbs, round and straight and glossy, served as rails wrapping around the deck. Wood smoke from the dying fire in the creek-boulder fireplace inside was chic Northwest ambience.

Scott and Dolores lived on twenty or so acres of secluded Salish County property that, along with the house, could have made the cover of an Eddie Bauer catalogue. This would be hard to give up if worse came to worst. In truth, I didn't see a criminal conviction in the cards. Maybe he'd get light probation and pay court costs. The biggest hit would be the huge loss of income if he didn't get re-elected.

"I think you told me your dad had property out here."

"He did. You're sitting on it."

I didn't feel out of place bringing up the subject since he had opened up to me once before.

"Ah, so the place is paid for."

"Thankfully. If you're wondering how we'll survive if I lose, Matt, we will. Tighten the old belts. Unless things get uglier than they are now, and I don't see how, I'll be able to practice law. By the way, how's that going?"

"You know what they say. Practicing law is easy. It's the clients that are a pain in the ass."

We laughed and Scott went in to fetch the coffee.

I thumbed through a magazine on the table that had a picture of another pretty vase on the cover.

When Scott got back, I said, "Every time I turn around, there seem like there are a lot more lawyers. I went to a Bar Association meeting and shook hands with a dozen people I'd never seen before."

He nodded and we sipped from heavy mugs.

"Matt, if you don't mind, I'm curious, how's that Bandolero case coming along?"

He was making reconnaissance easy.

"Funny you should mention it. Ever heard of a guy named Leonard Smart? He goes by the biker handle 'Mongo.'"

Scott answered without a pause. "I don't think so. Maybe. Bikers come through the system from time to time. Why?"

"His name came up. Seems the DEA knows who he is."

I didn't mention my interactions with Mongo. I was fishing.

"I also heard of him when I talked to Luke Barkley," I said.

Scott almost knocked his coffee mug off the arm of the chair. I knew what I was doing. Scott glanced back to be sure Dolores hadn't driven up.

"I'd appreciate it, Matt, if that cocksucker's name doesn't cross your lips again while you're sitting on my porch."

"My mistake." Not. "Sorry, man. I'd only been digging for information from local law enforcement."

Scott began breathing normally. I let him recover himself.

"So," he said, "what about this Leonard Smart character? What's your client's name? 'Gunk'?" Scott did a rictus grin thing right out of Stephen King.

"Scott, the ... uh ... unnamed county sheriff ..." and that's as far as I got. He couldn't control himself.

"Let me paint the picture for you, Matt. He fucked my wife! Can you even imagine what that was like?"

I held up my hand, tried to get him to stop.

"No, you can't imagine it! Jesus!"

He kept going. "I've always been aware that men like her. And she shines on to them. I'm sure you've noticed, yourself."

"She is attractive, Scott," I risked.

"Yes, and I was stoned. I passed out on our bed. Something woke me up. I went back out to the living room right as the front door slammed shut. Dolores was sitting on the sofa in a skimpy robe I bought her on a trip to San Francisco. She pulled it around her, covering up her legs. Mascara was running down her face, and she looked like she'd been ..."

I grimaced and shook my head, ran a finger across my throat. "Cut!" Didn't do any good.

"In my house. On my sofa. With me in the next room."

"Okay, okay, Scott. Enough!"

His arms were rigid. His hands clutched the chair. His lips were thin and white. Not his face, which was crimson. And his eyes! Tiny slits shot streams of yellow fire.

"Breathe, Scott."

He took a moment to calm down. In a quiet voice, he said, "He forced himself on her. Said he'd fallen in love with her and couldn't help himself. It didn't happen again."

I took note that this wasn't quite how Dolores had told it, or Luke. The common tendency of human beings to tell their stories as they themselves perceive them is axiomatic. The legal system accommodates the fact that each of three witnesses to the same traffic accident will swear under oath that it happened thus and so, all different. The syndrome is more pronounced, of course, when one's own petard is hoist, to wit, Scott Key's.

"Scott, I didn't come here to dredge all that up. I wanted to know if you'd heard of this guy Smart. It may be important to my case. You see more of the criminal element than I do. By the way, if you decide you want legal representation, I could run it by Jack Tulio?"

Scott winced but didn't say no.

"He might be okay," he said. "Jack and I have plenty of history, but it's always been between the lines—in court, as it were."

"He's good."

"Yes, he is. Go ahead and ask him what he thinks, if you would, Matt. Don't say I've decided."

"Got it."

We tried other topics—winter coming, logs that needed splitting, a tune-up for my ancient truck—but the earlier conviviality had disappeared like the wood smoke that I no longer noticed.

I asked directions to the loo. Scott had calmed down when I emerged. I declined his offer for more coffee. I was halfway to the truck, when out of the dim reaches of my caffeinated skull came a bolt—the mysterious, half-remembered connection that had eluded me. Draped over the back of Scott and Dolores's fireside sofa I'd seen a heavy woolen blanket, orange and white. Over the white silhouette of a longhorn were the words "University of Texas."

I felt two synapses in my brain exchange high-fives.

43

My phone was winking at me when I climbed back into the truck. Pepper Martin had left me a message suggesting I meet him at my office. Didn't say what about, and my journalist friend was already there when I arrived. His feet were up on the piece of furniture I charitably called a coffee table.

"I'm sorry, Mr. Martin, to be late for my appointment."

"You'll find my fees are reasonable, Mr. Archer. Like that lunch you owe me."

"Please take your feet down. I paid fifteen dollars for that beauty."

"You'll be happy to let me spill this coffee on it when I tell you what I found out."

There was already a wet ring where his mug had been—at least a Joltin' Joe monogrammed mug, I was pleased to see. I located a paper towel.

"Dolores Key went to the University of Texas."

I stopped wiping up, hand in midsweep. "Wow!" I feigned surprise, wanting to spring on him the connection I'd already made.

"She didn't graduate, though. Take a guess why she left UT and came home."

"Tell me."

He went on, "A little dust-up. An arrest, minor in possession, no conviction. The police report mentioned a Leonard Smart."

"How'd you—wait, I know better than to ask."

"Not that hard, Matt. It's called Google. You know, on computers." He waved at the ancient beige monitor perched on my desk, cathode ray model, aged-out last century. From Mick Malone, Pepper'd found out Mongo's age and had sleuthed a range of reports in Austin. The names popped up on some other guy's rap sheet: Leonard Smart and Dolores, a year apart in age, same police blotter.

"Jesus!"

"No, not Jesus, Matt. Heavier set, the same long hair but reddish blond. Poor Dolores. She lasted a year, away from her rural, far northern corner of the US. Being a pretty eighteen-year-old girl at a fraternity party during a drug raid added to her homesickness and brought an end to her brief college career."

"Pepper, you're looking at a Pulitzer."

He acknowledged my compliment with a tip of his coffee mug. But before he got too cocky, I told him about the comfy wool stadium blanket I'd seen at Scott Key's house.

Here in far-away Salish County, the word "Texas" does not lightly trip off the tongue in conversations. The place might be on another planet—which explained why the connection between a tidbit in a long-ago saga by Scott Key involving his ex-college wife had lingered somewhere in my brain. Now, more than one puzzle piece slipped into another.

Pepper shook his head. "Tell me, Matt, what are the chances? A Mongo connection, drugs. He shows up here. Dolores's husband is addicted to pot."

"Hardly probable cause."

"Do you want to know what else Mick found out? I should let him tell you."

"Pepper, time's a-wastin'. Out with it."

"Mick had a real police lab, not Yuri's chemistry set, take a gander at the phone you found. A partial print. Those magic machines that do a bizillion matches in ten minutes found ... Leonard Smart, who wasn't at the bust."

"It was a plant."

Pepper loved the moment. I tossed a twenty on the coffee table. I started for the door. He followed me, shoving the twenty into my back pocket.

"Down payment, Matt."

I thanked him and, to myself, upped his fee to dinner.

My optimism that morning had been justified after all, though nothing I'd planned. Just shoulders back and steps forward. I'd told off Deanna Mackenzie, gotten stopped by her boyfriend for a fake traffic infraction, then taken a flyer and visited Scott Key. Look what I'd found: Luke Barkley, Dolores and Scott, Leonard "Mongo" Smart, Bandoleros and Angels, even Deanna—jigsaw pieces spread out on a table, lying there in front of me. Only thing now was to assemble them in a way that'd spare Willard "Gunk" Carlyle from doing time.

I had an idea. It could wait till tomorrow.

I was jazzed. I called Yuri the next morning, filled him in, and he was impressed—until I told him it was time to talk to Mongo again and why.

"No way, Matt. He'll eat you for breakfast."

"You'll be with me. Two against one. Yuri, I feel like we're rounding third, heading for home."

Yuri, no fan of sports metaphors, said, "Maybe sliding into third. I'll see what I can do. Meet me at the club. I have a surprise."

I did need to calm down, so working out was a good idea. After an energy bar and glass of OJ from the stop-n-rob on the corner, I went to meet Yuri.

Being the buff faceman he was, Yuri Brodsky was a magnet for pretty women. At the club, for instance, lo' and behold an attractive woman would show up on the treadmill next to his and make a exaggerated show of hanging her towel on the handlebar and smiling a lot. Once, I observed a pair of ladies, maybe a tag team, one on either side.

When I caught up with Yuri at the gym, visual entertainment was not my purpose. As for him, I wasn't sure. After he and I took a few round trips up and down the stairs to work up a sweat, we stood by a drinking fountain and toweled off.

"God, Matt, look over there. Wearing that oughta be illegal."

The word "illegal" caught my ear, and my mind drifted away.

"Matt, you with me?"

I snapped to.

"Matt, my lips are moving. There are sounds coming out of my mouth. It's called talking."

"Sorry, man."

"Take a look at her! In the green leotard."

He had a point. Bending and stretching, all yoga-ista, on a mat past the racked weights was Reason Number One why guys choose coed athletic clubs. Of course, a woman like the one we ogled was complicit in voyeurism, knowing full well what she was doing. I'm not passing judgment, merely leveling the political correctness playing field.

I turned to Yuri. "Do you know her?"

"I do. That's Linda. Linda Cranston."

"A friend?"

"Perhaps a little more than that."

I knew better than to pry.

He continued, "We sort of spent the evening together last night. She works at North County Credit Union. Assistant Manager."

"Damn you work fast." I meant it a nonlibidinal sense.

Yuri Brodsky said, "You and I had the number off the cell phone. North County is the one and only credit union around here. I go there myself. I accidentally on purpose ran into pretty Linda after you and I talked last week and she and I went to dinner, then back to her place."

"Yuri, what are people for, except to help each other in any way possible? To go the extra mile. Make the ultimate sacrifice."

"Even if that means inventorying her purse after she fell asleep."

"Shit, man!"

"All I did was peek at her smartphone. Seems there's an access code number a bank officer can use to find individual accounts. Sort of a reverse directory."

Her smartphone. Was I an accessory?

"It's the twenty-first century, Matt."

He bent and took another swig from the drinking fountain. We stepped into the hall so Ms. Cranston wouldn't see us. I asked Yuri why he'd picked the gym today. He said he didn't think she'd be here after the previous night's calorie burning. Yuri, on the other hand, was indefatigable. Clearly.

"Of course you called the access number."

"Yes, I did. Hit pay dirt with Dolores Key's birthday. I got it off her Facebook page."

The whole scenario bothered me. Some people don't give a rip about protecting passwords, but burglarizing a woman's purse, invading privacy at a chartered financial institution. I told Yuri so.

"Hey, I didn't snoop Linda's account."

"I'll recommend you for a Good Conduct Medal. You have the chutzpah of a jewel thief."

"Comes with the territory."

"And the morals of an alley cat."

He didn't argue.

"So, are you going to tell me what you found out?"

"Dolores Key, stay-at-home unemployed wife, routinely

makes deposits in goodly amounts. Once a week, at least. In cash, not checks. The account is in her name alone. Every month or so, money goes back out in the form of a check. A counter check, I suspect. No name on it."

Snap! In went another puzzle piece.

"When do we see Mongo?"

"This afternoon, at that Betsy's place you like. The one where that waitress you know works."

Yuri peeked around at the yoga mats next to the stair-climbers.

"She's doing downward dog."

"Of course she is," I said.

Yuri said, "When'd you say you and Gunk are going to court? Next week?"

My stomach did a little flip of its own. "Yep. Lem said they could squeeze us in next week."

I left to change.

44

We reconnected at Betsy's, braving a gusty afternoon by sitting on the back deck like before. It was out of the way, not visible from the highway. Megan was off that day.

"Hey, Leonard. Have a seat." The use of his real name startled him.

He didn't smile, and sat down. "What's up, Counselor?"

We sat there like opposing chess pieces.

"A little conversation between us chickens. How's Dolores?"

I was rewarded with a twitch in his left eyelid. His enormous moon-face was drawn and stubbled. There was no longer the brash self-confidence I was used to. He looked at Yuri.

Yuri said, "Go with us for a minute, Mongo. Matt's just doing his job."

"This better be good."

I tried to look smug. "Oh, I think it is. You're a busy man, Leonard. In the interest of time, I'll lay this out for you. Does the name Agent Lockwood ring a bell?" I was making this up as I went along.

"Nope."

"Oh, he remembers you. But who doesn't? Maybe you remember a little dust-up in Austin a few years ago. Drugs, assault? Over a college girl you were hanging with?"

I had his attention. I went on. "Especially the drugs. Seems they were from south of the border so the DEA was involved, too. They saw a likely candidate, a biker dude and all, so they recruited you."

"You're making this up, Matt. Total fiction."

"Don't think so, Leonard. A cop gave me the story," I lied, sort of. The "Leonard" was starting to get to him. I was doing it on purpose; people slip up when they're angry, but I had Yuri for backup.

I reached into my pocket and pulled out my pint-sized, ancient Dictaphone. That got his attention. I opened it, pulled out the tape, and dropped it into my coffee. I wasn't even sure the batteries were charged, but as theater it had the intended effect.

"Okay, Matt, what's this about?"

"The only thing it's about, as far as I'm concerned, is keeping Gunk out of jail. To zealously represent my client, like we always say."

Mongo moved the coffee cup over in front of him and rattled the tape around in the coffee. "How do I know you don't have another one of these running?"

"He doesn't," said Yuri. "Just hear him out."

"What I know is this," I began. "You and the now Dolores Key had a thing going down at UT. For whatever reason, and I don't need to know, it ended. One way or another, the DEA got hold of you and enlisted you. You agreed, you were young, and it kept you out of jeopardy."

He was listening.

"You joined the Angels, moved up in the ranks—you were a natural—and finished law school, of all things. Whether they knew that or not, I don't know if that mattered to them. Doesn't matter now, does it?"

"They knew, and it was all cool."

I breathed an inner sigh of relief. My bluff was paying off.

"Did you take the bar exam?"

"I did, and passed. Also two others."

"That's more punishment than I was up for. Which ones?"

"This state. And California."

"Here? What on earth for?"

"How shall we say, my 'associates' thought it would be a good idea."

"So let's dial forward," I said. "The Texas Angels get wind of some internal dissension up this way, in British Columbia, in a chapter that's making a fine go of providing high-quality taboo products to the States. So, they deputize you to come up and check things out. You like the idea. For one thing there might be extracurricular fun with a sexy former girlfriend."

"Say, I almost enjoy spending time with you two, but where are we going with this?" He was recovering some of his braggadocio. "Why do you think this bullshit has to do with Gunk?"

"I'm almost done. Whatever the internal problem was with the B.C. Angels, you ironed it out. But they were annoyed, too, about a little penny-ante group of aged-out Bandoleros here in the States moving pot across the border. Not a large amount, but cutting into whatever profit they'd otherwise get. So you arranged a bust."

"How in the world do you expect to prove that, Matt?"

"I don't have to prove anything, Leonard. That's not why we're here. That device you planted? You didn't quite get all the fingerprints off it. We matched one. To you. And there were the bogus calls. That was clever. The DEA public number. So what. One to a number in B.C. that was out of service. And one to you, to throw us off. The puzzling part was the call to the credit union. Then we figured that one out."

He was definitely listening.

"Let's not forget the 'recreation' (I did the air-quotes thing) with your old sweetie-pie."

The anger gambit was working. He jumped ahead of me. "She's a bitch! Used me to make the contact with a supplier up north, over a year ago when she tracked me down and called me. I show up here, and is she warm and fuzzy? No way. Shook her little ass, then blew me off. Good little judgie's wife now. Dealing drugs? So I was, uh, displeased. And her old man, I find out, has his tit in a ringer already."

He was more agitated than was safe. We are all vulnerable to affairs of the heart and whatever other body organ.

He growled, "Okay, Matt, what next … assuming even a quarter of what you've said is true? Or verifiable."

"You're going to help me get Gunk off. And I'm not going to spread this around, verifiable or not, to some bad bikers up north with chains and guns who wouldn't take kindly to a double agent, a DEA nark, in their midst. Street cred, big and scary as you are, or not, I do recall Freight Train's comment about 'punishment,' or whatever he called it."

"I can take care of myself, Matt. Please don't fret on my account."

"Mongo, I'm not going to the law or anywhere else with this. I have a plan to help your buddy Gunk, and I'd like your assistance. He goes to court day after tomorrow."

He looked out at the river. So did we. I waited.

"All right, Counselor. I'll do it for Gunk. He's a sorry piece of work. I don't need the hassle. I'm going back home anyway. I'm bored as hell and I hate the rain. What do you want? Lay it out for me."

So I did.

Then I called Lem Fish and told him we were ready to go. He got back to me in fifteen minutes and said there was an opening, surprisingly, on Monday—eleven o'clock, Judge Stone's courtroom. I kept my voice level and said sure.

45

S howtime. Gunk's day in court was upon us.

I'd spent Friday and the weekend at the office checking and double-checking what we knew, including going online and doing actual legal research. I drafted the first honest-to-goodness legal memo I'd written in a while. I hadn't heard back from Gunk whether he was willing to take Lem Fish's plea deal, so after the meeting with Mongo on Thursday afternoon, I'd called him. I didn't give him all the details, just laid some legal mumbo-jumbo on him, and told him Mongo and I were on the same page.

"What's that mean?" He was understandably suspicious.

"Gunk, we're going to court. No choice. We'll play it cagey. We have some options open. Sometimes, the unexpected happens. We'll plead you to the government's deal if we have to as a last resort."

"When's the court date?"

"Monday."

Silence. Big sigh, then, "A whole weekend to sit and stew. Sheila probably shouldn't bring Gordon down tonight."

I said, "Probably shouldn't risk it this time."

"I'll ride down with you. Not take the bike."

"Good," again. "See you here Monday morning at eight."

He hung up.

∾

The US District Court building is on an elevated piece of ground in the state's biggest city, an hour and a half south of Church Harbor. The monument to New Deal architecture takes up an entire block. Gunk and I rode down together not saying much. The sky was blue, temperature in the thirties. Traffic was light so we made good time. Pricey parking, the buildings tall, the pedestrians numerous, street traffic noisy. We weren't in Kansas anymore.

This was a big deal. For all my usual bravado, I was nervous. I was on edge even if there wasn't going to be an actual trial. Any lawyer will admit that the quantum leap from state court to federal court is daunting. Our country's duplicative judicial system, the two-layer, federal and state court arrangement, isn't that hard to understand. Trials for kidnapping, racketeering, tax fraud, US Border violations are held at the federal level. Decisions at that level can go on to an appellate court, then in rare cases, to the Mountaintop, the Supremes. The same hierarchy exists in the state system, except the trials take place in the familiar confines of the superior court down the street from my office.

The Federal Building itself is large. Steep, wide steps ascend to heavy, metal-trimmed wooden doors with aged bronze inlays of scenes from the Nation's history. There was genuine security when we entered, metal detectors, scanners, and guards. We walked down a high-ceilinged hallway to Courtroom Number Two. In the quiet marbled corridor and hushed atmosphere, whispered conversations played out against the backdrop of centuries of Anglo-Saxon jurisprudence. Here is where the lowliest malefactor would await his or her fate, sometimes seated down the pew from a former captain of industry, both facing a seasoned judge or a jury of randomly selected citizens. If a person is in the position of appearing in the case of "The United States vs. You," it's not his or her best day.

Gunk was dressed in sensible khaki slacks, a long-sleeved

shirt and tie, and a dark sweater. His hair was washed to a sheen and in a ponytail. True, he looked a bit like my cousin the steelworker dressed up for my wedding, but I'd seen the "before" picture. I wore my go-to-court blue suit, a spanking white broadcloth shirt, and my best J.C. Penney tie.

The stakes were high, as Gunk realized. He'd brought with him a change of clothes, twenty dollars, and the obligatory toothbrush. If our strategy didn't pan out, he wouldn't be riding back with me. He'd be sentenced and remanded to the custody of the US Marshal. He also brought a book, *Zen and the Art of Motorcycle Maintenance*, which I would have wondered about, had I not known that it was as much about motorcycle maintenance as *The Grapes of Wrath* is about grapes.

We took a seat outside the courtroom on wooden benches, vintage World War II. The courthouse had been built years ago and endured periodic interior remodels to account for the population increase. The place was redolent of years of legal files and furniture polish. A row of suspended ceiling lamps shone with subdued incandescence. Ten or so people waited along with us outside the courtroom. Public Defender Rebecca Murray and Daniel Ray Higginbotham (aka "Butthead") joined us.

The tall courtroom door swung open and we walked in. It was imposing—the same twenty-foot ceilings, more shiny benches. Up front was the waist-high bar railing and beyond that stood a formidable judicial bench elevated a good ten feet above the floor.

Assistant US Attorney Lemuel Fish arrived. We shook hands. He introduced us to a Mr. Evan Wood, who he identified as a DEA agent. Mr. Wood went to an empty row behind us and sat. We didn't have long to wait.

"All rise," boomed the bailiff. We stood.

A little woman in a black robe strode in from a door in the front of the chamber to our right. She ascended to the high bench, disappearing for a moment then reappearing and sitting down. She ran a hand through her white hair and put on a pair of pince-nez which settled halfway down her nose. This was the Right Honorable Judge Marilyn Macy Stone, a fifteen-year veteran of the federal bench. The stories I'd heard of her playing with a tiny guillotine on her desk while a frightened attorney pled his case were no doubt apocryphal, but like all myths, sort of true. Judge Stone did not bite the heads off young lawyers, but no one had ever seen her smile. Not the clerk, not the bailiff, not the guy who swept up. Certainly not the attorneys. She was a good judge and fair, to be sure—gave prosecutors a rough time, too—but why not a sociable cup of coffee in her chambers when things were slow?

"You may be seated," called the bailiff. All of us complied, with a swish and shush of clothing and rearrangement of files. I looked around the courtroom. We were the only ones there. Our case was called. Gunk and I, Rebecca and her client, and Lem passed through the swinging gate and sat at our respective counsel tables.

"Mr. Fish, please proceed."

"Thank you, Your Honor."

Lem outlined the elements of the charges against Mr. Willard Carlyle. The accused was complicit in transporting a large quantity of a controlled substance across the international border in concert with four other members of a notorious motorcycle gang. Lem explained to the judge that a plea arrangement had been offered which he expected the defendant to accept. A plea would save the expense of a trial and the busy court's time, and would involve restitution of a sum of money and some incarceration. Judge Stone turned to me.

"Mr. Archer, welcome to our court. How does your client plead?"

I motioned for Gunk to stand.

Judge Stone said, "Mr. Carlyle, please approach the bench." We walked forward. My heart was galloping. Timing was everything. I glanced at the clock. What was taking him so long?

"Mr. Carlyle, the prosecutor is recommending a fine and jail time," she continued, "so, I have a few questions for you."

"Yes, Ma'am," said the florist from Salish County standing next to me and glancing at the court reporter to his right.

"First of all . . ."

And that's as far as she got.

46

The courtroom door behind us banged open. Heavy strides started up the aisle. Everyone turned around. In came Mongo.

Not the Mongo we knew. The mountain of a man was dressed in full courtroom mufti: a three-piece tan suit that had must have tested the inventory of a big-and-tall store, a bespoke brown-striped tie knotted perfectly, and shiny cordovan slip-ons. His reddish blond hair was parted in the middle and it draped his shoulders. A gleaming gold watch chain, of all things, strained across his massive belly and completed the ensemble. The chain was connected to a gold pocket watch which Mongo nonchalantly pulled out and glanced at, saying, "Judge Stone, may it please the court, I sincerely apologize for being late."

I don't recall which part of the frozen tableau I noticed first. The elderly five-foot something bailiff who seemed to shrink before our eyes? The stunned court reporter, hands motionless above her keyboard? Assistant US Attorney Fish who sat open-mouthed and, for the first time in our acquaintance, unable to say a word? Gunk, Rebecca, her client?

Judge Stone did not hesitate.

"It definitely does not please the court, whoever you are," said Her Honor with the severity that usually caused mere mortal attorneys to question their calling. "Bailiff, remove this ... person from the courtroom."

Mongo held up a hand.

"Your Honor, please. I am Leonard Smart, Esquire, and I represent Mr. Carlyle here today."

I risked a look at Gunk and held my breath. Whew! That had been close.

"So who is Mr. Archer?"

"He's co-counsel. I have the substitution of attorney form right here."

After a considerable and fraught pause, Judge Stone said, "Gentlemen, please be seated." She drew the words out slowly.

Three of us returned to the table, Mongo, Gunk, and me. Rebecca and client Higginbotham moved back to chairs behind us. Mongo—that is, "Attorney Smart"—put the substitution form in front of me and I signed it. So did Gunk, who remained remarkably calm.

The judge leaned forward and peered at her laptop. We waited while she punched in some information. She finished and looked up.

"I do see Leonard Allen Smart, member of the bar in good standing."

Mongo took the substitution form to the bailiff who handed it up to the judge.

"Mr. Fish," she asked, "were you aware of this?"

"No, Your Honor, and I strenuously object to this turn of events."

"I can understand that. For now, Gentlemen and Lady, I'm going to let this matter proceed. If you have a formal objection to make at some point, Mr. Fish, I'll hear you out. Mr. Archer, Mr. Smart, shall we continue with taking Mr. Carlyle's plea?"

"In fact, no, Your Honor," said Mongo, rising. "I have new evidence I'd like to offer, if it pleases the court."

Judge Stone peered over her glasses at one of us, then the other.

"I'm still not exactly pleased, Mr. Smart, but we don't have a busy calendar today. Let's say I'm intrigued. What 'new evidence'?"

"I'm handing up an affidavit by licensed Private Investigator Yuri Brodsky." He handed the paper to the bailiff. "As Your Honor will see, Mr. Brodsky describes a number of calls made from a cell phone belonging to my client."

This phone, not the one I'd found at the scene, did belong to Gunk, and Yuri'd traced the numbers. We were playing a long shot, a Yuri Brodsky patented two-hand set shot from beyond the key.

Attorney Smart continued, "Among the calls were ones to me, Mr. Carlyle's attorney, and to Mr. Higginbotham," he turned and pointed behind him, "who we submit is an informant."

Megan Janssen, waitress and charming dessert and movie-watching companion, had guessed right! I turned back to see Butthead, who had to be scared to death by this time, and Rebecca Murray whose jaw had dropped and was resting on that day's fashionable scarf.

"Both calls, Your Honor, we submit were illegally tapped, without proper warrant."

Lem Fish was on his feet. "Your Honor, I object. I have not seen this affidavit. I was entitled to see it before it was presented in court."

"Have a seat, Mr. Fish. First, let me read it."

"And while you are considering this, Your Honor," continued the enterprising Mr. Smart, "we believe the agent responsible for the illegal wiretap is here in court. Mr. Wood, seated back there."

We all waited. My heart was pounding.

Finally, the judge spoke. No, first she smiled. She honestly smiled, corners of her mouth spread, teeth appearing, eyes crinkling, and shook her head.

"You know, Mr. Smart, I haven't kept track of how many

cases I've heard in my years, but this is one for the books. I'm going to let you proceed. I warn you, this better be good. I'm guessing you would like to call a witness?"

Lem Fish, again on his feet. "Your Honor, I repeat. In addition to the entirely unorthodox nature of this proceeding, I am only now aware of what's ... I'm unaware of any of this!"

I couldn't blame the poor guy. Mongo the Lawyer called Agent Evan Wood to the stand. Under oath, Mr. Wood admitted that his office had "intercepted," was the word he used, Gunk's phone. I unclenched my fingers and placed my hands on my legs to stop them from shaking.

Agent Wood did claim that they had probable cause for a one-party consent to a wiretap. This was allowed under very precise circumstances, but under questioning by Mongo he failed the legal test. The tip-off had come from an informant, now revealed as the unfortunate Mr. Higginbotham (illegally in the country, after all) who'd told the DEA only that he *thought* something was going to go down and *guessed* at the place for the drug delivery. That wouldn't have passed muster with a judge for a one-party wiretap warrant, which was why the DEA hadn't bothered to seek one. Mongo didn't mention the tapped call to him. He didn't need to.

He called Mr. Higginbotham to the stand. That didn't happen because Rebecca had recovered enough to jump to her feet and object that any testimony by her client would violate his right against self-incrimination. Judge Stone agreed.

"Mr. Fish, Mr. Archer, and Mr. Smart, please approach the bench. You too, please, Ms. Murray."

We did and stood shoulder to shoulder before the raised pulpit and craned our necks up to the judge's face.

"Mr. Fish, how much of this did you know about?"

Lem replied, "None of it, Your Honor."

"Mr. Smart or Mr. Archer, why not?"

I said, "We only recently learned how Mr. Higginbotham was further involved. On a hunch, we checked out Mr. Carlyle's phone the day before yesterday."

I didn't look to see if Mongo had his fingers crossed behind his back on that one. We'd taken a flying leap and we might land on our feet. Plus, everything we'd said was pretty much true.

"Mr. Fish, did you know about the informant?"

"I did, but not who he was. As you know, when a criminal investigation is based on information from a confidential informant, that informant's identity must be protected."

"Until," continued the judge, "that identity is necessary to allow a defendant the right to confront witnesses against him in court. You remember the US Constitution, do you not, Mr. Fish?"

That was unfair. This seasoned veteran of the bench, whose word was law, literally, was having fun. Lem, for his part, seemed to be taking it well.

"Mr. Fish, I'm willing to continue this matter to give you time to respond to recent developments. Would you like to do that?"

Lem didn't take long to answer. This was not a murder trial. He had bigger fish to fry, so to speak. He also would have plenty to say to his coworkers in law enforcement.

"No, Your Honor."

"Gentlemen and Lady, you may return to your seats."

We did.

"I'm going to rule as follows: I am persuaded that there was a warrantless and illegal wiretap of Mr. Carlyle's phone. Pursuant to the Fourth Amendment and the doctrine of 'fruit of the poisoned tree,' the prosecution would not have known anything about the alleged transport of marijuana across the Canadian border, time or place, without that illegally obtained information. The charges against Mr. Carlyle are dismissed. Mr. Fish, prepare the order and submit it to me for my signature when it's convenient. Mr. Carlyle, you're free to go."

We stood. Judge Stone rose, too, lowered her glasses, and said, "One more thing." We paused before making our escape. "Mr. Smart and Mr. Archer, you can expect an inquiry from the State Bar. I'm not accusing you of anything, but I'm a suspicious old broad, and what took place here today has me, I must say, suspicious. We're adjourned."

Down came the gavel with a bang. Gunk, eyes wet, hugged Mongo, then me. I reached over the bar behind me, shrugged, and shook Rebecca Murray's hand. I avoided Lem, and we left. Criminal law is a bitch.

47

Not long afterward, the other shoe dropped. Less than a week, in fact. Shoes plural. High-heeled boots with fur around the ankles that she slipped off and set inside my front door when I let her in. She shook my hand lightly, shrugged off her parka, and settled herself in the easy chair, legs tucked under a too-short black skirt. It appeared she'd be staying awhile.

"Hello, Dolores."

She wore the tiny, diamond-encrusted Cartier cross I'd seen before. It draped into the *décolletage* the ever chivalrous Luke Barkley had alluded to. Her baby blue V-neck sweater looked like cashmere. The entire outfit might have been expensive, but Christian Dior meets sackcloth and ashes, it turned out.

She nodded politely when I offered coffee. Light snow was drifting across the window behind the sofa when I returned and sat down. I waited for her to talk.

"Matt, you've got me dead to rights, it seems." That was pretty close to true.

The last time I'd seen Leonard "Mongo" Smart was when he came by my house the Saturday after we'd gotten Gunk off. He wanted to say good-bye, of all things. I was touched. I'd grown fond of this big honkin' bad biker, licensed to practice law in three states, DEA undercover agent, and who knew what else.

He'd modified his big Harley ride to add a pair of expensive saddlebags with rivets all around, hard, glossy leather, brass snaps here and there, and matching grommets on belts securing the big outer pockets. Out of one of the compartments, Mongo extracted a package wrapped in brown butcher paper. Little bigger than a football, it was a token of our friendship, he said.

I unwrapped it. It was a Chinese or Japanese bowl, white with red and orange and yellow flowers on thin green stems. I'd seen it before. I remembered I'd knocked one off a shelf at Gunk's shop and broken it when I'd bowled him over. Another, pretty and intact, had caught my eye on the mantle at Scott Key's house. The pattern of both was identical to the cover of the ceramics magazine I'd leafed through on Scott's deck.

"Surely, Matt, you've asked yourself where Judge Scott Key gets the dope he smokes. He needs a safe source. And a safe place to stash it. How convenient to have an artisanal wifey. And she can supplement her walking around money by distributing Japanese vases around town."

This was not a farewell gift. This was a final shot at an unrequited love affair. Cupid's arrows are sharp and go deep.

"Mongo, you shouldn't have," I pretended.

"Not to worry. By the way, I washed this one out. I don't think a sniffing dog would notice."

"You are a true gentleman."

"Matt, do you ever go into antique stores?"

He named one I'd driven past a time or two called "Auld Junque," a name offensive in both Gaelic and Gallic. It slumbered, along with other establishments, in the old section of Church Harbor.

We did the fist-bump. Mongo zipped up his heavy-duty leathers, remounted, and gunned his V-twin pipes. I waved as he motored off. I'd forgotten to ask how he knew Butthead was the snitch. Or maybe it was that axiom about not asking a question if you don't have to.

That afternoon, I drove to Church Harbor's Old Town District, a historic area where the first streets and wooden sidewalks had been laid out in Ebie Church's day. Down by the wharf, fronting the street, were graying buildings that once upon a time serviced the fishing fleet and other waterborne trade. Now, these had been long-since abandoned and rehabbed into an eclectic collection of shops, a mixed bag, limping along, not on the usual tourist itineraries. I parked in front of a shabby convenience store and got out. Between it and an ancient dry cleaners was my objective. Further down was a pawn shop and The Mission, its sad derelicts lounging on the front steps smoking.

Auld Junque looked to be a respectable antique store despite its neighbors. I tried to be nonchalant when I went in. But big guy, hometown high school sweatshirt, not the usual clientele—I felt more than a little out of place. After "Can I help you?" from the proprietor who gave me a once-over, I grunted "just looking, for the wife" and said no thanks. I wandered through the clutter to the back of the store, squeezing past desks and chairs, floor lamps with shades askew, and tattered loveseats. I bumped my shin on a table that, for a fleeting moment, I considered buying to replace the cheapo piece at my house. The two-hundred-dollar price tag disabused me. Shabby would continue to be my motif.

On my way past the front counter, I had not failed to notice two very familiar pieces of decorative crockery on a shelf. I moseyed around and waited until another shopper arrived and the owner went to help her. With his back turned, I snapped a picture on my cell, shoved the phone back into my pocket, and let myself out. I risked a quick look back; the guy had seen me.

Scott Key had told me about Dolores's relationship with his

mother doing ceramics together; now, she had a workshop at their place. The rest was first-rate police procedural.

I sent the photo to Mick. Intrepid wife Pamela went online that night and matched what I'd seen to an Eighteenth Century Japanese pottery style called *imari*. Mick said he'd have our suspect tailed. I kidded that it must be a slow time in law enforcement, that the police blotter these days must read like an advertising supplement.

"Matt, that's a compliment. You know, what Church Harbor needs is a good old-fashioned crime spree."

This wasn't exactly a spree, but drug trafficking by the wife of an elected public servant, a judge at that, wouldn't be sloughed off.

Mick's tail didn't take long to take photos of Dolores Key carrying an ordinary paper grocery bag into Auld Junque and coming back out with the bag folded under her arm. An undercover cop dropped by the shop—not exactly a cop, rather a youthful loser who'd bought some judicial relief by continuing to keep tabs on the local drug scene. The fellow wore a wire, said magic words to the proprietor, a name he already knew, and took possession of a one-ounce baggie of "green vegetable material," like it says on search warrants— lifted out of a pretty Oriental vase. The proprietor wasn't fooled. Before the youngster was even out of the store, the owner made a phone call.

Sitting on my sofa, Dolores herself completed the scenario. She asked about my interest in antiques—trying to be coy, I guessed.

"Why?" I asked, playing along.

"Don't be silly, Matt." She got up and walked over to inspect my bright new gift sitting on the mantle. She ran a hand around the lid. "Scott told me you asked about Leonard, about my ceramics." She picked up the *imari* bowl and lifted the lid, I assumed to admire her handiwork. She looked at me and smiled. "Empty," she said.

"Of course."

"The owner of the antique store called me and told me about a recent customer who looked out of place, who browsed but didn't stay long. The description matched you. A day later, in came a customer he'd sold to before who said the right words, but he ... what, my accomplice?" she even giggled, "... my associate, was suspicious."

Pot in pots, I mused. An advertising slogan. I kept my mouth shut.

"Is there anything else you'd like to know?"

I couldn't think of anything.

She said, "I lied to you. What are you going to do?"

"It's not up to me, Dolores. Don't you know that?"

She came back and sat down beside me on the couch. She put her hand on my leg. I felt the warmth for sure, but the effect was more that of a call girl than respectable judge's wife, not that I'd know, of course. I removed her hand and set it back in her lap.

"Please, Matt. Gunk's situation turned out okay. Leonard, I mean Mongo, is out of the picture. I bet he's halfway to Texas by now."

She hesitated, then went on, "Scott's ruined, and there's nothing I can do about it."

She leaned into me and this time the tears seemed real. I let her cry for a bit but disentangled myself and found a box of Kleenex. She blew her nose in a decidedly unladylike manner.

"What are we going to do for money? I didn't make much. Do you know how much?"

"Yes, I do." That did startle her out of what to that point had sounded like a prepared script. She'd have done well on the stage.

"How?"

"Dolores, since this seems like as good a time as any, why don't you tell me the rest."

She sat back up, lowered her head for a minute. The snow outside was increasing. "Scott started using pot a few years ago. It can be pretty addictive. Not that innocent, natural substance the kids like to boast about. The powerful, smelly bud from up north."

I let her assume this was news to me.

"Leonard and I, um ... knew each other. You know about Austin. I was a little wild once in a while, down at Texas. One time it got out of hand. Leonard wasn't all that nice. I had to call the police. So I left and moved home."

Dolores was telling her story, so why interrupt? Her hands stayed in her lap like a penitent. A penitent who, under other circumstances, could adorn a fashion runway.

"Leonard and I did keep in touch by email from time to time. He told me about a year ago that he was coming up here. I knew he was a biker, a Hells Angel in Texas, and he said he had work to do or something like that with a gang in B.C.— needed to pour water on a little brush fire, is how he put it. I asked him to do me a favor and he said he would. I asked him to put in a good word for me with the guys who delivered pot from time to time. Business was picking up, so to speak, not to mention that I had to keep Scott supplied. The Japanese ceramics were my idea."

"They're pretty. And the right size. Pot in pots," I did say.

She laughed at that. "Leonard and I got together when he came here. One thing led to another. He wanted to start up with me again and I told him no. He's not happy with me, you know."

I didn't buy her denial, given what I knew. At least she didn't say that now she was a devoted married woman.

I changed the subject. "Do you take it in baggies or vases each time?"

"Are you gathering more evidence?"

"Not at all. Merely curious."

"I do—did both. Kept up my pottery skills. I've gotten quite good, if I say so myself." A little joke.

Maybe her sense of humor would help her in the days ahead, down the bumpy, bumpy road ahead. I chose not to ask how many drop-offs she used, nor how long she'd been in the biz. I didn't buy her version of the Mongo story. By then, why should I care?

She congratulated me on the result in federal court.

"What I think happened, Dolores, is that the bust of Gunk and the boys had nothing to do with you being supplied. The B.C. Angels worried that our feeble stateside Bandolero buddies were cutting them out of part of their livelihood, starting to poach. Neither, as it happens, was the case."

I got up and poked the fire. I set another log on the flames. Fire in the fireplace, cozy snowy day, nothing else planned, and a pretty woman on my sofa who needed consoling.

Possibly sensing an opening, Dolores said, "What should I do, Matt? What can I do?" She gave me a half smile that was supposed to be alluring. When I didn't answer, she sat up straighter and shivered. She ran a hand with brightly colored nails through her dark curls, arranging loose strands. In another context, the tousled effect might have been erotic but that day she just looked tired.

"Matt, come sit back down. Please. You have nothing to lose, right?"

"Just some self-respect is all, Dolores. I'm kinda low on that commodity these days, so I'm hanging on to what little I have."

I stayed where I was.

"Where's Scott in all this? How much does he know?"

"Doesn't matter, does it? Once this gets out, we're goners. For now, I don't know where he is. He's staying away somewhere. He knows something's up and doesn't want to be seen with me."

That moved me. Being alone, and guilty, and on the margins of what was once a marriage is an awful place to be. I knew how she felt. The situation was out of her control now. Was I sorry enough to offer comfort?

No way. The photograph on the mantle reinforced my willpower, new A-line haircut and all. So did the left-over Halloween candy in the bowl on the coffee table I'd persuaded Allie to leave with me for "safe-keeping." So did Megan Janssen's both-feet-on-the-floor, old-movie-watching time. And Ellen's recent goodwill. And Mick's and Yuri's trust.

We sat in the quiet for several minutes. Dolores sighed, a sigh of resolve, it seemed. She was a tough cookie.

"Dolores, as far as I'm concerned, I have no further part to play in this drama. If the cops decide to follow up on what they know, that's up to them. Get a good lawyer. I suggested Jack Tulio to Scott."

"Good advice, Matt."

Her purse was on the chair. She went to the door and slipped on her boots. I held out her parka and she slid her arms into the sleeves. I opened the door and let her out. There was no goodbye kiss on the cheek. She walked to her car, head down and leaning into the oncoming flurries. I hoped she had snow tires. It wasn't even Thanksgiving yet.

48

nd then it was.

Ellen confirmed that I was invited to dinner. She'd also invited Yuri and his mother. I called Megan Janssen, just to check in. I didn't want her to think I was ignoring her. She was doing the cooking for her brother who was in town with his roommate who she hadn't met. I told her Allie and I would come out to the animal shelter soon and look at dogs.

I got to Ellen's at three, pronto. Dinner was planned for five. Allie answered the door. She was wearing an honest-to-goodness dress, white, with a blue sash, and she looked awfully grown up. She watched with interest as Ellen and I shared cheek-to-cheek kisses, me safely holding a pumpkin pie in each hand.

Yuri and his mom arrived. Mrs. Brodsky handed Ellen a bunch of flowers. I took their coats. Yuri hugged Allie. He and Ellen swapped amateurish high-fives, frowned when they missed, and settled for a honest-to-goodness kiss. On the lips. I swallowed hard; she and Yuri looked good together. I wasn't suspicious, just envious. I hung up the coats and came back to hug Mrs. B and then her son.

I hadn't seen Mrs. Brodsky since I returned to town. Yuri's dad had passed away several years before. Far from the caricature little old Jewish lady with white hair, stooped and dressed in black, Mrs. B was almost Yuri's height, stood straight as a die, and was dressed in a stylish plum-colored pantsuit. Her hair was gray with streaks of blonde. She and Ellen ran into each other from time to time. They shared a fascination with the game of bridge, which I couldn't fathom, neither the game nor anyone's attraction to it.

Mrs. Brodsky patted the sofa beside her and she and Allie launched into conversation—gesticulating, laughing—like a couple of college roommates. Yuri poked at the fire and we watched the sparks flare up the chimney. He turned and stood in front of it, hands behind his back. I found a vase for the flowers. The house smelled welcoming as only a roasting turkey can make it.

I followed Ellen into the kitchen. She and I had always been a good team. We'd shared cooking responsibilities, and this afternoon was like old times, minus the accidental-on-purpose hip bumps or close-contact reaching around for something on the counter. We tended to the stuffing and mashed potatoes, gravy, Brussels sprouts, red jello-mold fruit salad, and black olives, as traditional as a Norman Rockwell cover. Ellen hadn't gotten rid of our wedding china, bless her. The table was set with the good silverware, matching sugar bowl and creamer, the gravy boat we'd bought that didn't match anything, pewter candlesticks, and starched linen napkins.

I decanted rosé-colored sparkling cider into an etched crystal pitcher, and we sat. We held hands and bowed our heads. I knew I couldn't make it through saying the prayer, so I'd fobbed that one off on Yuri's mom. She recited something in Hebrew, then translated: "Yea, though I walk through the valley ..." Dang, that David guy could flat-out write. Ellen and I both sniffled, in unison. Allie waited a nanosecond before reaching past the Brussels sprouts to the bowl of mashed potatoes. My dad had taught me how to carve a turkey and not have it look like a hand grenade hit it.

I can't say I tasted my dinner. Too many feelings were flooding my brain at once, so vivid was the scene before me, so thankful was I on that day of thanks, so wrapped up in emotion was I, that I don't remember how much or whatever course I ate. Except that it was delicious.

I do recall that before dessert, Yuri and I took a break and went outside. Liberated household or not, the women cleared and stacked dishes. I'd wash later. Mrs. Brodsky was in Allie's room, hopefully hearing about fifth-grade shenanigans and not about helmetless motorcycle rides.

I retrieved our coats and Yuri and I stood on the back stoop. It was snowing lightly. The first snow of winter had stuck around, and the easy wind and downy flakes (thank you, Robert Frost) settled on our heads, on the lawn and tree limbs.

I thought about Gunk and Sheila, and their son Gordon. Gunk had said he was going to try a border jump Wednesday night. If he was caught, he'd plead American Thanksgiving and hope for a forgiving cop. I said I'd get to work on Sheila's situation and noted that marrying her or at least planning to might help. He didn't talk about the result of his case, other than to thank me again.

"What a strange set of events," Yuri began, pulling his parka close and zipping it. "I began to think something was wrong with the picture when you told me about 'rendezvous' and 'pedigree' and all those other nonbiker words Mongo used. I'd heard of him but I hadn't met him—not much remarkable about just another biker around, even one who looked like he stepped off a movie set."

"So all that buddy-buddy camaraderie between you two at The Palms was fake."

"Sort of. Yeah. Part of what I do."

Ellen came out and joined us. She handed each of us a cup of coffee and retrieved one for herself.

"This guy Mongo, Matt," she said. "Gunk, Mongo? You do have interesting playmates."

I'd filled her in earlier about how the whole thing went down, and some of the background but not all of it.

"Interesting, yep. I think Leonard Smart is exactly what he appears to be, improbable as that is. Biker with the Angels, attorney licensed in three states, and on the feds' payroll. Just your everyday guy. He handles the moral and ethical, not to mention legal, ambiguities somehow."

Yuri stood across from Ellen and me, looking at us standing side-by-side against the porch railing. He lifted his cup as if to toast us. Ellen reached down and took my hand. I squeezed it, and she pulled it back like it was an accident. I chose to believe it was on purpose. Ellen didn't make mistakes. She did move a skootch away from me, but not that far.

Yuri said, "Old Mongo took care of an intra-tribe squabble in B.C. and stifled what the Angels feared was an end run by the Bandoleros. He got everything he came up here for."

Not quite everything. I hadn't told even Yuri the more sordid details of Mongo and Mrs. Judge Key. I hated the gossip trade.

He went on, "You dragging him in as co-counsel was brilliant."

"So was your brainstorm." I turned to Ellen. "It was Yuri's genius to think of Gunk's cell phone. Maybe the government had tapped it. It was a gamble and I prayed the DEA would have a guy in court to watch how things went down. So we ran the bluff. If it failed, we'd lose."

Ellen said, "But why the Mongo brouhaha in court? All the theater? If I'm following you, you could have done it by yourself."

"The diversion, the confusion is why. The element of surprise. We had to catch Lem Fish off-guard. If I'd have pulled the rabbit out of the hat earlier, Lem would have asked for a continuance, and I'd have had to agree. He and I have known each other a long time. Adversaries who are also friends don't do that to each other."

Ellen frowned, tracking my chronology.

"Okay, okay, I took liberties, but I hope I stayed within the lines."

"Weren't you misleading the judge, too?" Ellen asked.

"Nope. She made the right ruling. Bad wiretap. Case dismissed."

Yuri said, "So poor old Higginbotham, Butthead the butthead, was the snitch."

"And you always have to chase down an informant," I agreed. "They lie, have ulterior motives—well, look how this turned out. Mongo was all over it. So, yeah, it was a long-shot. We gambled that Ms. Murray'd never let Butthead take the stand."

"What was, er, Mr. Higginbotham's story?" asked Ellen with a wrinkle of her nose and a pair of air quotes.

"Dunno. And I'm not going to ask the boys over at DEA. Here's a guess, though. He used to be a north-of-the-border Angel, too, but got crosswise with them. The gang stripped him for some infraction and the Mounties were on his tail besides, so he flees down here where he has some measure of safety. If he gets busted for Gunk's little caper and has to do jail time, he's better off here than having to worry about unannounced and very messy Hells Angels wrath. Maybe the government would have put him in a witness protection program in another state, which he'd go for like a free round at happy hour."

I added, "Poor Rebecca Murray, though. At least she's well paid."

"And she's pretty, right?" Yuri said. "Perhaps you could introduce us."

"You never quit, do you?"

Yuri let the implications of that comment hang in the air without replying, with the lady I was still married to standing beside us. We went back inside. We hadn't brought up the recent judgeship election, still too close to call. A recount was underway and neither Judge Key nor his opponent, who should not be named, had declared victory.

❧

The group reassembled in the living room for my world-class pumpkin pie adorned by globs of vanilla ice cream.

Allie said, "Hey, you guys. Wanna hear a joke Gunk told me?"

I'm sure Ellen joined me in offering up a silent prayer to the Goddess of Appropriate Holiday Dinner Table Conversation. Allie took her time putting a chunk of vanilla ice cream on a slice of pumpkin pie, ignoring the four pairs of eyes paying close attention.

"Sure, honey," said Mrs. Brodsky.

"How do you tell the difference between a happy motorcycle rider and an unhappy motorcycle rider?"

Yuri was slowly shaking his head. Mrs. Brodsky, a veteran in these matters, said, "I give up, Allie. How do you tell the difference?"

"Look for the bugs in his teeth."

Ellen narrowly avoided losing her coffee into her lap. The rest of us dissolved. How do you follow that line? You don't even try, Dad.

$$\sim \sim \sim End \sim \sim \sim$$

Acknowledgments

My first thank-you goes to writer Dani Shapiro who gave me confidence, at a workshop many years ago in the lovely Rocky Mountain town of Ouray, Colorado. She told me that in fact I did have something interesting to say and wrote well. Keep at it, she said.

More recently, at a conference in Marin County, California, overlooking the blue Pacific Ocean, writers Tom Barbash and Pam Houston and fellow attendees read my umpteenth draft, laughed at the right places, and offered helpful advice.

My writing groups in Bellingham include PenUltimate Writers, Red Wheelbarrow Writers, and Whatcom Writers and Publishers. No fledgling author should leave home without one of them. Their support kept the keys a-typing.

Skilled and encouraging, my editor Virginia Herrick persevered through every rewrite, punctuation gaffe, and misplaced modifier.

And last, truly heading the "without whom" list is my patient wife Cherie. I've lost count of how many times she's proofread the manuscript and offered helpful suggestions. That said, any glitches that remain are my fault. I probably chose to keep them.

Retired attorney and lobbyist Richard Little lives and writes in the Pacific Northwest. His work has been published in the *Seattle Times*, the *Seattle Post-Intelligencer*, the *Santa Fe Writers Project*, *Cirque Literary Journal*, and *Clover, A Literary Rag*. He has also published two collections of short stories, *Postcards from the Road* and *Jakey's Fork - A River's Journey*. Further writing can be found on his blog, "The Write Stuff," at http://pepys2000.blogspot.com.

Made in the USA
Columbia, SC
08 September 2018